"So," Dr. Rankin went on sternly, "I wouldn't be too critical of her clothing."

Daisy glanced down at her decrepit thongs, wrinkled shorts and juice-stained top. No wonder Daddy Big Bucks in his fancy suit had been so disapproving.

"*If* she's my daughter?" Wyatt snapped. "What do you mean, *if?*" He pulled a leather case from his pocket and reeled out an accordion row of pictures. "See? Rebecca most certainly is my daughter."

Wyatt's attitude ticked Daisy off—although she was impressed that he carried so many pictures of his child. She found herself hugging Becca closer. "I'm a shrimper by trade," Daisy informed Wyatt with a touch of pride. "I own a trawler that I usually contract to a larger fleet." Her voice grew cool. "Sorry I don't meet your dress code."

Oh, she'd met his type before. Men who conquered worlds—and women. And, she told herself, she *wasn't* impressed.

Dear Reader,

I can't tell you how pleased I am to have been given the opportunity to write Temple Wyatt's story for Superromance's "Family Man" series.

Have you, by chance, ever heard a snippet on the news and not caught the end? That happened to me some time ago, while I was on vacation. I heard on a radio broadcast that a yacht had disintegrated in a sudden squall and that a woman—a "fisherman"—had, at great risk to herself, saved a young child believed to have been thrown from the yacht. For whatever reason, the youngster was unable to give authorities any personal information and refused to let go of the rescuer. Broadcasters begged anyone who might know the craft or the child to please contact them.

I never heard how the story ended. For me, that poor child remained in a sort of limbo. Not only did worries about the actual outcome haunt me, but from time to time I'd make up an ending. What if the child had been kidnapped? What if one parent had been searching all along? *The Water Baby* is that story.

By the way, the incident *didn't* occur off Galveston Island. (But it's such a beautiful place!) And there was no hint of foul play in the real episode. But I love an air of mystery. And a happy ending. I mean, what's the use of being a writer if you can't tidy things up in the end?

Roz Denny Fox

P.S. I love to hear from readers. I've moved—my new mailing address is: P.O. Box 17480-101, Tucson, Arizona 85710

Roz Denny Fox
THE WATER BABY

Harlequin Books

TORONTO • NEW YORK • LONDON
AMSTERDAM • PARIS • SYDNEY • HAMBURG
STOCKHOLM • ATHENS • TOKYO • MILAN
MADRID • WARSAW • BUDAPEST • AUCKLAND

ISBN 0-373-70686-3

THE WATER BABY

Copyright © 1996 by Rosaline Fox.

This edition published by arrangement with Harlequin Books S.A.

® and TM are trademarks of the publisher. Trademarks indicated with
® are registered in the United States Patent and Trademark Office, the
Canadian Trade Marks Office and in other countries.

Printed in U.S.A.

THE
WATER BABY

CHAPTER ONE

THE FIRST DAY Daisy Sloan let her Boston trawler stray into Rum Row, she was looking for solitude. Today, she'd come back deliberately—because she'd stumbled on the largest shrimp bed she'd ever seen.

As a rule, locals who contracted their boats to the larger Mosquito Fleet shunned the area. Daisy would be the last to deny there was an air of danger about the Row. She'd grown up listening to the legends of pirates' booty and prohibition, from which the cove had derived its name and reputation. Currently a plethora of whispered rumors regarding the exchange of contraband out here kept the feelings of uneasiness alive. Drugs. Guns. Artefacts. Anything illegal.

Daisy wasn't the type to thumb her nose at danger. If she'd seen anything suspicious yesterday, she'd have hightailed it back to Galveston faster than you could say "Papa Rose Maseo," long-time boss of the Island's underworld. And she certainly wouldn't have come back a second day.

It hadn't hurt that both days a cloudless blue sky met jade water without interruption. Daisy figured either the sinister stories were blown out of proportion or the people who traded illegally did so under cover of darkness.

Luckily neither Daniel Coletti nor his brother, Sal, who fancied themselves her protectors, had asked where she'd landed such a rich catch. Their egos had suffered when she'd weighed in higher than anyone in the fleet. Especially as she'd managed without the help of Loren Bonner, the college student who normally pulled nets for her. It was, in fact, her daring to shrimp alone that had made Daniel throw a royal fit and sent her seeking solitude in the first place.

They'd known each other forever and had fallen into a pattern of going dancing together on Saturday nights, but that didn't give him license to be so bossy. Things were financially tight for her right now because of bills accrued during her father's long illness. And then she'd had to buy out her sisters' share of the house—even though Violet and Jasmine had both married men with lots of money.

As the hot June sun beat down on Daisy's back, a gulf breeze scooted across gentle waves, cooling the air enough to make her chosen profession about as close to a permanent vacation as any paying job could get.

Uh-oh. Today it appeared she had company in the cove. A fancy yacht floated above her shrimp bed. The kind worth big bucks. Daisy cut her engines and eyed the anchored craft warily. A little girl with shoulder-length blond curls hurried to the bow rail, leaned over it and waved. A man and a woman sat at an umbrella table in the stern eating what was probably breakfast. Equally wary, they studied Daisy for what seemed a long time. Then the slim dark-haired woman picked up a coffeepot and replenished the mug her companion held.

"Phew." Daisy released her breath. A family. People bent on mischief surely wouldn't bring their child along. Relieved, she dropped her first set of nets. Strangely, the adults on the yacht seemed relieved, too.

The child watched the entire process with serious blue eyes.

Trolling slowly into the current—and closer to the yacht—Daisy felt the nets begin to swell. By the time she cranked the winch designed to hoist the heavy load, she'd gotten involved in a conversation with the curious child. The elfin-faced girl asked a million questions about the crustaceans Daisy pulled from the sea. The kid might look dainty in her flowered sundress, but she wasn't the least bit squeamish. Grinning, Daisy tossed the girl a soft-shelled crab to examine up close.

At twenty-six, Daisy wasn't so old she'd forgotten her own fascination as a child with sea urchins and the like. Fondly she recalled the patience with which her father had answered her endless questions.

The little girl's curiosity about sea creatures reminded Daisy of an old story she'd loved when she was young. A wonderful, magical tale of the sea written by Charles Kingsley. *The Water Babies*. A much-read copy still claimed a prominent place on Daisy's bedside bookshelf. So she was a bit disappointed, yet not really surprised, to learn that the child from the yacht had never heard of the story. Daisy knew children today spent much of their free time in front of a TV. That was certainly true of her own nieces and nephews every time she saw them—although that wasn't often.

Daisy shot another surreptitious glance toward the girl's parents. They'd cleared the table, donned sunglasses and now lounged close-by in deck chairs, soaking up the sun. If this was typical behavior, no wonder the girl's knowledge of the ocean and its creatures was sadly lacking. Not that Daisy didn't like to veg out. She did. But she wasn't a parent. Parents should spend quality time with their kids.

Two hours sped by as Daisy entertained the wide-eyed child with excerpts from Kingsley's yarn. As a result, her own workday passed quickly, too. She examined her catch for fish that needed tossing back, and at the same time, made a game out of pretending to search for the elusive water babies. Careful to point out that they didn't actually exist, she painted a colorful fantasy about the marvelous fairy isles where the babies lived.

It seemed a harmless enough way to help a solitary child pass the time. Besides, Daisy hadn't had so much fun in a long while. She felt a niggle of disappointment when the girl's father called her for lunch.

Still enthralled, the girl skipped off, saying she couldn't wait to share the tales of the water babies with her mother.

Daisy listened unabashedly as the dark-eyed beauty—who obviously wore the label Mom, in addition to those of top fashion designers—declared the whole notion of water babies to be utter nonsense. In the next breath, she ordered her daughter to go below after lunch and play with her dolls or puzzles. She did her best to quell any further contact with Daisy, bestowing her a dark look.

As it happened, neither Daisy nor the girl paid the woman's decree any mind. If the child slipped below at all, she soon made her way back to the bow. "I wish I could swim," she whispered loudly to Daisy. "I'd go find those water babies."

"You can't swim? For goodness sake, why aren't you wearing a life vest?"

"They're hot," the girl complained.

"We humans need help staying afloat." Daisy pointed to her own waist belt. "Water babies have gills, sort of like fish. Wait—I hear them talking." She cocked an ear toward the sea. "They're telling you to go get your life vest."

The blue eyes clouded with doubt as the girl knelt in the very front of the bow. "Do you *really* hear them? Where are they? I don't see them. My mother said there's no such thing."

Daisy was relieved to see the child jump up, dart away and shrug into a bright orange vest. Her eyes, though, were still shadowed with disbelief when she returned.

Daisy had always believed in the power and comfort of imagination. So she felt no compunction in saying, much like the original storyteller, that just because people say there are no such things as water babies—just because you've never seen one—who's to say there are none?

That chased the shadows from the blue eyes and made the girl laugh. Within a few minutes, she and Daisy agreed conspiratorially to keep the existence of water elves their special secret. She even blew Daisy a big kiss.

Daisy loved kids. They were totally guileless. However, being single, she had no immediate prospects of having a child of her own. Someday, when she found the right man to father them, she wanted a houseful of kids. In fact, if she could, she'd put in her request here and now for a daughter as charming as the girl from the yacht.

Becca was the name Daisy had heard the parents call her. The child was precocious, using a sophisticated vocabulary well beyond her years. She was five, six at the most, Daisy guessed. At that age, kids got bored easily. Daisy thought the parents should've invited one of Becca's friends along, so the poor kid wouldn't have to strike up conversations with strangers. Not that Daisy minded. For the first time, she wondered where the family lived.

It was pretty plain that the girl's parents—a dark-haired man on the downhill side of forty and his beautiful wife, closer to Daisy's age—were too wrapped up in each other to pay proper attention to the child. A second honeymoon, perhaps? The adults had the starry-eyed look of new lovers, and they tended to ignore everything around them for long periods of time. Including—after that first close inspection—Daisy's trawler. A honeymoon would explain why the yacht had chosen to anchor in such a secluded cove, too.

Whatever the reason for the yacht's presence, Daisy was glad of it. Now, she'd not only enjoyed a few hours of lighthearted banter, she'd managed to put her own problems on hold. If she hadn't spent time telling the lonely child stories, she would likely have spent it juggling bills in her head—an exercise in futility.

Returning to Rum Row had netted her an extra-good catch and a pleasant day. But then, she believed wholeheartedly in serendipity. All things happened for a reason.

"WHAT DO YOU MEAN, you lost her, Boggs?" Temple Wyatt, thirty-four-year-old CEO of Wyatt Resorts, shouted at the private investigator on the other end of the line. He paced his San Francisco penthouse, going as far as the phone cord would allow. "Friday you assured me that Miranda and my daughter were headed for Domingo DeVaca's estate in Rio. I just finished filing a flight plan for Brazil. Five minutes more, and I'd have been out the door on my way to meet you there. What makes you think they've flown the coop again? If you somehow tipped them off, I swear I'll wring your scrawny neck."

Temple passed a hand over his freshly shaven jaw as he listened to Jack Boggs. Wyatt's heart sank in despair even as he cursed his ex-wife under his breath. She had no right to take Rebecca. The courts had given him full custody. For weeks he'd had Miranda followed while waiting for her to name her game. Always before it'd been money. But now with Domingo in her corner, Temple didn't know what her motive was. He knew it wasn't a burning desire for custody of Rebecca; Miranda had made her lack of interest in motherhood quite clear from the outset. So her motive must still be money. More money. DeVaca made millions from his Monte Carlo casino, and his string of posh resorts were wildly successful. Counting family money, the Brazilian could buy and sell Temple twice over. God only knew why such a man would elect to help Miranda—except that she was beautiful and adept at lying.

"I see, Jack," Wyatt murmured, listening more carefully. "You say the estate seems to be vacant today? Is there anyone you can question? I know you don't speak Portuguese. I don't, either. But I've visited Domingo's place a few times and made do. He has a big staff. Some of them speak English." He sighed. "Well, give it a try and call me back. I can always change my flight plan and intercept them elsewhere."

He hung up the phone and dropped tiredly into the maroon leather chair that sat behind a battered oak desk. The chair was new, one of those ergonomic masterpieces made for busy executives. The desk was an antique. His mother had given him the chair and a matching modern desk last Christmas to improve his decor. She'd almost had apoplexy when he returned the glass-topped desk and kept the one that had been his grandfather's.

Temple leaned both elbows on the scarred surface and raked his hands through his recently trimmed hair. He glanced up when the door opened and his housekeeper slipped into the room. Her crepe-soled shoes made no sound on the thick carpet as she collected a tray that held an empty coffee carafe and Temple's uneaten breakfast.

"No breakfast again, Mr. Wyatt? It won't do our little sprite a bit of good if you get sick." She cocked her head and studied him. "Is something wrong? I thought you'd be on your way to get Rebecca by now."

"Boggs tells me Miranda disappeared with her again. I'm fresh out of ideas, Maddy. I've been one step behind them for months. Domingo has properties all over the world. He could hide them indefinitely if he chooses."

"Maybe it's time to involve the police," the woman ventured hesitantly.

Temple didn't reply right away. He gracefully unfolded his rangy athletic body from the chair, straightened his tie and wandered over to stand beside a fully decorated artificial Christmas tree. The tree, loaded with bright lights and shimmering angels, looked out of place in the late-spring sunshine streaming through the window. Even more out of place because of the still-wrapped gifts beneath it. Temple knelt and picked up a package that contained a doll his daughter had begged Santa to bring. His thoughts drifted back to Thanksgiving weekend, when he'd stood in line at the mall for an hour just so Rebecca could tell Santa in person exactly which doll she wanted. He'd had no way of knowing it'd be the last weekend he'd spend with his child.

Damn Miranda. She'd never wanted the child she'd schemed to conceive—other than as a means to marriage. Nor had she shown more than a tepid interest in motherhood in the four years since the divorce. She'd ignored the open house at Rebecca's kindergarten in October. And the school's Thanksgiving feast, even though Rebecca's teacher had sent her a personal invitation. Then, *wham!* During her routine monthly visit conducted at his mother's condo, Miranda had taken off with their daughter.

Temple set the package carefully back where it belonged and moved away from the tree. Whenever he tried making sense of his wife's latest escapade, his gut churned with fury. In the past she'd always dragged him into court hoping to increase the alimony he paid her. This time she'd made no such demand.

"I keep thinking this is about money," he mused to the woman who'd been his housekeeper since before his marriage. Before he'd stepped forward voluntarily and assumed responsibility for an unborn baby's paternity—judging wrongly that babies brought out nurturing instincts in all women. "As you know, Maddy, from the minute Miranda discovered Wyatt Resorts' net worth, she's only ever been motivated by cash. Which is why I've tried so hard to keep this incident out of the news. But maybe it's time to go public and offer a reward."

"I wouldn't know about that, Mr. Wyatt. I just know you can't go on the way you have been. I haven't seen you smile in months. You hardly touch your food. Dr. Davis has given up asking you to play handball with him. And your poor mother, cries her eyes out blaming herself."

"I don't know how else to reassure her, Maddy. I told her I probably would've let Miranda take Rebecca out to her health club, too. They were supposedly going to get one of those damned fresh-carrot, cultured-yogurt shakes." He couldn't keep the sarcasm out of his voice, although he'd considered Miranda's health-food kicks the least of his problems. "If only I hadn't pushed for her to stay involved with Rebecca. I honestly never suspected she'd take our daughter on a ... spree."

"It's kidnapping, Mr. Wyatt. You should call it like it is."

He sighed. "I know, Maddy. Technically it is. I guess it's past time to run this by my attorneys again."

As soon as his housekeeper left the room, Temple placed the call. The Wyatt name opened doors in the law firm he kept on retainer. Temple was put through immediately to Patrick Marsh, senior partner of Marsh, Marsh and Schatz.

"Patrick, it appears Miranda's gone underground with Rebecca. I'm considering offering a reward to smoke her out. I think a million dollars would get her interest, don't you?" Temple slipped out of his jacket, unbuttoned his vest and rolled up the sleeves of his snowy white shirt while Pat Marsh reeled off thirty reasons it wasn't wise to stir up what he called the money vultures.

"It's easy for you to say hold off, Pat. Your daughter sleeps in her own bed every night. I think I'm as familiar with money vultures as anyone around. After all, I was married to one. I want Rebecca home. That's the bottom line."

He leaned back in his chair and rested his feet on a corner of his desk. Closing his eyes, he digested all the dire warnings his friend continued to spout. When the veteran attorney finished his spiel, Temple opened his eyes and said, "The P.I. you recommended can't nail Miranda down. Domingo DeVaca's got friends everywhere. I know him fairly well. He probably fancies himself Miranda's savior in all of this. Who knows what lies she's fed him? Yes, I've met several of his hotel staff. I suppose I could try greasing palms." Straightening, he let the chair snap forward. "I'll give your suggestions a try, Pat, then I'm going to leak news of the kidnapping and the reward."

He frowned as he listened. "Domingo and Miranda a romantic item? Yeah, I've thought of that, too. I'm not sure, though. I'll grant you, she's probably enamored with his money. But she also knows I'd pay a bundle to get Rebecca back. I'm sure she knows I'm getting damned tired of pussyfooting around. I'm running out of patience, Pat.'' With a terse goodbye, he slammed the phone back into its cradle, then snatched it up again to call Brazil.

Over the next few hours, many people jumped to Temple Wyatt's beck and call, yet no one turned up a single concrete lead. Boggs managed to find out that sometime earlier in the week the Brazilian's sixty-foot yacht, the *Isabella*, had left port for an unknown destination. Reluctantly he admitted to Temple that he suspected DeVaca and his two female guests had flown out by helicopter to join the boat en route to the States. The trail was stone-cold by the time Temple followed up. Nor was he able to unearth a soul who could—or would—confirm where, or even if, the *Isabella* went through customs to enter a U.S. port.

Beaten and exhausted, Wyatt called his lawyers again. His legal advisers still urged him to hold off going to the police—to wait for Miranda to break her silence. There was little doubt among those who knew Temple's ex-wife that she'd eventually ask for money: A lot of money.

Temple stood at the window overlooking San Francisco harbor—a sight he'd once loved—and worried. It was June first, and Rebecca had already missed half of her first school year. How much longer could anyone expect him to wait before he charged Miranda and Domingo with kidnapping?

He would give Miranda two more weeks.

SHORTLY BEFORE two o'clock on her second day in Rum Row, Daisy hauled in a net that finished filling the fore hold with fat juicy shrimp. She jockeyed the trawler west of the yacht and prepared to drop her aft nets when all at once, a swift-moving boat with a deep hull approached the yacht from the sea side and doused her engines. Daisy caught a fleeting glimpse of three swarthy men.

Great shrimping or not, she couldn't haul anchor fast enough. The chain squeaked and her knees quaked. Rendezvous with speedboats spelled trouble with a capital *T* in Daisy's book. Though disappointed at having to leave before her aft hold brimmed with shrimp, Daisy lost no time taking the trawler to full throttle. She aimed her craft toward patrolled waters and her home port on Galveston Island. Over the growl of her boat's engines, Daisy heard the speedboat leave the same way it had come— fast. She couldn't resist darting one last sympathetic glance toward the forlorn waif who leaned far over the bow rail, frantically waving goodbye. The orange life vest made Becca easy to see, even from the increasing distance between them.

Daisy lifted a hand to return the wave. After all, the poor kid wasn't to blame for her parents or the company they kept. If the truth be known, Daisy didn't want to think about what the speedboat might be picking up or dropping off in such a hurry. They hadn't had time for more than a quick exchange. No matter what contraband was loaded aboard the yacht, it was a shame for that sweet child's sake.

At least now it was no longer a mystery how the couple could afford such an expensive yacht—sixty feet if she was an inch, and every inch riding regally high in the jade green water.

As Daisy turned away, a tremendous blast rent the air. Stunned and horrified, she whipped back around to see the craft blow thirty feet high and splinter into a trillion pieces across her trawler's wake.

The scream that tore from her throat danced away on the sudden hot wind. In a reflex action born of a lifetime working the sea, she shut down the *Lazy Daisy*'s engines and scanned the choppy waves for any sign of survivors. She swallowed a sob. That little girl...

Through a giant swell, Daisy saw the speedboat idle briefly along the shore. She was too far away to identify any pertinent markings—not that she would've gone in hot pursuit. Her first priority was to save anyone who might have survived the blast. As if confident no one would fit that description, the powerboat revved up and disappeared—into thin air, it seemed. In the same heartbeat, Daisy spotted a bright orange life jacket bobbing a safe distance away from the rapidly sinking debris.

Before she could think twice about her own safety, she dropped anchor, shucked her deck shoes and leapt into the frothing whitecaps, her heart in her throat.

She swam toward the blob of color being buffeted to and fro. It seemed to take forever. At last she was there and she reached out and grabbed the life vest with both hands. Hanging on fiercely, she began to kick her way back toward the trawler.

"I've got you, my sweet water baby," Daisy said between gasps as she towed the terrified little girl to safety. "I won't let you go. I promise..."

CHAPTER TWO

"I NEVER DREAMED Becca would refuse to let me out of her sight, Dr. Rankin." Daisy spoke softly, ever mindful of the child sleeping in the oversize hospital crib. "Not that I begrudge her anything, mind you. But it's been two weeks, and I'm going stir-crazy being cooped up."

The slightly stoop-shouldered gray-haired man scribbled on the chart. "When you pulled her out of the water, Daisy, you became her lifeline. There's still so much we don't know about the mind. A consensus among the staff who've examined her is that she's suffering some type of trauma-induced shock."

Daisy shivered. "That's no surprise. She had a pretty shocking experience."

"And you were her savior," the doctor said. "A real heroine."

Daisy shrugged the praise away. "I was hightailing it out of there. And what kind of heroine shrimps near a pricey yacht in Rum Row and doesn't get the name or call letters? Still, it's odd the authorities haven't turned up more, a yacht that size."

It was the doctor's turn to shrug. "I suppose one bit of debris is much like another. Anyway, I detect a bit of our local look-the-other-way attitude, don't you?"

"You . . . you mean no one's searching?" Daisy stammered. "Why?"

"Daisy, Daisy." The doctor closed the chart. "You know our history as well as I do. Galveston's withstood Jean Lafitte's pirates, takeovers by both the North and South in the Civil War, horrendous acts of God and scoundrels of all sizes, shapes and colors. What's one yacht? I'm not condoning it, mind you. And don't forget—there've been no inquiries." He arched a brow and returned the gold pen to his breast pocket. "*Accidents* happen in the Row. Some think the less said, the better."

Daisy drew a hand through her tangled strawberry-blond curls. "What about Becca?" Her sad gaze flicked to the child again. "She's lost both parents. Surely there are aunts, uncles, grandparents—someone." Daisy paused to rub her temples, aware she was beginning to sound hysterical.

"The news is getting around. Maybe a relative will show up soon and you can get back to your own life."

Daisy nodded. "My sister, Jasmine, read the story in the Houston paper. But my other sister, Violet, who lives in New Orleans, apparently hasn't heard a word."

Dr. Rankin smiled sympathetically. "Well, Daisy, I hate to run. But I still have half my rounds, and I teach a pediatrics class in less than an hour." He paused at the door. "The thing about shock is that Becca could wake up from this nap and remember everything. She suffered a nasty bump on the head. Will you stay at least until the swelling's completely down?"

"Of course. I feel guilty complaining. Only, I have a house, a dog, a cat and a boarder—a very busy medical student who's been forced to look after everything. And tons of bills, yet I'm missing the best shrimping in two years." She followed him to the door. "What if we asked Jana Jefferies to do a network television appeal?"

The doctor tugged at one ear. "I've got no objection, as long as Jana tapes it here. Who knows? It might work. Otherwise, I'm afraid the next step is foster care. So far, with you here, I've managed to stave off Social Services."

"Foster care? Oh, no." Daisy turned back to the child. "I'll stay for as long as you need me."

"You've already given more than we had a right to ask. Do call Jana, and good luck with your search," he said as he withdrew.

Daisy gazed thoughtfully at Becca. The child screamed the roof down if Daisy left her side. Neither of them could handle this indefinitely. Daisy craved the sun and the sea; she needed to get out of this room. And Becca— they knew nothing about her, not even her age.

Taking a deep breath, Daisy reached for the phone and dialed the local TV station.

MORE THAN A WEEK had passed since Jana Jefferies's moving interview had aired in neighboring states. Daisy prowled the stuffy hospital room and grappled with the fact that no one had come forward.

The taping had been difficult. The lights and cameras had terrified Becca. If anything, she'd drawn deeper into her shell. Now Daisy feared that their efforts had been for naught. But there was still *some* hope; a few days ago Jana had called to say her boss had sent the tape to an international wire service.

She was just too impatient, Daisy decided. Pressing her nose to the window, she gazed longingly at the sun. Her arms still ached from having rocked Becca to sleep for her afternoon nap. There seemed so little change, even though Dr. Rankin had pronounced the girl physically recovered.

Daisy intensely disliked the two women who'd come from Social Services. They seemed to consider Becca just another case—not to care about her *personally*. What would happen to the girl if they placed her with total strangers?

Daisy sighed and watched her breath steam the window. Suddenly she sensed another presence in the darkened room.

Whirling, she noticed a tall broad-shouldered lean-hipped man silhouetted in the partially open door. "You have the wrong room," she said softly, moving quickly to intercept him. People were always stumbling in here, looking for some other patient. Becca hadn't been asleep ten minutes. If he awakened her, she'd be too cranky to eat supper.

Daisy's next words stuck in her throat as she found herself skewered by arctic blue eyes.

"I recognize you." The man surveyed her from head to toe. "From TV."

Surprised, she clung to the doorknob. Her own eyes followed his sweeping survey of the room, and she reflexively blocked his passage. Something in the way he homed in on Becca's crib frightened Daisy. Had one of the men from the speedboat come back to finish what they'd started? Without hesitation, she forced him out, closed the heavy door behind her and promptly hailed a passing medical student.

"Please call security," she implored.

The student dropped his textbook and gulped. He shoved dark-rimmed glasses back on his nose and puffed out a skinny chest. "Okay, buddy. No need to involve security if you quit buggin' the lady and leave quietly."

"Lady or vulture?" The stranger raked that laser-beam gaze over Daisy's decrepit thongs, wrinkled shorts and juice-stained tank top. "The lawyers warned me."

Daisy studied his impeccable three-piece suit. Lawyers. Had Social Services sent a man this time? Well, she wasn't going to apologize for insulting him. Talk about vultures...

Summarily dismissing her, the stranger again addressed the student. "Listen, I've traveled a long way to get here. I'm Temple Wyatt." His tone implied that the name alone opened doors.

When no one moved, he seemed annoyed. But Daisy relaxed. So he was just lost. Thank goodness, he wasn't from Social Services. Before she could direct him to the nurses' station, he backed the student to the wall. "I spent half the night flying through a thunderstorm from San Francisco. First I want to see my daughter. Our pediatrician is on his way, but until he arrives, I'll have a word with the doctor assigned to her case. Is that clear?"

The student bobbed his head repeatedly, while Daisy stood by feeling sorry for whatever poor soul was handling his child.

A sudden commotion near the elevators claimed Daisy's attention. Jana Jefferies and an entourage of cameramen spilled out into the hall. Jana swept right up to the stranger, gushing as only Jana could in her most affected Southern drawl. "Y'all must be Temple Wyatt. You talked to my boss. Guess we missed you at the airport. But, sugah, I'm just so proud to hear my little ol' interview reunited you and your long-lost baby." Spinning, Jana hissed at her gawking crew in an altogether different tone, "Roll those cameras, you fools."

Light bars sprang instantly to life, blinding Daisy. She recovered long enough to ask, "What baby, Jana? Not Becca!"

"Why, of course. Temple Wyatt—of the world-famous Wyatt resorts—is that darlin' child's daddy." Jana ignored Daisy's confusion. "Don't frown so, hon. You'll wrinkle." She straightened a strap on Daisy's tank top. "Now, sweet thang, when you set hands on that *big* reward, don't forget who did the interview that brought Daddy Bigbucks to town."

The man identified as Temple Wyatt let his lip curl contemptuously. So, his legal counsel had pegged these bloodsuckers right. The blonde with the frizzy hair probably figured she'd landed on a gold mine. Like hell! Temple knew her kind only too well.

Daisy was still chewing on Jana's astounding revelation when Becca began to scream. Not bothering to excuse herself, Daisy raced back in to the room and scooped up the frightened girl.

Just as the sleep-groggy child snuggled into Daisy's shoulder, Temple Wyatt strode through the door and held out his arms. "Rebecca, sweetheart. Daddy's here, Sunshine," he crooned. "Everything's going to be all right."

Becca arched away from him and let out a blood-curdling shriek. Her eyes were blank and uncomprehending.

"Is she in pain?" Wyatt demanded of Daisy. "What in hell do you have her on?"

Daisy had her hands full holding fifty pounds of thrashing child. And Jana's camera lights were heating her body to match her temper. "She's not on anything. Can't you see she's scared to death? Get out. Everyone get out and leave us alone." Her mind raced. She'd seen

Becca's father on the yacht—or maybe not. Who was this man?

A harried-looking Dr. Rankin rushed into the room. "Everyone out!" he shouted, and began shooing Jana's crew toward the door. "That means you, too." He motioned to the man claiming to be Becca's father. "Staff at the information desk said they asked you to wait in the lobby until they found me. Are you hard of hearing?"

Temple's eyes never left the woman rocking his sobbing child. Then, although he wanted to rip Rebecca from her slender arms, he turned his attention to the doctor. "Are you Rebecca's physician?" It hurt Temple to hear his precious girl scream so. "Would someone mind telling me what's going on?"

"Rebecca?" Dr. Rankin squinted up at the suntanned tawny-haired stranger. "It's true, then. Our Daisy's fishing netted someone who knows our little mermaid."

"Our water baby," Daisy murmured as she moved away.

"Her name is Rebecca. Rebecca Maria Wyatt." Temple's lips thinned bitterly. "My ex-wife took her from my mother's home. Kidnapped, I should say." He raked a hand through his hair. "Rebecca was a year old when Miranda and I divorced," he clarified. "I don't know exactly what's happened to my daughter in the last few weeks, Doctor, but before I take her home, I'd like a full report. She seems...disoriented." Wyatt's brow furrowed. "The person I spoke with at the TV station didn't mention injuries. I'd planned to fly home this evening." He glanced at his watch as if willing the hours away.

"I see." Dr. Rankin massaged his jaw. "Quite a tale there, young fella. So I guess your ex remarried? Must've been her new hubby Daisy saw on the yacht before it blew up. We naturally assumed it was Becca's daddy."

"Yacht?" Temple blinked. "DeVaca's? I'm afraid you have me at a disadvantage, Doctor. I left San Francisco the minute I saw Rebecca on TV. Is Miranda here in the hospital, too?" He glanced from one to the other. His daughter was calmer, at least, which eased the knot in his stomach.

Dr. Rankin sent the man a measured look. "If Miranda was the woman with Becca, I'm sorry to say there's been no trace of either adult since the accident."

The news staggered Wyatt. He paled beneath his tan, closed his eyes, bowed his head. Then he reached blindly for a chair and sat.

"Becca doesn't seem to know this man, Dr. Rankin." Daisy spoke from the shadows where she'd gone to rock the child.

"Is that a fact? Maybe you'd better come down to my office, son. I think we've got some sorting out to do."

"Why, Doctor? Why doesn't my daughter know me? And I don't understand about Miranda." Wyatt rallied enough to square his shoulders. "I want to see someone in authority." He slanted a distrustful glance at the woman who held his child.

Dr. Rankin pulled his stethoscope from around his neck and folded it into the pocket of his less-than-lily-white lab coat. "I'm afraid you're still stuck with me. I'm chief of staff. Shall we...?" He opened the door. "Daisy, we'll talk later."

Temple took two steps, then stopped. "What kind of hospital is this? If that woman's a nurse, why isn't she dressed like one? She looks like a...." His gaze bored through Daisy, but he let his sentence hang.

Dr. Rankin brought him up short. "Mr. Wyatt. *If* Becca is your daughter, you owe Daisy Sloan for saving her life. I wouldn't be too critical of her clothing."

"What do you mean, if?" the younger man snapped. He pulled a slender leather case from his inside pocket and reeled out an accordion row of pictures. "See? Rebecca most certainly is my daughter."

Wyatt's attitude ticked Daisy off, even though she was impressed that he carried so many pictures of his child. Even at that, she seriously doubted it made him a better human being. She found herself hugging Becca closer. "I'm a shrimper by trade," Daisy informed Wyatt with a touch of pride. "I own a trawler that I contract to a larger fleet. Sorry if I don't meet your dress code. You'll have to take my wardrobe up with Daniel Coletti. He docked behind me the day I fished Becca from the sea, and he was nice enough to go by my house and pack me a bag. Guess he plumb overlooked my gold lamé. I've been playing catch-as-catch-can ever since." Breaking off, she crooned to the girl who'd begun to whimper again. "Hush, my water baby."

Temple leveled her one last stare before Dr. Rankin firmly ushered him out the door.

Daisy stuck her tongue out at his broad back. She was fully aware that it was a childish thing to do, yet she was surprised to find her grip on Becca not quite steady. It was Wyatt's eyes. They were clear and blue as the Texas sky on a summer day, but below the surface they simmered dangerously, like an approaching hurricane.

Oh, she'd met his type before. Men who conquered worlds—and women. After all, both her sisters had married corporate sharks. Daisy wasn't impressed by men like Temple Wyatt. All she could think was, Poor Becca. When parents were handed out, this kid really drew deuces.

Drained from crying, Becca fell back into a restless sleep. Little sniffles escaped her tiny body every so often. Daisy was reluctant to lay her down. With one hand, she smoothed matted curls off the flushed, tearstained cheeks. Something like a lead sinker settled in her stomach. It wasn't right that so small a child be a pawn in her parents' games. Who would hold Becca and dry her tears if she was sent back to San Francisco with the resort czar?

Daisy tried to tell herself that everything would be hunky dory. No doubt Becca would have the best money could buy. Nannies by the score. Round-the-clock nurses. But what about love? Daisy sighed. Maybe the kind of love she believed in was nothing more than a pipe dream, like her sisters claimed.

She shook herself out of an uncharacteristic gloom. Both Violet and Jasmine had long poked fun at her ideals. They maintained that the best way to choose a life partner was based on preset criteria. In college they made "perfect husband" attribute lists—"rich" was at the top—and only dated men who fit the bill. Were their marriages as hollow as they seemed? Daisy rose from the rocking chair and placed Becca in the crib. Strangely her arms felt empty. She shivered, missing the child's warmth.

The door opened and a student nurse tiptoed in. "Oh, good," she said, "the kiddo's asleep. Dr. Rankin wants you in his office for a conference. I'll stay and buzz you if Becca wakes up."

"A conference? With me?" Daisy pulled at the tank top, which remained molded to her breasts from Becca's hot little body.

The nurse smiled dreamily. "Lucky you. Dr. Rankin's with the most gorgeous man ever to set foot on the island. I wish he wanted a conference with me."

Daisy pursed her lips. So Temple Wyatt was still here? Her first thought was that she wasn't dressed to go through the lobby. Now Daisy took perverse delight in knowing her rumpled appearance would annoy Mr. Three-Piece-Suit.

She took her time getting there, too. After a cursory knock, she popped into the chief of staff's office.

Both men rose.

In spite of Daisy's resolve to shake up Wyatt, she feared she was the one who'd been shaken. He was too good-looking, too masculine, too...everything. She sank silently into the nearest chair. The next instant she hardened her resolve; he was, after all, only a man.

To equalize power, she resorted to her usual method for dealing with obnoxious dock workers—she deliberately visualized Temple Wyatt wearing Donald Duck shorts beneath his sharply creased Italian wool trousers. She smothered a laugh.

He shot her a dark look before returning to his seat. "How is Rebecca?" he asked, thrusting out his chin enough to loosen a silk tie patterned in muted blue shades that matched his eyes.

Daisy was surprised by the depth of concern in his voice. "As well as can be expected," she said evenly, "considering how upset she was. She's dozing again. But she rarely sleeps long. I need to get back. What is it you want from me?"

Wyatt stood and rubbed the back of his neck as he paced the width of the room, struggling to articulate what was on his mind. Dr. Rankin had sung the praises of this blond woman with the strange dark eyes. Temple wondered how much, if any, of this praise was true.

The doctor cleared his throat. "Daisy, Mr. Wyatt believes his ex-wife and daughter were with a Brazilian hotelier by the name of Domingo DeVaca. He claims that, as far as he knows, DeVaca's business dealings are, er, were on the up and up."

Wyatt turned and impaled Daisy with pain-filled eyes. "If you were close enough to pull Rebecca from the water, you must have been close enough to see or hear more than you reported." He grabbed a wrinkled newspaper from the edge of the doctor's desk and shook it. "This story you fed the authorities is vague at best. I want the truth, Miss Sloan." Anguish made his eyes turn to flint.

Daisy rose and faced him across the desk. "What are you saying? That I lied? Why would I, for goodness sake? I told the police everything I know."

"A million dollars is a lot of reward."

Daisy pulled back, aghast. The amount stole her breath—and so did the accusation.

Dr. Rankin leapt to his feet. "Wait a minute. If I'd known what you were about, Wyatt, I'd never have asked Daisy here. Her honesty is above reproach!"

Daisy flashed the doctor a look of gratitude.

Temple snorted. "Come on. I heard what that TV woman said to you about the money."

Daisy clenched her fists. "You think I saved that precious child's life for a *reward?*"

"*If* you saved her."

"Has anyone ever told you how contemptible you are?" Daisy almost choked on her anger.

But the man in the designer suit wasn't giving an inch. "My ex-wife and I may have had our differences. But shallow vain gold-digger that she was, Miranda would never have placed Rebecca in danger. I think you know exactly what happened out there, Miss Sloan. And I'm asking questions until I get the truth."

Daisy reached behind her for the doorknob. She tucked a corkscrew curl behind her ear with the other hand. "I don't know," she said coldly. "You can believe me or not. I've heard, however, that people who ask too many questions around Rum Row sometimes flat-out disappear. Now excuse me, I'm going back to Becca. She panics if she wakes up and I'm not in the room."

"Are you threatening me, Miss Sloan?" Wyatt stiffened a moment, then he threw back his head and laughed. A row of even white teeth made his tan seem darker.

"Why, no. That wasn't my intent." Daisy drew in a breath. "But now that you mention it, for all I know, you could have blown that yacht yourself."

Temple's smile froze. "Try that tack and I'll sue you for slander." Who in blazes did this person think she was dealing with? He hadn't made it to the top of the international-resort business by bending to pressure.

Daisy yanked open the door. "So sue me. All you'll get is a twenty-year-old trawler. Frankly I can't see you busting your butt hauling in shrimp nets." All at once she gave a guilty flush. She'd forgotten the Sloan family home on the West Bay. It also belonged to her—and to the bank.

Wyatt saw and misread her guilty expression. He cut off her exit by trapping her against the wall, an arm on either side of her. Dr. Rankin was watching with wary eyes. "In that article, you told the police you were shrimping alone," he said with silky softness. "If the work is so butt-busting, why don't you have help?"

Daisy didn't like the way he was invading her space. She flattened her back against the wall, only to jump when her head accidentally brushed his hand. "I...I..." Looking directly into the bottomless blue eyes left her breathless. She glanced away to break the hold he had on her senses. "I do have a helper—a college student. Aubrey Bonner's son, Loren. He was sick that week." Darn, she was babbling. For pity's sake, she didn't owe this jerk any explanations! Deliberately she opened her eyes and glared back. "Feel free to check, Wyatt. Now if you don't mind, I'm outta here."

"I *do* mind," he said, loud enough to stop her. "Your story is too pat. It's got too many holes. Considering what I've heard about this town's history, all of you could be in cahoots to bilk me." His angry eyes connected with those of the doctor. Abruptly Temple straightened away from Daisy and returned to his seat. Getting into a shouting match with a woman wasn't his style.

"Miranda tried taking me to the cleaners repeatedly," he said curtly. "I don't bilk easily. As I said, Rebecca's pediatrician is flying in from San Francisco. Until Dr. Davis arrives, a member of my flight crew will sit outside Rebecca's door. So don't get any cute ideas about going underground with her, Miss Sloan. I'll not release one dime of that reward until I have her safe at home."

"I'll tell you what you can do with your reward," Daisy sputtered. "Shove it. I don't want one penny of your stupid money."

Dr. Rankin threw his pencil down on the desk. Normally soft-spoken, he roared, "Call in a hundred consultants. That child's in shock. I'm telling you, Wyatt— tear her away from Daisy and you'll only prolong her problems."

Sitting back, Dr. Rankin took a calming breath and steepled his fingers. "We know enough about shock to know that whatever the victim selects as an anchor must remain steady. For some reason, Becca has made Daisy her bridge between this world and the world she's retreated into. Remove Daisy, and your daughter may never come back from the other side."

Wyatt swallowed hard, and Daisy stifled a protest. Dr. Rankin had never been quite so blunt about her role. Daisy didn't know if she wanted to be anyone's anchor. Especially not anyone of paramount importance to a man like Temple Wyatt. She'd planned to march upstairs, collect her belongings and leave Wyatt to handle his daughter's terror however he saw fit. Now she had to do some hard thinking. Bestowing a final troubled gaze on Wyatt's disbelieving features, Daisy left the room, slammed the door—and pinched herself hard, so she'd start breathing again.

The minute she stepped off the elevator, Daisy heard Becca screaming. Fully expecting to encounter resistance at the door, she was relieved to see that Wyatt's guard hadn't arrived yet.

"Thank goodness you're back," the young nurse cried, gathering her things to rush away.

Daisy acknowledged her with a bare nod. She already had Becca's arms wound too tightly around her neck. "Oh, my water baby," she murmured. "Your daddy's here to take you home." She felt the little body relax, but knew it was because of tone, not what she'd said.

Trying to be optimistic about the inevitable, Daisy reached for a hairbrush and sat in the rocker, Becca in her lap. "Let's make you beautiful for that San Francisco doctor, shall we?" She smiled into the vacant blue eyes. "Who's to say you won't recognize him and come out of this slump?" But her voice wobbled.

Becca liked having her hair brushed. She sat quietly and let Daisy secure it in a long ponytail with a pretty bow that one of the night nurses had given her. Everyone on staff had taken an interest in trying to spark awareness in the child. That was another reason Daisy could kick Temple Wyatt for his rude unfounded allegations.

Fortunately Becca's father only appeared once more that day—when he stuck his head inside to announce that his guard was in place.

Less than an hour later, though, Wyatt's great California pediatrician swept into Becca's room with a reluctant nurse in tow.

Becca was in the middle of eating.

Daisy didn't like anything about the new doctor. It was hard enough to get the kid to eat, and this evening the dietitian had sent tuna noodle casserole, which Becca seemed to enjoy. At least she did until Dr. God of the Brooks Brothers suit and salon-styled hair made the mistake of ordering Daisy to leave the room.

She started to, but Becca went wild. The meal tray flew, drenching both Daisy and the child in milk and noodles. The visiting doctor wrested Becca away as he instructed Daisy to clean up the mess.

"Clean it up yourself," she snapped. "You caused the problem." Snatching a towel, she scrubbed at the stains on her shirt as she stalked out. It didn't help her disposition to be stopped by the guard and then practically bowled over by Temple Wyatt himself.

"What's going on in there?" Temple grabbed a fistful of Daisy's shirt.

She twisted free. "Ask your marvelous consultant. He has all the finesse of a Kentucky mule."

Puzzled, Wyatt drew back. "Dr. Davis is here? Then why's Rebecca throwing a fit? She adores him. Glendon and I are old friends. He's like her uncle."

Daisy treated him to a mutinous expression and continued to scrub at the sticky noodles.

"Oh, for God's sake, stop that. You're only making it worse." Temple jerked the towel out of her hands and reached for the doorknob. "If by some remote chance you own a piece of clothing with more material in it, please go put it on. I think you should hear what Dr. Davis has to say about Rebecca's condition.''

Daisy struggled to keep from slugging him. This was his second snide comment about her clothing. The man was obsessed by some puritanical view about what women should wear. Daisy marveled that he even had a child. No doubt he made love with his clothes on and the lights off.

Suddenly that notion struck her as funny. Temple Wyatt had the Ivy League look most women drooled over. Not Daisy. She didn't care if he owned every hotel in the world. His holier-than-thou arrogance was a big turnoff. Who cared what he thought? She glared at the door that swung shut on his polished heels. Darn, but she did want to hear what Dr. Know-It-All had to say.

She whipped around and started in, only to be stopped by the gleam in the guard's eyes. Daisy was contemplating washing her hands of the whole mess when Dr. Maris Sandeford, a quiet pediatric resident Daisy knew and liked, came to her rescue. She offered Daisy her lab jacket.

"Thanks, Maris, you're a lifesaver." Daisy pulled on the jacket and buttoned it up. Both women cast concerned glances toward the door as Becca's screams continued.

"I don't care if that man *is* Becca's father," muttered the young doctor. "I can't believe anyone who loves her would condone upsetting her like this. Scuttlebutt says he's planning to take her back to California before she comes out of shock. Someone should stop him."

"Dr. Rankin, you mean?" Daisy asked absently. "Does he have that authority even if Becca's father wants to sign her out?"

"Dr. Rankin would need to make some corroborating statement. But in some cases the courts advocates for children, usually those instances where parents make unwise medical decisions."

The noise escalated. "In Becca's case," she murmured, "who would approach the court if not Dr. Rankin?"

"You." Maris's answer was deceptively simple.

"Me?" Daisy flinched. "Wait a minute. Who am I? A college dropout, for goodness sake, who runs a not-very-profitable shrimp boat."

Her friend shrugged. "It's an option, that's all. We don't know what Mr. Wyatt will do yet, do we?"

"No," Daisy muttered. But she knew Temple Wyatt intended to take Becca back to San Francisco. "I should go see if I can help. Would you hunt up Dr. Rankin and tell him the consultant has arrived?" Daisy asked as the door flew open and a harried-looking Wyatt stuck his head out.

"There you are, Miss Sloan," he barked. "Dr. Davis is having trouble getting close enough to Rebecca to do a comprehensive exam. The nurse seems to think you might have better luck calming her."

"Go," Maris whispered. "I'll find Dr. Rankin."

"Hurry, please," Daisy begged as she shook off a shiver of apprehension and walked toward the man with the disturbing eyes. Reaching him, she saw his lips compress in the tight line she'd come to associate with disapproval. "*Now* what's wrong?"

"Is that coat all you have on?" His eyes locked on the jacket hem, which barely skimmed the bottom of Daisy's shorts.

She flushed. When she'd buttoned the coat she hadn't thought how it would look to the casual observer.

The hot flare in Temple Wyatt's normally icy eyes wasn't the least bit casual, however. For all his city style, Temple Wyatt was no different from the lusty shrimpers who crowded the dock giving wolf whistles every afternoon when Daisy unloaded her day's catch. Except they were more honest.

Lifting her chin, she marched past him. It irritated Daisy that he could make her blush. If she prided herself on anything, it was her ability to ignore the cruder side of men. Any man who finally got under her skin would be funny and sensitive and romantic. So why did Wyatt's gaze send chills chasing up and down her spine?

Daisy blanked her mind to such unsettled feelings and, instead, reached for the sobbing child, who'd just landed a solid kick in the good doctor's midriff.

"Rebecca, this behavior does not become a kindergartner," Dr. Davis said, sounding somewhat winded. "Remember at your last visit we discussed how big girls don't throw tantrums?"

Rebecca kicked him again.

"So she's five, then? We wondered," Daisy murmured.

"Didn't you ask her?" Dr. Davis said haughtily as he placed his stethoscope to the sturdy little back, now that Daisy held Becca securely.

"She hasn't spoken since the accident," Daisy said, tucking the child's head protectively under her chin. "Surely you've read her chart."

He waved a hand. "I checked her thoroughly before school started. She was doing fine." He deftly took her pulse. "Rebecca seems robust enough, despite her experience. It isn't as if she was kidnapped by strangers. She'll snap out of this as soon as Temple gets her home into familiar surroundings." He stepped away and removed the stethoscope from around his neck.

"Are you certain of that, Glendon?" Wyatt slipped into the circle of light. He was beginning to be unsure of anything where Rebecca was concerned.

Daisy heard the worry in his deep voice, and his stock went up a notch with her. Perhaps he did love Becca. She rocked the whimpering child. Maybe things would work out, after all.

Dr. Rankin and Becca's psychiatrist burst into the room just as Dr. Davis clapped Wyatt on the back. "As usual, Miranda has spoiled Rebecca rotten. You know what I've said about you two trying to outdo the other. Bright kids learn to manipulate early. Rebecca's just in one of her sulks."

"You think?" Temple's voice still held shreds of doubt.

"Bank on it," Davis said, slicking his neat hair back with a palm. "We're dealing with the Royal Princess Syndrome."

"We're dealing with latent shock," Dr. Rankin said stoutly from across the room.

The visitor turned and gave the local doctor a condescending look that Daisy didn't like at all. He shrugged lightly and said with a polished smile, "Well, Temple, it seems we're of two opinions here. Believe whom you will. Of course, I've been Rebecca's physician since she was born."

Daisy felt that sinker in her stomach again as the team's psychiatrist broke in and cautioned Temple against removing Becca from Daisy's care.

The sinker grew heavier as Wyatt studied her with those awesome blue eyes for a moment without blinking, then said, "I appreciate your interest, gentlemen, but I'm inclined to go with Glendon's recommendation. How soon can you have Rebecca ready to leave?''

Daisy's knees gave way. She sat down abruptly in the old rocker. Imperceptibly her arms tightened around the girl. It was *wrong* of them to take her. Temple Wyatt was making a big mistake. She knew it in her heart.

In some cases, the court advocates for children. The resident's words echoed in Daisy's head.

Maybe they did things differently in California, but Daisy Sloan had been born on Galveston Island and islanders stuck together. Since it was her fault Temple Wyatt had found them, perhaps it was up to her to set things right.

Beyond her dark thoughts, she heard Wyatt announce he'd give them three days to prepare for Becca's discharge. "I need to speak with the police about Miranda," he said. "And we'll have to notify her parents. They aren't well. I can't leave them to deal with this alone. Besides, I'd like to be sure that everything possible has been done to locate the . . . the wreckage.''

Daisy ignored the tremor in his voice. She, who rarely stuck her nose in other people's business, had just made up her mind. Tomorrow she intended to see a judge about protecting this defenseless child.

CHAPTER THREE

EARLY THE NEXT MORNING while Becca slept, Daisy slipped from the hospital, armed with a host of carefully worded depositions from Becca's medical team. By eight-thirty, the deed was done. She'd lodged a petition to stop Temple Wyatt from taking his daughter; if she won, *she'd* be looking after Daisy.

By nine, the island was abuzz with the juiciest scandal since the 1957 raid on the Maseo brother's slot machines. Always champions of their own, the islanders had had the last laugh back then, too. Old men still sat on park benches and chuckled about the hundreds of fruity-eyed slot machines a greenhorn government agent had hauled out and dumped in the bay to impress a *Life* magazine reporter. Or, rather, they boasted about the stir it caused when the machines bobbed back to haunt him, floating down the causeway on the evening tide.

The islanders loved scandals they could sink their teeth into. Daisy's battle with the upstart city fella hit the rumor mill with the speed of a Coast Guard cutter and beat her back to the hospital where she continued to camp out at Becca's bedside.

Daisy never ceased to be amazed by how quickly gossip spread. She had to admit it kept her on the straight and narrow—which certainly wasn't for lack of Daniel Coletti's trying to talk her into bed. Daisy would be darned if she'd let her love life be bandied about the next morning over breakfast in all the Island homes.

Why such a thought would pop up now, Daisy couldn't say. Maybe it had to do with the questions they'd asked at the courthouse about Becca. Questions that made Daisy reflect on her singlehood, and her desire for marriage and children in that order.

Islanders tended to assume she'd give in and marry Daniel one day. She enjoyed Daniel's friendship, but he wasn't the man with whom she wanted to spend her life. She couldn't help thinking that when the right man came along, a little thing like gossip wouldn't keep her from his bed. Making love with the right person would be beautiful and spontaneous, she was sure of it.

There she went, off on a tangent again. Sighing, Daisy tried again to interest Becca in lukewarm cereal and watery apple juice.

The child dawdled, and Daisy's mind returned to its wandering. The truth was, Daniel didn't set off any bells and whistles when he kissed her. But maybe, as her sisters said, that was silly. But she— Daisy was startled out of her musings when the door to Becca's room crashed open.

The girl scrambled into Daisy's lap and began screaming. For the second time in as many days, Daisy found herself wearing food down her front in the presence of Temple Wyatt.

His glacial gaze skipped over the mess. "What in hell is the meaning of this?" he shouted over his daughter's screams. Still not believing the woman's audacity, Temple shook some papers under her nose. The summons he'd been delivered.

The racket brought a nurse on the run. "Do you need help?" she asked Daisy.

"I don't think so." Daisy stood, though not without some difficulty, considering that Becca was clinging to her neck. "I should have foreseen this visit," she said, calmly retreating to her usual spot beside the window, Becca's screams now only whimpers. She'd known, of course, that he'd be furious.

"I'm sorry for upsetting Rebecca." Temple got a grip on his fury. "My dispute is with you, Miss Sloan." He crushed the paper in a large fist. "Is this some kind of joke?"

Daisy hauled in a deep breath and ignored the pain that darkened his clear blue eyes. This wasn't the time to waffle. She'd set her course last night. "Take a good look at your daughter," she said, facing Wyatt. "The sight of you terrifies her. I filed that petition, hoping to buy her some time to get well."

His stormy gaze settled on his child. It softened a little, giving Daisy hope for a rational outcome. Then his eyes hardened, and she knew there'd be no compromising with Becca's father.

"Lady, you're crazy. Last night I actually thought about forking over the reward to you. Now you'll play hell collecting one red cent."

Fury ripped through Daisy. "I said I don't want your money." Her voice rose. "I think you've lost sight of what's best for Becca. For your information, Mr. Wyatt, not everyone has a price."

"We'll soon find out, Miss Sloan. In court." He stalked out and slammed the door so hard the overhead fan swayed.

Daisy winced. She hugged Becca tight, uncaring that the wet cereal seeped through to her skin. What if she *wasn't* doing the right thing? What did she know about what was best for shock victims? More to the point, what did anyone know? Dr. Rankin had as much as said that Becca's team was shooting in the dark.

All at once the small body snuggled against Daisy, and she had her answer. For the moment, at least, she was the best shot this kid had. "Yes," she muttered, bending to pick up the tray. "I will see you in court, Mr. Wyatt."

However, Daisy could have used more time to gather her courage. Within the hour her summons came—for the next afternoon at five. An enclosed note said it was to be an informal hearing in Judge Forrester's chambers. Daisy latched onto the word "informal." It made the prospect of facing Wyatt less daunting.

Unfortunately she barely slept that night, tossing and turning on the cot in Becca's room. The time of the hearing couldn't be worse. The child was always restless in the late afternoon. Yet there was no question of leaving her at the hospital. Her fixation with Daisy was the whole point of the hearing.

All day she worried and fretted about the fact that no one had seen or heard from Becca's father since he'd stormed out yesterday. Where was he? Plotting against her, no doubt, she thought, stifling approximately her thirty-thousandth yawn.

Later, on the ride to town, Daisy voiced those same concerns to Dr. Rankin, who, thank goodness, had elected to accompany her.

"According to the grapevine," he said, "Wyatt's been closeted with his attorneys, who flew in late yesterday on a private jet."

Daisy absently combed her fingers through Becca's clean bright curls. "Attorneys? As in, more than one?"

"Two for sure. Maybe more."

Now Daisy wished she'd worn a skirt, instead of going on the assumption that informal meant clean jeans. Wyatt would be sure to disapprove of jeans.

Soon she had more to concern her than blue jeans. Daisy was forced to listen as a court clerk read, in a nasal twang, documents proclaiming that the case brought by the state of Texas versus Temple Wyatt concerned the health of a minor—and had been initiated by one Daisy Sloan.

She felt like an ax murderer. Wyatt's two lawyers skimmed her attire and dismissed her with a glance. They each wore three-piece pinstripe suits.

Only Temple Wyatt looked worried. But didn't he look glorious in his powder blue suede sports coat and knife-creased pearl-gray slacks? Daisy knew she wouldn't look that put-together no matter what. She'd always dressed casually, unlike her sisters, whose color-coordinated clothing was never less than elegant.

When the clerk finished reading, she took a seat behind a transcribing machine, and Daisy began to sweat.

Judge Forrester began proceedings by asking Wyatt why he thought he should be allowed to go against medical edict to take Becca back to California. Except that the judge looked over the top of his Ben Franklin glasses and referred to the girl as Rebecca Maria Wyatt.

Daisy wondered if anyone besides her noticed that Becca didn't so much as flicker an eyelash on hearing her full name. Wasn't that significant?

If so, no one mentioned it. Instead, one of Wyatt's attorneys stood and said he'd speak for his client.

Daisy was surprised Wyatt didn't do that for himself, since he was so adept at expressing his displeasure. Nevertheless, his lawyer—the more senior one with the weasel eyes—read a three-page dissertation on Temple Wyatt's attributes.

Daisy was impressed. Then she squirmed. Did they have to keep looking at her like she was some...some lowlife? How could she possibly compare favorably with a multimillionaire jet-setting hotel mogul?

The answer was she couldn't.

Daisy was relieved when the state's attorney said he'd be presenting her rebuttal. She could have hugged him. Thing was, she didn't think it boded well that he tore one sheet of paper off his pad to the other lawyer's three.

Of course, he *was* young. Wouldn't those expensive California lawyers just know he was free, she thought miserably as he ran a nervous finger beneath his worn shirt collar.

She'd almost convinced herself he'd do just fine when he cleared his throat and announced in a loud voice, "Daisy Sloan is BOI." Then, smiling ear to ear like the Cheshire cat, he sat down. Daisy's jaw went slack.

Temple Wyatt jumped up. He impaled the youngster with those fathomless blue eyes. "What in hell does that mean?"

His lawyers, too, demanded clarification.

Daisy wished she could sink through the floor.

The judge banged his gavel and sent Becca tunneling into Daisy's neck. Scowling, Judge Forrester barked, "It means Daisy Sloan was *born on the Island.* In case you didn't know, we spell island with a capital *I.* Recommendations don't come any higher than BOI in my court. Now, shall we get on with this? I don't have all day." Bang went the gavel again.

Temple motioned for his lawyers to huddle. The way all three gestured made Daisy's heart gallop. She wasn't surprised when their attack turned personal.

"Fact is, Judge," the younger attorney said smugly, "if Miss Sloan takes Rebecca, it means she can't go out and fish. That leaves her with no viable means of support."

"I don't fish, I shrimp," Daisy interjected even as Forrester looked to her for an answer. "And I do have other means of support. I have a boarder—a medical student. Normally I have two, and no doubt will again next semester," she rushed to say, knowing full well that rent from one boarder didn't cover her expenses.

It seemed they knew, too. Weasel Eyes read what amounted to a very black look at Daisy's total financial picture. More like a *red* look. Without shrimping, her outgo was definitely more than her income. Be that as it may, she didn't want the world to know the state of her finances. Embarrassed, she studied her sneakers.

The judge merely rapped his mallet harder and said he took exception to the men's tactics. "Miss Sloan isn't starving. She owns a piece of prime Island property. Confine yourselves to valid objections, please." He paused, then added, "In any event, I'm sure a man of Mr. Wyatt's...stature would want to make financial provisions for his daughter's care."

"No!" Daisy objected loudly. "That's not necessary."

Dark looks and more heated discussion between Temple and his henchmen. After a few moments, Weasel Eyes got to his feet. "Outside of the fact that my client has already been separated from his daughter far too long, Temple has a very real concern for Rebecca's personal safety. Can Miss Sloan guarantee that you won't have a devastating hurricane if the child remains in her care?"

Daisy shifted Becca to her other hip. Her laughter exploded; she couldn't help it. "You're kidding! Last week

I read that San Francisco hired a special team of seismologists to do nothing but sit around and watch the San Andreas fault. You guys live in a city waiting for the next earthquake—the big one—and you're worried about a little hurricane? Give me a break.''

"Good point." The judge smacked his gavel. "Next issue."

Weasel Eyes placed his palms flat on the table. He loomed over Daisy. "It's news to us that you can read anything beyond the Sunday comics, Miss Sloan. Why don't you give up this charade and spell out exactly what it is you want from my client?"

"I don't know what you mean. I *said*—I don't want anything except for Becca to get well." She dropped a kiss on Becca's nose. "What I've proposed is a short-term arrangement. Until she comes out of shock. Goodness, I'm not asking for anything permanent." Tears sprang to her eyes, and she lifted a hand to brush them away.

As though feeling Daisy's sudden tension, Becca started a low keening wail.

Temple's other attorney rose. "How very touching. You should do Hollywood, Miss Sloan. You've missed your calling."

"Or maybe not." Weasel Eyes leaned forward and snapped his fingers. "Picture this. A yacht supposedly disintegrates, yet no wreckage is ever found. It's a B script if ever I heard one, Temple. This wouldn't be the first off-the-wall scheme Miranda cooked up to get you to fork over higher alimony. Could be she hired the Sloan cookie to fleece you good this time."

"Now just a darn minute!" Daisy endeavored to stand, but Becca only wailed louder. She did manage to look Temple in the eye, however. "I am not an actress. And if you want to be sued for slander, let that man call me a cookie again.''

Judge Forrester pounded his gavel. Everyone except Temple and Daisy gave him their undivided attention. Those two continued to glare at each other—until Wyatt frowned, rubbed his jaw and made a second long slow inspection of his opponent.

Daisy bet he didn't miss so much as a freckle on that leisurely perusal of her body. Her skin prickled uncomfortably, before his gaze shifted to Becca and softened visibly. Daisy suddenly felt weak. She did her best to concentrate on what Wyatt's lawyer was saying—about how he was a pillar of the community and how a virtual stranger stood between him and his duty as a father.

Daisy thought about that as she gently removed Becca's thumb from her cupid's-bow mouth. Daisy didn't feel like a stranger to this child. But to be fair, she tried placing herself in Wyatt's shoes. That was when she noticed the pain in his eyes—a dark despairing kind of pain.

Lord, what have I done? She'd never intended to hurt anyone. Daisy opened her mouth to say as much, to withdraw her petition and let him take Becca home if that was what he wanted. But before she could, Wyatt stood and began gathering his papers.

All eyes shifted. Talk stopped. His attorneys seemed perplexed. ''What are you doing?'' one hissed. ''We're not even close to a settlement.''

''It is settled,'' Temple stated, pausing to slant another troubled look at Daisy. ''We've all overlooked one thing. Whatever anyone else might be, Rebecca is definitely no actress. See how she clings to Miss Sloan? As if her life depends on it. I want my daughter fully recovered, gentlemen, whatever it takes.''

Daisy almost wept at the anguish on his face. She knew then how much Temple Wyatt loved his child. Enough to step aside. A lump rose in her throat, and she couldn't have spoken to save her soul.

Fortunately Dr. Rankin jumped to his feet and shook Temple's hand. "You've made the right decision, son. All along we've assumed that if she had a little stability with someone she trusts, Becca, er, Rebecca may snap out of this. It might speed the process if you could supply Daisy with a few of your daughter's favorite toys."

Temple's gaze again strayed to Daisy, but he didn't say yes or no to Dr. Rankin's request.

This time, however, Daisy thought she glimpsed deeper emotions overshadowing his pain. Anger. Distrust. Jealousy. Not that she could blame him. He didn't know a blessed thing about her. Plus, it had sounded as if he'd been betrayed by a woman. One he'd loved enough to marry.

For just a moment, Daisy wondered how a man of Wyatt's sensitivity could have loved such a woman. But then, never having been in love herself, she was hardly in a position to judge what did or didn't spark that level of passion. Still, duplicity of the magnitude he'd suffered would leave scars.

She stood and began to move toward him, wanting to say something to allay his fears. It happened again, as it had the day before—when she drew near, all her senses first heightened, then failed. Around Becca's father, Daisy found herself either tongue-tied or hostile. Right now, her knees threatened to fold and her throat felt tight. A stuttering stumbling woman wasn't exactly the image she wanted to leave him with.

Slowing her steps, Daisy let the moment pass. She fell in behind Dr. Rankin in time to hear him tell Wyatt that it would simplify things if he'd sign Becca's discharge papers now.

Wyatt considered the suggestion, then nodded. Dr. Rankin clasped his hand briefly, then ran to catch the state's attorney.

At that moment, the seriousness of what she'd done hit Daisy. After tomorrow, there'd be no more twenty-four-hour nursing care for Becca. No team of doctors dashing in and out offering encouragement and suggestions. Soon, she alone would be responsible for the well-being of another person. A tiny fully dependent person. Fleetingly Daisy was swamped by utter panic.

Temple seemed to pick up on it. "Having second thoughts, Miss Sloan?" he asked. Although in truth, he didn't know what he'd do if she suddenly backed out. Rebecca seemed totally reliant on this . . . floozy.

"N-no." Daisy croaked out a hasty assurance. But she *was* having second thoughts. And third. True, she'd cooked, shopped and cleaned house for her dad and herself. Had done a bit more when he'd taken ill. But he'd been an independent old cuss. (Some said she took after him.)

Surely this panic was a perfectly normal response. But if that was true, why couldn't she meet Wyatt's all-knowing gaze? Darn, what was there about the man that he could send her into a tailspin at a mere glance?

Wyatt's lawyers were still arguing. "Giving up like this is stupid, Temple," Weasel Eyes said. "We didn't even present Glendon's statement. That would've impressed the judge."

"Thanks, but no." Temple shook his head. "I probably shouldn't have asked Glen to come. He's been too close to Miranda's and my problems to be objective."

"Nonetheless," the younger attorney cautioned, "as Rebecca's custodial parent, you have certain rights."

Temple turned and made another lengthy survey of Daisy and his child. "Yes," he murmured, "I do have rights."

Daisy battled a quick stab of discomfort. What did he mean by that? She might have asked had Dr. Rankin not called to her from across the room, saying he was ready to leave. She made a conscious decision to circumvent Wyatt completely. With any luck she wouldn't have to undergo his scrutiny ever again. At least not before Becca was completely well and ready to return home. Even then, busy as he sounded, he might send a member of his staff to collect his daughter. Daisy didn't want to examine why she found that thought depressing. So she just wouldn't think of him at all.

And later there wasn't time. When she arrived back at the hospital to collect their things, more bad news awaited her. The ward clerk handed Daisy a note from her boarder. Stephen said that he was failing med school, he was sorry to have missed her, but he had a ride home to El Paso. She'd known his grades last semester weren't good, but he'd worked harder this term. Daisy hoped his caring for her house and her animals hadn't been to blame.

Her spirits plummeted. Not just because she felt vaguely guilty about Stephen's dropping out. Not just because she needed the income from his rent, although it would be tough until she could advertise in the next college paper for a new tenant. She might need money, but the one thing she wouldn't do was accept payment for Rebecca's care. Even when times were tough, she'd always managed to get along—she managed and didn't worry about money too much. No, Daisy's discontent went deeper. It had to do with her unsettled feelings about Temple Wyatt. And with his lawyers' assessment of her net worth. She, too, had dropped out of college and later regretted her hasty decision.

At the time, her sisters and their friends used college as a place to land husbands. Daisy had scoffed at this and vowed to be a shrimper all her life. Later she'd discovered it took more than simply hauling in nets to make the job pay.

Becca stared vacantly into space as Daisy packed their few things. Was this just another whim—this decision to take Rebecca Wyatt home with her? "No," Daisy said, answering her own doubts. She sighed. Would Temple Wyatt go back to the coast? she wondered, feeling a little catch in her throat. That was what she wanted, wasn't it? To never lay eyes on him again? "Yes!" And that would be accomplished if Becca got well. Then her bold action would be justified, leaving her with a story to tell her own grandchildren—if she ever had any.

SHORTLY AFTER DAISY tucked Becca into bed the second night the girl was spending in her home, the doorbell pealed.

Pipsqueak, Daisy's fox terrier, tore downstairs.

Daniel. Darn, he'd wake Becca. Daisy rushed to the door. Earlier, when he'd phoned, she'd expressly told him not to stop by.

Daisy snapped on the porch light and opened the door. Pipsqueak nudged the screen ajar and escaped. As Daisy was about to give chase, she was stunned to see that it wasn't Daniel leaning on her bell. Instead, standing knee-deep in boxes, was none other than the man Daisy had convinced herself she never wanted to see again. Temple Wyatt.

"You!" she exclaimed.

He smiled. "Interesting house," he said. "Are you adding a basement? Is that why it's on stilts?"

"It's built on pilings—to avoid flooding during hurricanes. Many homes in Galveston are."

Wyatt lost his grip on a box he'd picked up. "You're joking."

"No. Mercy, are these all Becca's favorite things?" Daisy craned her neck to see.

"More or less," Temple muttered, beginning to move the crates into her tiled entry.

Daisy stepped aside to give him room. Her black cat, Troublemaker, walked over, sniffed a box, then strolled out. She shrugged, knowing both dog and cat would soon return. "I must say," Daisy groused good-naturedly, "I expected a doll and maybe a few stuffed animals, but this—" she considered a fair-sized crate "—what's in it? Her canopy bed?"

Temple ignored her. When the last carton was safely stacked inside, he closed the door and took out his wallet. "How much is rent? Give me a round figure."

Daisy blinked. She'd been trying to read the printing, but the boxes were all turned upside down. "What?"

He gave her another crooked smile. "Do you require first and last month down, plus a cleaning deposit?"

"You can't believe I'd charge for keeping Becca. What kind of person do you think I am?"

"Not for Rebecca," he said, his voice falling to a rough whisper, "although I insist on at least paying her expenses." He shook his head. "No, this is for me. Didn't Dr. Rankin tell you? He showed me your ad and told me about your boarder leaving. I'll rent both your spare rooms. One for an office and one for sleeping."

Daisy couldn't mask her shock. Suddenly the neat print on the boxes blazoned out at her. Words like Monitor, Keyboard, 600 MB Hard Drive, CD-ROM, Model 4790 Fax. Why, the nerve of the man! He planned to set up his business here in her home.

"No, you won't," she declared. "Not one square inch will I rent to you."

"Two rooms." He flashed two fingers in front of her nose, then peeled several one-hundred-dollar bills from his wallet. "This should cover a bed and a second room for my computer, a fax machine or two and a desktop copier. I won't need phone hookup. I have a cellular." Folding the greenbacks, he tried to press them into her hand. "I'll plan on two months. After that we'll see."

Daisy pulled back, and the money hung between them a moment before it floated to the floor. "No," she said again. "No way. You cart these things right back out, mister. I won't rent to you."

"On what grounds?" This time his smile didn't quite reach his eyes.

"I beg your pardon?"

"I asked, on what grounds won't you rent to me?" He started ticking things off on his fingers. "You didn't specify only a female in your ad. I have the money and the references. I've never filed for bankruptcy. I have no criminal record. You need a reason to turn me away."

"Hold it right there." She jabbed a finger in his chest. "I don't care if you're an Eagle Scout. This is *my* home and I don't want you here."

He crossed his arms and shook his head. A sun-bleached curl fell rakishly across his forehead. "I'm afraid that's discrimination, Miss Sloan." He shrugged and reached into his pocket, pulling out an official-looking document. "Discrimination of any kind is prohibited under the Fair Housing Act. Besides, if you don't take *me,* you could get the next Hillside Strangler."

Face paling, Daisy put a hand to her throat.

A dimple creased his cheek briefly, then disappeared as he handed her a copy of the act.

Recovering, she batted the pages from his hand. They'd no more than joined the money on the floor when the doorbell shrilled. Daisy jumped a foot. "Oh, for crying out loud, you've made me a nervous wreck. This time it's got to be Daniel."

Temple scooped up the money and tucked it into Daisy's hand. "The boyfriend, huh?" he said cheerfully as she shrank from his touch. "Well, point me toward those rooms and I'll make myself scarce."

Exasperated, Daisy stepped over a box and jerked open the door. As she suspected, Daniel Coletti lazed there, one hand resting casually on the doorframe, the other tucked into the back pocket of worn too-tight jeans.

"Hiya, babe." It was his standard greeting, but it ticked Daisy off. Especially when he opened the screen door, grabbed her around the waist, pulled her close and nuzzled her ear. Daniel glanced up about then and caught sight of her well-dressed guest. He released Daisy abruptly. "Who's the fancy pants?"

"Shh." Daisy flushed. "Keep your voice down. Becca's asleep. Why are you here, Daniel? I distinctly remember telling you I wasn't up for company tonight."

"I really wish you'd call her Rebecca," Temple told Daisy as he hoisted a box on to one shoulder. "Dr. Rankin said to offer her the familiar. At home she *always* went by Rebecca. Now about those rooms..."

Daisy's back stiffened. "On the yacht, her mother called her Becca. I heard her myself."

"Oh, I get it." Daniel snapped his fingers. "The kid comes with her own shrink. Cool, babe. Now we can still go dancing Saturday night."

Daisy ran a hand through her untidy curls. "No, Daniel. This man isn't a doctor. He's Becca, er, Rebecca's father. Temple Wyatt, uh, meet Daniel Coletti, my, uh...a fellow shrimper," she ended lamely. She knew it must be obvious that she begrudged the introduction.

Temple steadied his burden and extended a hand. His narrowed gaze ran swiftly over the visitor's close-fitting jeans, striped tank top and on up to the small gold cross that dangled from Daniel's left ear. "Ah, yes," Temple murmured, "now I recall the name. Miss Sloan's fashion coordinator." He smiled then, and his solid handshake took Daniel by surprise—not a fact Daniel could hide.

Drawing back, the younger man turned an accusatory gaze on Daisy. "What's he mean, babe, your 'fashion coordinator'?"

"Nothing, Daniel. It's his warped sense of humor. Mr. Wyatt didn't care much for the shorts I was wearing the other day. I explained how you packed my suitcase. And don't call me babe again. You know it makes me see red."

Daniel appeared to digest everything she'd said before he reassessed her guest, his straight black brows drawn together over suspicious eyes.

Temple grinned an all-over grin.

Daniel placed a proprietary hand on Daisy's shoulder. "I'll just bet he didn't like those shorts, babe. What's he doin' here, anyway?"

"Trying to rent a room. Honestly, Daniel, keep calling me babe, and I'll toss you out on your ear."

Temple snickered as he shifted the carton to his other shoulder.

She wheeled on him. "And you'll be next."

Daniel set Daisy aside. "You won't have to dirty your hands, sweet thing. I'll be happy to get rid of him for you. What's he think—you run a hotel, for crying out loud? You stick to medical students. Those kids are still wet behind the ears. I'm not trusting any big-city dude with my girl."

Daisy all but stamped her foot. "I'm *not* your girl. Just your friend—though maybe not for much longer. And since when do you tell me how to conduct my business affairs, Daniel Coletti?"

Daniel puffed out his chest. "Since now."

"This box isn't getting any lighter," Temple said softly. "Name a room, Miss Sloan, and I'll get this stuff out of your way so you and the boyfriend can kiss and make up."

"For pity's sake! Go up the stairs. Take the first two rooms on your right. The bath is at the far end of the hall. And get this, Wyatt. Whoever I do or do not choose to kiss is none of your concern."

"Whomever." Temple grinned, shifted the box and touched two fingers to his brow in a mock salute. "If you're going to be a role model for Rebecca, you should try to use good English."

Daniel had disappeared during that last exchange. He returned holding a can of beer. After popping the top, he tucked one hand in his belt, leaned back against the doorframe and scowled.

Hands on her hips, Daisy was snarling at the man standing two steps above her, "So *that's* it. You think you can come here and prove me unfit to care for Becca."

Temple's eyebrows rose as he surveyed the pair below. Daniel's muscles bulged and his earring glittered in the light. Daisy's autumn-gold locks stood out wildly around her head, and the shorts she wore were, if anything, shorter than the ones she'd worn the day they met. Only these were gold, like the flecks in her brown eyes.

Then his lips thinned and he edged up another step. "Let's just say I wouldn't willingly leave Rebecca in the care of Bonnie and Clyde. But because of whatever cruel twist of fate I've been dealt, my daughter's definitely bonded with you, Miss Sloan. More's the pity." With that, in spite of the cumbersome carton, he took the remainder of the stairs two at a time and disappeared from sight.

Daisy smoothed a hand over her hair and down her blouse, as if doing so would rub away the trail of Wyatt's gaze. He'd made it plain what he thought of her. And she'd heard it all before from a mother who'd wanted *frilly* daughters. In the end, Rose Sloan had had to settle for only two—Violet and Jasmine. Daisy's father, bless him, had been willing to let his youngest daughter make her own choices.

Frankly Daisy liked being a free spirit. She didn't care what Wyatt thought.

She kicked at his copy of the Fair Housing Act, then picked up the pages and put them in order. This was her home. Her sanctuary. Which he'd invaded. Except that... she'd do all that and more if Becca were *her* daughter. She couldn't blame him.

"So you're going to let that joker stay?" Daniel spoke from the doorframe, and Daisy whirled, having forgotten he was there.

"A shrimp in hand's worth two in sea." She gave him a peek at the cash.

Daniel touched the edge of his beer to his forehead in a mock salute and opened the door. "If you get any time out from your baby-sitting, whistle. Otherwise, I'll see you around. Lori Gilbert's been all over me lately. Maybe I'll ask her to the dance on Saturday."

The screen door banged shut, and Daisy's frayed nerves sent a jagged burst of pain to her head. For a moment she stared into the darkness after him. Then she walked over and held the screen ajar for Pipsqueak and Troublemaker to come back inside.

Daniel should know she didn't respond well to threats. Lori Gilbert was all over everyone. If he preferred her type, they were welcome to each other. Daisy slammed the door.

"Boyfriend leave already?" a gruff voice asked behind her. "I hope it wasn't on my account."

Daisy jerked around and collided solidly with Wyatt, who was practically camped in her hip pocket. Her internal radar zoomed straight to where their bodies touched. Her heart rate soared; Daisy gnashed her teeth until it slowed. "Don't delude yourself, Wyatt. Daniel gets up at four in the morning to go shrimping. This is late for him."

"Terrible life," he murmured seductively. "Myself, I prefer sunsets."

"Shrimping is a *great* life," she insisted. "Morning's the very best time of day. And a person can be his or her own boss. Not that I owe you any explanation."

"You're absolutely right. You don't owe me a thing. I came to ask what room Rebecca's in. After I take the last load up, I'd like to look in on her."

She purposely avoided his direct gaze. "Maybe that's not such a good idea."

"Why not?" he flared. "Before..." Temple coughed, apparently unable to bring himself to finish the thought. Instead, he shrugged and said, "I used to read her a story every night. But that can wait. In one of these boxes is her favorite stuffed toy.'' His voice faltered and he looked away. ''I thought I'd give it to her tonight.''

Daisy cleared her throat. ''I only meant that I put her in a small room connected to mine. It used to be the nursery, but after my father died, I turned it into a dressing area. I moved a twin bed and small dresser in there so she'd be close to me in case she wakes up during the night. You'd have to traipse through my room to get there is all I meant.''

''I see.'' It was Temple's turn to study his toes.

Daisy thought about the mess her room was always in. Not dirty, just, well, sort of lived-in. And she wasn't sure she wanted Wyatt in there making more judgments. But on the other hand, if Becca had been *her* daughter... Just as quickly she relented. ''I've been staying up pretty late,'' she told him. ''At least I did when I bunked at the hospital. I suppose we can work something out.''

''Anything's fine. I'm a night owl, too. Say, what time is breakfast? I like my coffee black, my toast wheat. And I prefer egg substitute over real eggs. High cholesterol runs in the family,'' he said.

Daisy's eyes widened. ''Why are you telling me?''

''Your ad says room and board.''

''Yes, but I don't cook your meals.''

''Excuse me, Miss Sloan. What does 'board' mean?''

''It means you add what you want to my grocery list, and when I shop, I pick up your stuff, too. Within reason,'' she added, noting a hint of one of his devilish smiles. ''No lobster, no caviar, and no food to feed your friends. Got that?''

''Ah. What about weekends?''

''What about them?''

"Do we dine together on weekends? I assume you don't shrimp seven days a week."

"You assume wrong. When the shrimp run, we do. Which is precisely why I rent rooms to medical students. They keep crazy hours at the hospital, and half the time they eat in the cafeteria."

"Well, I'm not a medical student. When I'm not traveling I like home-cooked meals."

"So, find a bed-and-breakfast. Anyway, isn't this entire conversation pointless? I won't be out shrimping until Becca regains her memory, will I? And the minute that happens, you'll be out of here. For the time being, Mr. Wyatt, if you want something to eat, fix it. All seven days of the week."

"I get the message. But if we're going to be housemates, don't you think you should call me Temple? And are there other rules I should know about in this so-called boardinghouse?"

Daisy took a step back. Taking in boarders had always been something she kept low-key. She didn't advertise widely, only in the campus paper to get nursing or med students. And she didn't like his tone of voice. "Yes, *Mr. Wyatt,* there are other rules. I am not your secretary, so don't expect me to take your calls. Nor am I your tour guide, your dishwasher or your laundress. In short, do your best to stay out of my way. Understood?"

"I think that about covers it," he said. "You didn't mention mistress, but I suppose that goes without saying."

When she drew in a sharp breath, made a strangled noise in her throat and stormed off into the kitchen, he called after her, "Do I get clean towels, at least, or will I need to provide my own? And a key. Don't forget a key."

Daisy stood just inside the kitchen door, grinding her teeth. She rued the day she'd sailed into Rum Row. Damn the man. He was *so* annoying.

He was also very good-looking. And sexy.

She stood there and shredded his copy of the Fair Housing Act, still not believing that she, of all people, had fallen for his razzle-dazzle charm.

CHAPTER FOUR

DAISY REFUSED to term what she was doing in the kitchen "hiding," although she *had* planned to let the dishes soak. Anything that smacked of housework she stored until the mood struck her. Her long-term renovation plans called for a dishwasher, but it wasn't a high priority. Not like modernizing the one antiquated bathroom had been.

Tonight, though, on the evening of Temple Wyatt's unexpected arrival, Daisy felt a curious satisfaction at being up to her elbows in dishwater. She wasn't giving him a chance to make snide remarks about her stacked dishes. Bad enough to have him correcting her grammar.

She lifted a handful of soap bubbles, studied their iridescent colors under the light, then idly blew them into the air. Two large bubbles popped instantly. One floated lazily toward the kitchen window that faced the inlet, where, in the moonlight, silvery water lapped a weathered dock. Daisy saw that her favorite deck chair still sat close to the end of the pier. This time last month, she would've said to heck with clean dishes and kicked back out there, counting dimples in the moon's face.

Not tonight. Now everything about her carefree lifestyle had been altered—which would please at least one person she could think of. Rinsing the last pan, Daisy set it to drain. Her mother would've been delighted that something had finally brought some discipline into her youngest daughter's capricious life. "Bohemian" was how Rose Sloan—now Nettleton—tended to describe her.

But discipline of any sort was confining. Confinement didn't suit Daisy. It hadn't suited her father, either, which was why Rose Sloan had left to become Mrs. Archibald Nettleton when Daisy was a rebellious thirteen.

Her dad had claimed he understood.

Daisy never had. Everything she'd ever wanted or needed could be found in Galveston—or not far beyond her shores.

Daniel Coletti, now, dreamed of winning the Texas lottery and blowing town. His big plans included leaving the sea to conquer worlds not yet conquered. Which was another reason Daisy wasn't willing to bind herself to him with words that promised forever after.

Daisy scooped up bubbles with both hands and crushed them together until not an unbroken one remained. Her mind anywhere but on clean dishes, she pulled the plug and let the dishwater gurgle out. The soft sound was punctuated now and again by a solid thump from overhead—a reminder that Temple Wyatt was unpacking and making himself at home.

Daisy slanted a dark look at the ceiling. Maybe he had his Italian silk tie caught in his model 4790 fax machine. Wouldn't that be a sight? She smiled. Well, he'd better not wake Becca with all his thumping and bumping, or the great man himself could spend his evening logging in his daughter's reactions to her new surroundings. Dr. Rankin wanted every nuance, every response to Becca's change in habitat recorded in a journal.

A sigh escaped Daisy's lips. The truth was, there'd been precious little to log in Becca's diary. The poor mite hadn't even seemed to care that she'd been moved to new surroundings.

Shock was an awful thing, Daisy reflected. It held the mind captive. If this was hard for her to accept, it must be doubly hard for Wyatt as a parent. Perhaps she shouldn't be so resentful of him. Maybe his presence here would succeed in breaking through Becca's shell where all else had failed.

Not that Daisy imagined it would be an easy breakthrough. Even she awoke in a cold sweat some nights—hearing that speedboat, reliving the horror of the unexpected explosion. Unlike Becca, she hadn't been hit on the head or tossed about in the ocean. And what had Becca been doing when Daisy hauled anchor to leave? Daisy hadn't seen anything, but had Becca?

Suddenly restless, Daisy snatched up a sponge and scrubbed her kitchen counters until they gleamed. She'd bet cleanliness was next to godliness with Temple Wyatt. Wouldn't her mother adore that man? Wyatt had discipline enough to counteract a dozen Bohemian Daisy Sloans. He was probably a lot of things Rose's daughter was not. Neat, stylish and well organized, to mention a few. Come to think of it, frustrated as Daisy was over the changes in her life, a man like Wyatt must be more so. After all, he knew how little the landlady and the tenant had in common.

Nada. Zero. Zippo.

Wyatt had to have figured out before he showed up on her doorstep that they wouldn't get along for five minutes, let alone twenty-four hours a day.

In a way, though, Daisy admired him for placing his child on, at the very least, a par with his business. She didn't think either of her sisters' husbands would do that for their children. With those two, business always came first. Daisy remembered when her nephew, Jasmine's son, Talbot, was born. Jasmine had developed eclampsia. Her obstetrician put her in the hospital and took the baby early. Everyone in the family was worried sick—except Jasmine's husband. He was in Memphis closing a big industrial-park deal. Daisy had been the one charged with calling him. When she'd finally insisted they interrupt his meeting, he informed her that women had been having babies for years without men's interference. The jerk actually thought the statement made him an enlightened male.

Ha! Daisy knew then and there that if she'd been the one married to him, it would have been *sayonara* time.

Pausing in her cleaning frenzy, she wiggled her bare toes against the cool tile floor. She'd been comparing him with Wyatt. In fact, neither of her spoiled brothers-in-law would give up the easy life to live in a rented room like Wyatt was doing.

Violet's husband was never home. He'd never been to any of his kids' birthday parties. Too busy making money. *Things* were important to him.

Was Wyatt any different underneath?

It was only a guess, but Daisy thought he was. Still, she'd be willing to wager that he'd never lived a day in his life without amenities, either. Lots of amenities. Temple Wyatt had that "born to the manor" look about him.

She rinsed the sponge, tossed it back in its holder and stripped off her rubber gloves. Was he in for a shock at Sloan House, she mused as she squeezed lotion on her hands—soft hands which were one of her few concessions to femininity.

Daisy paused and smoothed one of those hands lovingly over the aged wood cabinet. Her family home had been built in the late 1800s. Before the great hurricane of

1900, the event by which everything on the Island was measured. Facilities in these old homes weren't necessarily up to modern standards. Despite all the work she'd already had done on her house, the pipes sometimes backed up and the electricity wasn't always reliable.

But Grandfather Sloan and his twin sister had been born upstairs in the master suite the very night of the hurricane. This house had withstood a storm that virtually leveled Galveston Island. Daisy loved the story. In truth, she loved every nook and cranny of Sloan House. Which meant she was willing to cope with whatever small inconveniences occurred while she earned the money to restore and renovate.

Why hadn't she thought of it that way before? She'd simply consider Temple Wyatt another inconvenience. Grinning, Daisy poured herself the last cup of coffee and rinsed out the pot. It was suddenly suspiciously quiet upstairs. She decided to peek in on her new boarder before heading to her room to take a long look at her finances. The shrimp Daniel claimed were running so well weren't going to come knocking at her door, but maybe she could lease out her boat for the remainder of the season. The idea popped into her head out of nowhere.

Of course, she wouldn't let just anyone handle the *Lazy Daisy*. There were one or two seamen she might consider. Daniel's younger brother, Sal, for one. He'd been saving up to buy his own craft. Sal was more serious and maybe more responsible than Daniel. Loren Bonner was another possibility. He'd been itching to take her boat out alone for a year now. But Aubrey wouldn't want his son giving up college to shrimp full-time—which pretty much left her with Sal. Daniel would have a blue-cow hissy fit if she stole Sal off his crew.

Daisy plodded up the curving stairs, careful not to spill her coffee. Leasing out the trawler to anyone would be traumatic. Her dad had bought the boat the summer Rose Sloan walked out on her family. Violet and Jasmine had had their boyfriends and parties. Daisy...well, the trawler had become her refuge, the one place she felt safe from the emotional storms. It was sort of like the role Dr. Rankin said she played for Rebecca. Funny, seen from that perspective, Rebecca's behavior made more sense.

Caught up in her thoughts, Daisy paused on the top step. The door to the smaller of the two rooms she'd rented out to Temple Wyatt stood open. A shock wave passed through Daisy like a school of minnows swimming upstream. Her Ivy League boarder was no longer wearing a jacket and tie. He'd changed into soft blue jeans, deck shoes without socks and a short-sleeved pullover.

It was as if her breath stalled. Gripping the hot coffee cup, Daisy forgot her finances and stared at Wyatt's tousled sun-streaked hair. She liked him better this way, looking less than perfect, as he struggled to connect a series of extension cords that didn't quite reach any of the room's outlets. A sheen of sweat darkened the fine golden hair on his forearms. For some reason, Daisy found that amusing. So the great Temple Wyatt could actually sweat. What a concept.

"Dammit!" Unaware he had an audience, Temple sat back on his heels and raked a hand through his hair, sending a new lock tumbling across his damp brow. His display of temper made him so much more human. Daisy enjoyed the sideshow so much she didn't realize he'd attached the cords to a four-way connector plucked from another box and had once again aimed the prongs toward an outlet.

"Don't!" she shouted as he plugged in the whole mess. Her warning came a fraction too late. Every light in the house winked out.

"What in hell?" Wyatt roared.

She heard him stumbling about in the dark. "Stop!" she yelled. "Let me get a kerosene lamp from my room." But that word of caution also came too late. Wyatt blundered into the hall, crashed into Daisy and sent hot coffee flying everywhere, including over her arm.

She couldn't contain a yelp of pain.

"What happened? Are you all right?" he asked as he clutched at her and made things worse.

Daisy didn't try to mask her irritation. "Besides overloading the circuits and frying all the fuses in the house, you mean?"

"I know that," he snapped. "I was asking if I hurt you."

"For your information, Wyatt, I was carrying a full cup of coffee when you stampeded out of your room and mowed me down."

"I'm sorry. Are you badly burned? Tell me where the circuit-breaker box is and I'll have the lights on in a jiffy. Then we'll get you taken care of."

"There *are* no circuit breakers," she told him. "At least not yet. The fuse box is downstairs in the kitchen closet." She hesitated. "I hope I still have some spares. Fuses are getting scarce as shrimp's toes on the Island. After the last hurricane, I had to order them from a hardware store in Houston. Spent two weeks without electricity."

"Whoa! Back up a minute," he said. "What do you mean, no circuit breakers?"

"Shh. You'll wake Becca."

"Sorry. And I wish you'd call her Rebecca. But, back to our problem. I thought all fuse boxes had been replaced with breakers years ago. Fuses are a fire hazard, you know."

"It's not your problem, bucko. It's my house." She made her way unerringly to the bathroom and felt around for the aloe spray. As she doctored her minor burns, she went on, "Fuses are okay if you don't put pennies behind them when they blow out. It helps," she drawled scathingly, "if they're not overloaded, too. What were you setting up in there? NASA Mission Control?"

"Very funny, Miss Sloan. I'm trying to set up an office so as not to interrupt the flow of my business. By the look of your financial statement, someone in this household had better be earning a living."

Daisy didn't like the underlying implication—that living under one roof made him responsible for her, made them beholden to each other. Her voice was cold. "I'll go get that lamp." With sure steps, she turned toward her bedroom.

"Hold on. There's greater danger of fire using a kerosene lamp. I have flashlights in my toolbox. Let me get them." Temple grasped her wrist to stop her.

Jet streams of heat shot up Daisy's bare arm. She was startled, and also a little amazed, by the fact that his hands weren't altogether smooth but slightly callused, as if from manual work. And he didn't smell all flowery and dandified like the uptown crowd, either. She detected a subtle scent of suede and maybe a hint of sage. To keep from showing that she was affected, she turned to sarcasm. "Is there some reason you're so hung up on fire, Dogberry?" An avid fan of little theater, Daisy used her pet term for people who made "much ado about nothing."

"Yes, as a matter of fact there is," Temple responded gruffly.

"Really?" Why had she wasted her breath on a clever theatrical reference? He probably hadn't recognized the bumbling constable's name—probably had never even seen the play.

His tense words cut through the darkness. "My father died pulling me out of a burning hotel in Aruba."

The breath slipped from Daisy's lungs in a hiss.

He went on, more to himself than her. "Dad intended to tear the old structure down. I thought it would be a lark to sleep in the penthouse that night, where I'd heard kings had slept. Like most dads who spend time on the road and rarely see their kids, mine did his best to indulge my whims."

She wanted to stop him; he sounded so anguished, so full of guilt. But she didn't know what to say.

"When my father discovered the elevator didn't work and there was only one usable set of stairs, he tried to talk me into pitching a tent outside. I wouldn't listen. I was twelve and unfortunately never far from my portable tape player. His warnings about the building being tinder dry didn't mean a thing to me. I wanted electricity so I could listen to my tapes. Later I heard there was a short in the wiring. It was the first and last trip I ever made with my father...." His voice tapered off into nothingness.

A knot of sorrow for the boy he'd been twisted in Daisy's stomach. You could certainly never tell about a man by looking. Temple Wyatt had lost so much. His father. His wife—first through divorce, and now she was gone forever. Goodness, his only child had been kidnapped; now that he finally had her back, she didn't even know him. No wonder he was suspicious of everyone and slow to trust.

"I'm sorry," she said quietly. "I didn't mean to bring up bad memories. Get your flashlights. I'm sure I have enough fuses on hand to change the lot."

For a moment he was silent, then she heard him swear under his breath. "Have you ever wondered if you're a jinx, Miss Sloan? Forget it. I don't usually unload my life story on strangers."

She'd be willing to bet he didn't. Temple Wyatt didn't seem the type to admit to any weakness. Not even a small one. And she'd guess that he generally didn't accept sympathy, either, no matter how well meant. But he was right on target about their being strangers. Which was, in the end, what made Daisy bite her tongue and keep further compassionate words to herself.

She thought about him, though, in the few short minutes he was gone to get the flashlights. Wyatt was a man who fished in deeper more troubled waters than she'd ever suspected from their earlier encounters. It was plain to see he hadn't had the easy childhood she'd assumed.

Well, her sisters always accused her of shooting her mouth off first and asking questions later.

Temple returned, a flashlight in each hand. Their fingers brushed as he passed her one. Shaken by the suddenness of his touch, Daisy almost dropped hers.

"Careful," he cautioned. "Here, let me lead the way. I have the larger beam."

Again Daisy pulled from his grasp. "No need. I know the way blindfolded. This happens a lot during storms. I'll go alone."

"It does? Why haven't you had the place rewired, then?"

Daisy glared through the circle of light. "Oh, I can give you about eight thousand reasons. Which is, I believe, the last estimate in dollars for rewiring."

"Money well spent if you ask me."

"Nobody did. My banker has this funny quirk about depositors not spending funds they don't have. Stay put until I get back. And don't plug anything in when the lights come back on. Got it?"

Temple clicked his heels and bowed. "Yes, ma'am. But how will we discover the weak link in the system?"

From the landing below, her voice floated back. "Easy, Sherlock. Look in the mirror. Then repack half of those fancy electronic toys you unboxed."

Temple leaned over the railing to watch the progress of her flashlight. Quite the repertoire for a shrimper—from Shakespeare to that classic children's story, *The Water Babies*—right? Not to mention Sherlock Holmes. He sighed. Why hadn't his daughter bonded with someone more...predictable? Someone who wasn't so damned eccentric? Daisy Sloan was not only unconventional, she was careless. And careless spelled danger, of which the Wyatts had had enough.

Maybe he'd shell out part of the reward money, after all. With a few stipulations of course. Temple wondered what else this odd house on stilts needed to make it safe. Fuses, indeed! Even his resort in far-off Tonga had circuit breakers. Or had Daisy Sloan planned this display, hoping to put the bite on him? Like Miranda had done so many times.

The lights sprang to life, erasing unhappy memories. Temple blinked, closed his eyes and massaged away the strain. It had been a long tiring day. Perhaps he'd forget about setting up his office tonight and just hit the sack. His father used to say that everything looked better in the light of day. Of course, he'd never met Miss Shrimp Boat here.

Speak of the devil... Temple heard her whistling off-key as she took her sweet time getting back. On second thought, his optimism about daylight was probably misplaced.

Temple was still scowling when Daisy reached the top step.

"Now what?" she demanded. "I had a whole box of fuses. Nary a copper penny did I use. Just please refrain from plugging in all of those machines at one time."

"But I need all of them to run my business."

"Then pay a visit to the Strand. It might appeal to you since it was once the greatest backing center between New York and San Francisco. I'm sure someone there has commercial space they'd love to lease you."

"That isn't an option. My resorts are in different time zones. The staff needs access to me at all hours of the day or night."

"Twenty-four hours a day? But when do you sleep?" She sounded annoyed again.

"I'm a light sleeper. Insomniac might be a better word for it."

"Oh, great. That's what I hated at the hospital. People prowling around keeping me awake. I really wish you'd find another place to rent." As if to underline her statement, Daisy yawned. "Sorry," she muttered. "It's been a long day."

"I was just thinking that myself," he said, rubbing the back of his neck. "But if you don't mind, I'd still like to look in on Rebecca before I turn in."

She did mind. Her room looked like the wreck of the *Hesperus*. But he had those wounded shadows in his glacial blue eyes again. How could she, in good conscience, refuse him? "I, ah, no. I don't mind. Follow me."

"Thanks. I found her koala bear. Straylia, she calls him. One of my resort managers in Brisbane sent him to her. She was too small to pronounce Australia." He smiled. "Let me get him. I'd like her to have the bear when she wakes up in the morning. Who knows, it may trigger some memory. Dr. Rankin said she'll be most susceptible to remembering during the first few minutes after waking."

Daisy nodded absently. Why hadn't Dr. Rankin told her that?

"This way," she mumbled, discreetly trying to snatch up the pair of shorts and grimy tank top she'd discarded on the floor earlier. At least she'd picked up the tackle box and put it on top of the chifforobe. She hadn't wanted Becca to get hurt on any of the barbed hooks. For sure, if Wyatt was planning on making a habit of traipsing through her bedroom every night, she'd have to change her ways.

With a wry face, Daisy hurried past the bed, which still sat unmade. Making her bed wasn't any higher on her list of priorities than washing dishes. But Wyatt didn't say a word about the clutter. Daisy wished she knew what he was thinking.

In truth, Temple gave no more than a cursory glance at the big four-poster bed. His eyes were glued to the wall of windows, through which a giant moon glowed, looking for all the world as if you could reach out and touch it. The two opposite walls were paneled in some dark wood. The fourth held an inviting brick fireplace. On the polished teak mantel sat a replica of a three-masted clipper. There were others, but the one on the mantel was the most impressive. His gaze straying to it again, Temple ran smack into Daisy. He hadn't seen her stop.

She grasped his arm and held a warning finger to her lips.

Temple stiffened and drew back. Her hands were warm, and—surprisingly—well kept. Frowning, he clutched the koala to his chest as he breathed in the subtle scent of magnolias the woman exuded. Moonlight and magnolias were two weaknesses of his. Weaknesses he hadn't indulged in for so long he was surprised his body remembered how to react. And who would've thought he'd feel this punch to his midsection at the touch of some...some seafaring siren? It darn sure wasn't smart. Not when the siren clearly belonged to one of the rough-and-tumble pirates of Penzance.

"You needn't act so horrified." Daisy saw the way he'd studied her room, and she'd seen the look on his face. "I'm well aware my bedroom isn't up to Wyatt Resorts standards. Just don't say a word. Not one word. I'll give you a few minutes in here with Becca now, but tomorrow, we'll set down some rules for visitation."

Rules. Temple was jolted out of his stupor long enough to nod and turn his gaze to the bed where his daughter lay curled, sucking her thumb. The slight sexual stirring he'd experienced toward Daisy had faded, and in its place he felt a surge of love for his curly-haired daughter that weakened his knees. With shaking hands, he bent and propped the bear against the bed rail.

Temple was glad to see the sturdy oak rails on either side of the narrow bed, although he hadn't liked seeing his daughter in a crib at the hospital. She was too big for a crib. Too independent. And if she'd been herself, Rebecca would have been the first to object to being treated like a baby. Nevertheless, after all she'd been through,

Temple knew he'd rest easier with the rails. He didn't want her falling out of bed. A strange bed, in a strange house. Rebecca had never liked sleeping anywhere but in her own bed. Or rather, she used to feel that way. But look at her now. Sound asleep.

He knelt, reached out a hand to touch her bright golden curls, then drew back without disturbing her. An unpracticed prayer stumbled through his mind.

Daisy saw the motion and his hesitation. She experienced his anguish and felt compelled to help. "Her medical team is quite sure she'll regain her memory and her speech," Daisy whispered. "It's only a matter of time."

Temple glanced up. "And then I'll have to find a way to tell her about her mother," he said haltingly. "What'll happen then? Will she have a relapse? Lose her speech again?" His fingers curled around the wood railing. "Will you have answers for my daughter *then* Miss Sloan?"

Daisy fell silent. She felt a shiver of unease and rubbed her arms to ward off the chill. He still thought she knew more about the accident than she was telling. But she didn't. "Stay a bit longer if you like, but try not to wake her," she said in a soft voice. Then she left.

SOME TEN MINUTES LATER, when Temple walked back into her room, Daisy Sloan was seated at a battered roll-top desk. The top half of an old buoy had been made into a lamp that hung down and shed light over her right shoulder. As he approached, she picked up a worn brass propeller, about five inches in diameter, and plunked it down on the papers she'd been sorting.

Bills, Temple decided when he drew closer. A passel of them by the look of it. And she looked pale in the light. Exhausted. Vulnerable. Which dumbfounded him. He'd pegged her as the tough sort. The type to play the best odds and always come out on top. Now he wasn't so sure.

When he'd first entered the room, he'd intended to press her about the accident. To hammer at her until she broke down and told him what she'd been holding back. The question that came out of his mouth, however, made no reference to the accident. "What time is Rebecca likely to be up in the morning, Miss Sloan?" Temple saw that she'd expected something else, too, and that she was relieved.

Daisy smiled. The smile transformed her face and chased the fatigue from her eyes. Temple felt momentarily bewildered, but glad he'd let instinct lead him.

"Rebecca's been waking between six-thirty and seven," Daisy said, glancing up at the battered ship's clock that graced the wall above her desk. "Oh, and don't be concerned if she cries out in the night." A slight frown creased her brow. "I'm never sure if she's awake during those spells. The nurses didn't think so. She seems to drift off again if I just rock her." Daisy's brow lost its pucker. "Those nightmares have decreased in the past week. Now if we can just keep them on the run..." Her smile spread. "Call me Daisy, please. After all, we're going to share a bathroom. Frankly it makes me nervous sharing a bath with someone who calls me Miss Sloan." She mimicked his serious tone.

"Share a..." Temple flushed. "Miss Sloan," he stammered, "I—"

Daisy laughed aloud. "See? There you go again. Well, work on it tonight—seeing that you're an insomniac and you don't have your fax machine to keep you entertained."

She tipped back in her chair and let her laughter flow freely. Then she sat upright and said, "Good night,

Wyatt. You'll find your room in perfect order. I stripped that bed today and remade it with clean sheets myself. Oh, and Becca helped. So you won't find a snake waiting beneath the covers. Besides, I didn't know you'd be its occupant.''

Curious feelings washed over Temple as he pictured Daisy Sloan's small capable suntanned fingers smoothing the crisp sheets of his bed. Suddenly it wasn't his sheets her hands were caressing but his skin, and the air between them seemed to grow thick and warm.

Did she know what he was thinking? He tugged at the neck of his knit shirt, his eyes seeking a quick exit.

It was stress, he told himself. Caused by long months of worry over Rebecca and then finding her in shock, his ex-wife probably dead. Miranda's lovely face haunted him at night. Something about this story didn't ring true. He and Miranda had their differences, but he couldn't believe she'd put herself or their daughter in danger. He edged back toward the door until he felt the cooler air from the hallway. It cooled his skin and restored his sense of logic.

Why should he trust this woman? He was here only because the kangaroo court in this town was biased in her favor. Maybe he wouldn't share her damned bathroom. There was always the filling station down at the corner.

No way in hell did he plan to get chummy enough to be on a first-name basis—even though he'd suggested it earlier himself. *Daisy*. The name was all wrong for her. Someone named Daisy should be sweet. Sweet, wide-eyed, delicate. Not a tough babe who hauled in smelly shrimp nets out in a cove called Rum Row. Judging by her own words, anyone who did that courted trouble. Her mother would have done better to name her Pandora. Troublemaker. Pain-in-the-ass troublemaker, at that.

Temple roused himself to find that he was hovering in her doorway, sweating. He brushed his palms down the sides of his jeans to rid himself of the shivery sensation left by her melodious laughter. She was his landlady. Period. Nothing more. And there was distinct reluctance on both sides of this arrangement.

"Good night, Miss Sloan," he said stiffly. Then he was out the door and gone.

Daisy stared after him. Well, if that didn't beat all. For a minute she'd thought there was a slim possibility Temple Wyatt might turn out to be an okay guy. Apparently not. Oh, well, why did she care? It wasn't as if she needed him for a friend or anything.

Daisy yawned twice in a row, then shook herself awake enough to return to the task of figuring how to pay her bills.

Two hours later, after covering half a notebook with numbers, it became painfully evident that, to make ends meet, she did need Wyatt's rent money.

Daisy Sloan didn't like needing anyone. She threw her pencil down on the pile of bills and spent the next hour staring disconsolately at the moon. At last she picked up the phone and dialed Sal Coletti—to offer him her boat. He wouldn't mind being awakened for a reason like that.

And Daisy wouldn't need Temple Wyatt nearly so much if she could get her boat back on the water.

CHAPTER FIVE

WARM RAYS OF SUNLIGHT streamed in through the window in Daisy's bedroom and awakened her from a dream. She sat up and squinted, disoriented by the familiarity of her own room. Having grown accustomed to tossing about on the hard narrow hospital cot, Daisy couldn't believe she'd slept so soundly last night. She would have snuggled back to enjoy it a moment longer except that her thoughts suddenly leapfrogged to the reason she'd been bunking at the hospital.

Becca. Daisy stopped in the middle of a stretch. "Look out, Troublemaker," she warned the cat occupying the end of her bed. She threw back the covers, her feet already on the floor feeling for evasive slippers.

Panic gripped her. Not once during the night had Becca cried out. Nor was there a peep out of her now. And the time must be—what? Daisy grabbed for the captain's desk clock that sat beside her bed. It had been one of her father's prized possessions. The worn gold hands showed a few minutes after eight.

Daisy dashed for the alcove. She skidded to a stop beneath the archway, awash with relief. Becca was sitting up in bed, awake and well. Blond curly locks tumbled about her tiny face, and blue eyes stared solemnly at Daisy over the top of the fat brown koala bear.

A smile began at Daisy's toes and worked its way up. Did Becca recognize the stuffed toy? Was this the breakthrough the doctors had hoped for? Her heart pounded excitedly. Could recovery be this simple? If so, Daisy's tenure as Temple Wyatt's landlady would come to an abrupt end. Why did the notion cause her a moment's regret? After all, what mattered most was that Becca emerge from her shell, a whole and happy child.

Bending slowly, Daisy pushed visions of the child's father aside. She lowered the bed rail and gently combed her fingers through Becca's curls. "Good morning, sweetheart. Look who's come to visit. Is it Straylia?"

Becca promptly stuck a thumb in her mouth and held up her other arm, begging Daisy to pick her up. Straylia fell off her lap and hit the floor.

"Uh-oh." Even as Daisy said the words and knelt to retrieve the bear, she froze and stared at Becca. Was it her imagination, or had the girl exclaimed, "Uh-oh," too? Hardly daring to hope, Daisy got slowly to her feet, waiting to see if the sound would be repeated.

Instead, Becca lunged for the bear and almost fell out of bed.

As bad luck would have it, the girl's father chose that moment to make an appearance. Cellular phone glued to his ear, Wyatt strode through the door in time to see his daughter take a header.

"Catch her!" he shouted. Dropping the cordless phone, he covered the distance to the bed in one giant leap.

The suddenness of his move frightened Becca, and she began to scream.

Daisy, who'd lunged at the same time, slipped and landed ignominiously at Wyatt's feet. At least she'd succeeded in preventing Becca's fall.

The terror on his daughter's face drove Temple back again. He tripped over Daisy's fox terrier, who'd stuck his nose in to investigate the commotion. Temple wavered, windmilled his arms, but still lost his footing. He landed hard, his left hip crushing the case of his cellular phone.

Pipsqueak yelped and dashed into a corner.

Over the din of his barking and Becca's wailing, Daisy heard the unmistakable crack of plastic. She winced.

Wyatt grimaced in pain.

"Good going, Your Grace," she grumbled at Wyatt's lack of poise as she scrambled toward the startled but uninjured child. Pulling Becca into her arms, Daisy crawled on her knees to the far corner of the room. "Quiet, Pipsqueak," she ordered the dog in the same tone she'd used to scold the man.

Temple's left hip was so painful he wasn't sure it would ever function again. But even if he'd been mortally wounded, no way would he allow Daisy Sloan or anyone else to call his sweet little daughter names.

"Why is it, Miss Sloan," he managed at last through clenched teeth, "that you can't ever seem to use anyone's proper name? My daughter is *Rebecca*. Not Becca and not Pipsqueak." Propping himself up on one elbow, he frowned. "Why's she still crying? Is she hurt? Hungry? I'll bet that's it. Rebecca's always starving when she wakes up." He grasped the bed and tried to stand, but couldn't and dropped back to the rug with a moan.

Daisy stared at the man stretched out on her pink braided rug. "For your information," she drawled, "I didn't call her Pipsqueak. I was talking to my dog."

Temple blinked. "Dog?" He looked around, then drew back from the animal who'd quit barking, but now stood behind him with bared teeth and a growl bigger than the pooch himself.

"I do see a decided resemblance to his owner," he muttered. Then louder, "Have you been inoculated against rabies? *Both* of you?"

Vexed, Daisy set Becca aside, stood and reached out a hand to help Wyatt up. As if dealing with a stubborn shrimp net, she gave a good solid yank on Temple's arm.

"Ow!" he bellowed, clutching his left hip, which refused to straighten. In a half crouch, he suddenly choked on what he'd been about to say. From this angle, the view had changed dramatically. Temple found himself staring through his shapely landlady's almost transparent white cotton nightie.

Daisy heard his loud gulp. She noticed the problem at once. Not only did she release his hand, but she shoved him back to the floor and took satisfaction in hearing him groan. Gathering up the child and her stuffed toy, Daisy stepped over Wyatt's writhing body and swept from the room.

By the time he'd recovered enough to hobble after her, Daisy had donned her robe. Still clutching his daughter, she stomped down the curved staircase.

Temple clung to her bedroom door and measured the angry set of her shoulders. "Wait!" he called. "I apologize."

Shaken and embarrassed, Daisy continued toward the kitchen. Temple Wyatt was a lecher. If he tried something like that again, he'd be feeling pain in more than his hip.

Once in the kitchen, however, she stopped short. A mouth-watering cinnamon aroma wafted from her oven. Whatever could it be? Daisy hadn't shopped for groceries in more than a month.

Closer inspection revealed a quiche on the top rack, and on the lower a pan of cinnamon rolls. Not pop-from-the-can cinnamon rolls, either. These looked home-made.

Still in Daisy's arms, Becca leaned forward and reached a small hand toward the pan of rolls. Daisy jumped back just in time to keep Becca from burning her fingers.

The girl buried her face in Straylia and sobbed as if her heart would break.

Even more of a shock than finding fresh-baked goods in her oven, was Becca's reaction. Nothing they'd fixed her at the hospital held any interest for her. Not pizza, not hamburgers, not even ice cream. None of the foods that most kids loved.

"Oh, sweetie." Convinced they were making head-way, Daisy danced Becca around the room. "I'm with you. They look dee-licious. Mrs. Parsons from next door must've brought them over. Bless her. Look, Becca— when this bell rings, they'll be ready." She pointed out the timer, its hands nearly at zero, before resuming their dance.

In the midst of their two-step, Temple limped into the room. He tossed the mangled pieces of his cellular phone on the counter, plucked a pair of oven mitts from a drawer and said authoritatively, "Step aside, please. My breakfast is almost done."

"Yours?" Daisy's feet stopped moving.

"Yep. That was one of the terms of our agreement, right? I do my own cooking?"

Daisy didn't reply. She could practically taste those rolls.

"No wonder you're skinny as a post," he muttered. "All you had in the house was a chunk of moldy cheese. I've already been to the store and back."

Daisy's stomach tensed as he took out the quiche and set it on the counter, followed by the delicious-smelling rolls. But now Becca no longer seemed to want them; she did her best to shinny up Daisy's torso and get as far away from the man as possible.

Daisy jiggled the child to calm her. "You made these?" she asked Wyatt, sounding skeptical.

"You think it was a ghost?" Temple stripped off the mitts and set them aside.

She shook her head, licking her lips when he picked up a saucepan of glaze and proceeded to drizzle frosting over the hot rolls. She hadn't even noticed the pan on the back burner.

"This, and a tall glass of milk, is Rebecca's favorite breakfast," he said, eyeing his daughter sadly. "I used to fix it on weekends when I was home." With a resigned shrug he put the pan in the sink and ran it full of water. Then he opened the refrigerator and brought out a carton of milk. After filling the two glasses that were on the counter, he hesitated, and reached into the cupboard for a third glass. Cocking an eyebrow, he said, "You're welcome to share. I made plenty."

Daisy feigned disinterest. "I'm not hungry," she declared. But it was impossible for either adult to ignore the loud rumble of her stomach.

"Look, I really am sorry about what happened upstairs. It won't happen again." Temple looked Daisy in the eye and handed her a glass of milk. He hoped she'd take it as a peace offering. "I'm afraid I haven't lived with a woman in a good long while."

"And you're not *living with* one now." Daisy snatched the glass, plunked Becca into a chair and placed the glass in front of her. She continued to glare at him as she seated herself. "I thought you said your mother took care of Becca."

"*Rebecca,*" he reminded Daisy patiently. "I said that's where she was when Miranda took off with her. Miranda claimed it upset her to visit my penthouse—she thought it should've come to her in the divorce settlement." Casting a glance toward his daughter, he murmured, "I wish now I'd given her the damned place."

"Sure you do," Daisy shot back. "Kids usually come after money in a divorce."

"I beg your pardon," Temple said angrily. "Rebecca was *always* my first consideration. But Miranda's trips to court invariably had to do with money. I pressed her to continue the visits—I didn't care where. Miranda's parents weren't in very good health, so my mother offered her town house. The visits went okay for about four months. I had no reason to believe that particular day would be any different. Neither did my mother. Miranda usually showed up after lunch and spent an hour or two playing with Rebecca. She rarely stayed long."

He took down plates and cut three pieces of quiche. "That visit Rebecca wanted chocolate ice cream. Miranda didn't approve of sweets, but she said her health club made a carrot shake." He shook his head as he served up the rolls. "I think it was spur of the moment. That's how Miranda was. My mother blames herself. Frankly I probably would've let her take Rebecca, too." Looking distant, he set a plate in front of Daisy.

She tore off a hunk of the roll and tested it to make sure it wasn't too hot before she gave it to Becca. Daisy didn't *want* to feel sorry for Temple Wyatt. She wanted to think he deserved whatever he'd been dealt by his ex-wife; however, she doubted it. Plus, the picture she was beginning to get of Miranda matched Daisy's own mother a little too closely.

"We don't need to make idle conversation about your divorce," she said primly, keeping her gaze on the quiche she was cutting up for Becca. "And from here on, ask before you enter my room." She had to insist on it for her own preservation.

Temple wadded his napkin into a ball. "All right," he said, after studying her at length. "I've noticed you're skittish around men. Why? Is your boyfriend jealous?"

Daisy hadn't intended to eat any of his blasted food, but it had looked so good. She'd barely sneaked a bite of roll and now she choked on it. "I don't have a boyfriend," she informed him the minute she drew a clear breath.

"What's Coletti? Last night he sounded plenty possessive."

"Yes, well, Daniel has big ideas about a lot of things. But whatever our relationship, it doesn't concern you. You rent rooms from me. Nothing more."

His eyes still bored through her with the intensity of a laser.

Flushing, Daisy concentrated on feeding Becca the last of the quiche. "Look at that, will you?" she said, indicating Becca's empty plate. "I think this is the most I've ever seen her eat. If you'll tell me what else she likes, I'll go for groceries right after I bathe her."

Temple set his fork aside and rubbed a thumb thoughtfully across his lips. "She used to like flaming things—peach flambé, cherries jubilee, baked Alaska. Of course I limited her rich foods." He smiled at his daughter. "She was fond of mahi mahi dipped in basil and butter. Oh, and artichoke hearts. Then there's kiwi fruit, endive and banana salad."

Daisy's mouth fell open and her eyes rounded. "Yuck." She smoothed a hand over Becca's curls. "Are you putting me on?"

Wyatt shook his head. "It tasted a hell of a lot better than the wheatgerm and brown rice Miranda tried to serve her."

Daisy pushed back from the table and stood. "Tonight she'll get jambalaya. Tomorrow, maybe, blackened redfish. I cook Cajun."

"I thought you Texans were into beef, thick cut and rare."

She snorted. "Texas. I've been meaning to visit there someday."

Temple looked confused.

Grinning, Daisy balanced Becca on her hip and started for the door. "Galveston's an island. 'A waif of the ocean waiting to be reclaimed'—that's what one historian called it in the nineteenth century." She paused. "Didn't your Yankee textbooks tell you anything? Tax collectors and our esteemed governor are the only ones who consider us part of Texas."

Temple watched her dramatic exit. He couldn't help being irritated by her flippancy. But he liked the sway of her hips beneath that old jersey robe. The woman was an enigma. A sailor with perfume and soft hands. He found himself wondering about the rest of her family. Had one of her ancestors been Acadian? Or maybe Creole? It might explain her unusual coloring—that mop of tight blond curls and the darker eyebrows. If Temple had to put a color to her eyes, he'd call them burnt umber. Her temper, though, defied description.

He sat back and poured himself another glass of milk. It wouldn't do to think about her at all. He'd been burned once. Wasn't once enough? He should stick to building resorts. It was safer. Speaking of building, he wanted someone to check the wiring in this old house.

After he cleaned up his mess in the kitchen, the first thing he needed to do was get his phone fixed. On second thought, if the islanders were as tightknit as his landlady insinuated, he'd better just buy a new one, rather than try explaining what had happened to his. Potentially embarrassing—for both of them.

Temple's mind kept straying to Daisy Sloan. She could deny all she wanted having a relationship with that muscle-bound Coletti. But Temple had seen the look in his eye. A smart man wouldn't risk having his nose bashed in to test the waters. No siree!

IT WAS AFTERNOON before Daisy's path crossed Temple's again. Becca was napping, and Daisy was storing her groceries when Wyatt walked in, a spanking new cellular phone at his ear.

He reached around her, opened the refrigerator and shifted things until he came up with a bottle of mineral water.

Daisy sniffed as she donned her rubber gloves. Her feelings on the subject of mineral water were easily read. It was a sissy drink. "Galveston's drinking water is the best in the world," she stated flatly.

Temple uncapped the bottle, tipped back his head and drank thirstily before he straightened and let the phone slide down his arm into his hand. In a fluid motion that spoke of practice, he hit the off button and tossed the instrument down on the counter.

"What's with these local contractors?" he complained as he recapped the bottle. "Don't they need money?"

Daisy glanced up from the bowl of shrimp she'd begun to devein. She wiped her chin across her shoulder and darted him a puzzled look. "What are you building?"

"Nothing. Your wiring is deplorable. I can't function without computers and a fax. Not to mention the safety risks in this place. You'd think these guys would beat a path to the door. No one'll give me the time of day, let alone an estimate."

"You're asking for estimates to rewire *my* house? What gall. No wonder no one'll talk to you."

"I said I'd pay cash up front."

"I pay my own way." She tapped a wet-gloved thumb to her breast. "Everybody on the Island knows that."

"Then they must know you haven't earned a dime this month. Are you going to let pride get in the way of good sense?"

"Now, wait just a darn minute," she said as a shrimp shot through her fingers and landed in the sink. "How would you like it if I waltzed into your house and started calling electricians?"

"You wouldn't have to. The wiring in my house is perfect." He sidled past her and returned the bottle of water to the fridge.

"Brother!" She jabbed the knife into the belly of a fat shrimp and blew at her bangs, which had fallen over her eyes. "In case it went over your pointed head, Wyatt, I got along *fine* before you blew into town."

"Are you saying you don't want this house rewired? You told me you'd had an estimate of eight thousand dollars." He stepped forward and sighed. "Give me that shrimp. You're butchering the damned thing." He took the glistening shrimp out of her hands and deveined it with a quick flick of his thumb.

Daisy saw purple, then red. "I can devein shrimp that way. It's just hard on fingernails." She felt like dumping the whole bowlful over his head. He was saved by the musical chime of his telephone. As he rinsed his hands and picked it up, she wondered if he had any idea how close he'd come to wearing the main ingredient for her jambalaya.

He talked business for a few minutes while Daisy fumed silently and mutilated seven more shrimp. The instant he clicked off, she turned from the sink and let him have it with both barrels. "You just don't get it, do you? You can't bulldoze your way into my home and take charge. I'll wire this house when I can pay for it. Not before."

A look of surprise crossed his face as he closed the phone and clipped it to his belt. "I thought you'd be pleased."

"Well, I'm not." She whirled back and ran water over the shrimp, her body tense.

"I can see that." Temple stepped up behind her. After a moment's hesitation, he placed both hands on her shoulders and massaged the tense cords that lay along her neck. "You refused the reward," he said quietly. "Is it so terrible of me to want to help someone who's put her life on hold for my daughter?"

Daisy stiffened a moment, then she relaxed and let the lethargy wrought by his clever fingers steal over her. "I guess not," she murmured. "If that's really what's behind your offer. I'm afraid I thought you were motivated by something less charitable. Like personal profit."

A wave of guilt swept over Temple. Had the art of saying what needed to be said to get what he wanted in business become so second nature that he let it spill over into his personal life? She had him dead to rights. In the beginning his main purpose had been to keep his business operations running smoothly while he suffered through his self-imposed exile. Now, feeling the softness of her flesh under his hands and smelling the subtle scent of magnolias on her skin, the reasons blurred.

However, he was saved a confession when Daniel Coletti burst through the kitchen door without knocking. A dirty, bloody, smelly Daniel Coletti.

Temple found himself recoiling from the odor of dead fish or, in Daniel's case, probably dead shrimp. At any rate, the smell was godawful.

Daisy took a step toward him, then she, too, pinched her nose. "Ugh! Why haven't you gone home to shower?" Suddenly she stiffened. "Has something bad happened on the wharf?"

"You bet it has, babe." Dark eyes glittered with anger. "I understand you called last night and offered Sal your boat. What are you trying to do? Steal my help?"

"You know Sal wants his own boat," she said defensively. "He almost has enough saved. He wouldn't be hauling nets for you next season, anyway."

"Next season," he snapped. "Not this season."

"Could we continue our discussion out on the back porch?" Daisy asked, her chin jutting to a stubborn angle. "I've had my fill of men ordering me about today."

Daniel's lip curled in a sneer. "I'll just bet you have." His gaze shifted to Temple's hand, still resting on Daisy's shoulder. "I got eyes, babe. I can see what's goin' on between you and the prissy dude."

Temple snatched his hand back, at the same time drawing himself up to his full six feet. "Who are you calling prissy? I believe the lady asked you to step outside." He took a menacing step toward Daniel.

Daisy slid between them. "Pulleeze!" she drawled. "Give me a break, you two." She motioned Daniel out and glared at Temple. "I am perfectly capable of handling this. I don't need a man to fight my battles. The deal on leasing the *Lazy Daisy* is between me and Sal. It doesn't concern *anyone* else."

The doorknob refused to give under Daniel's slimy hand, even though he yanked at it several times. "Sal's just a kid. He's already more than half in love with you, Daisy. But maybe you like having a school of men panting at your heels." His gaze swung to Temple.

Picking up a dish towel, Daisy strode past the burly shrimper. With a flourish, she wiped the knob, then jerked the door open. "Goodbye, Daniel. Go home and clean up. Rethink what you're saying before you destroy a life-long friendship."

"I thought we were more than friends." He threw a last bitter glance at Temple before he stalked out.

Daisy's voice turned gentle as she followed him. "Let friendship be enough, Daniel. Your soul's too restless for me. Mine finds peace standing still."

A look of chagrin creased his brow as he shifted from one foot to the other. "I don't want to die on a trawler like my old man did. Just once in my life I'd like to come home from work not smelling like a dead mackerel."

"I know that, Daniel. And you should find a way to do that."

"I've got almost enough saved for me and Sal to get outta here. Enough to take you, too."

"I love it here. Anyway, I'm not *selling* your brother my boat. I offered to lease it to him for the rest of the season. You'd really better go, Daniel. That muck is drying on your skin."

"Yeah, I'll go. But I'll be back. So don't be going to the bank with your part of Sal's catch. If I can't talk sense into him, I'll beat it into him."

Daisy crossed her arms. She leaned against the screen door. "Listen to you, Daniel. You've got a man's head and a boy's brain."

At the bottom of the steep steps, Daniel's irritation overflowed. "I suppose you think you've found your ideal man in Wyatt. If you figure Mr. Megabucks will sink roots in Galveston, you're nuts. But don't come crying to me when he breaks your heart." Spinning on his heel, Daniel stalked off toward the pier where he'd tied his small runabout.

Daisy's fingers curled into her palms. "I don't know what you mean, Daniel Coletti! I'm my own woman! You take that back!"

"You think I'm blind?" he yelled over the roar of his runabout's motor. "I saw you two. Thick as mosquitoes over a shrimp hold."

"Men!" Daisy growled as she stormed inside. They were all petulant boys when women didn't fall into line to suit them. Well, tough. She would've slammed the door had she not seen Temple at the sink, a satisfied smirk twitching his lips. She caught the door in time and closed it quietly. "Don't you have something better to do than hang out in my kitchen?" she demanded.

He grinned and held up the bowl of shrimp. "I thought someone should finish these. Frankly I wasn't sure Coletti wouldn't haul you off by your hair."

"Not bloody likely. Quit smirking and go foreclose on somebody's resort."

"I try to keep them afloat. I don't foreclose on them."

"Out of my kitchen, Wyatt, or I'll put a double shot of Tabasco in your jambalaya."

His laughter was full and deep. "I thought you didn't feed your boarders."

She stared at his well-shaped mouth a moment, tucked a loose strand of hair behind one ear and coughed. "Consider it a fair trade for the leftover cinnamon rolls."

Temple felt himself being pulled into her warm dark eyes, and he swallowed his laughter. "Coletti's right," he muttered. "I *would* break your heart."

By the time Daisy gathered her wits, she heard his tread on the stairs. Stepping into the hall, she shouted after him, "You arrogant jerk! What makes you think I'd let someone with your conceit get anywhere *near* my heart?"

"I don't know. Maybe because I'm having a run of bad luck lately."

"Of all the egotistical . . ."

While she ranted, he continued upward. Outside his bedroom, he paused and snapped his fingers. "Forgot to tell you," he called down. "While you were chasing Danny-boy, I got hold of your electrician, Jeb. I convinced him you were ready for that new wiring. He'll have a crew here early tomorrow." Temple saw that she was gearing up to explode. "Listen. I transferred funds from my bank to yours. It gives you complete control of the project." With that, he went inside and closed the door.

Daisy would've followed him and settled the money issue once and for all, but Becca cried out. Stomping upstairs, she smacked on the lights in her bedroom as Wyatt's fax machine whirred—and another fuse blew. Dammit! She did need new wiring. But she hated being indebted to anyone—especially to that overbearing resort mogul. She'd already told him she didn't have a price.

Maybe she could call Jeb and delay the work until after Becca made her breakthrough, Daisy thought as she rushed into the alcove. The child stopped crying instantly and held up her arms. So, no breakthrough yet. Daisy was still Becca's anchor. That meant she wasn't going to be rid of Wyatt and his equipment anytime soon.

As she settled Becca on her hip, another thought struck. Island gossip had probably already made the rounds about that blasted money he'd put in her account. She frowned. No way would she take money for saving this child.

Day care now—that was a different matter. Wyatt probably shelled out plenty for summer day care. Eight thousand dollars would buy a lot of baby-sitting. A Cadillac job. And she'd pay him back the balance with her next income tax refund. Satisfied she'd hit upon a solution, Daisy took Becca downstairs to play.

CHAPTER SIX

DAISY FOUND it wasn't easy being the perfect baby-sitter. She knew next to nothing about what kept kids occupied eight to ten hours a day. Inside, they lacked the tide pools and sea creatures that had once held Becca's interest. So she'd picked up a few toys to entertain her, instead. Granted, not the caliber her sisters bought their kids at FAO Schwartz, but she'd selected a few simple sticker books, several puzzles, coloring books and a super-duper box of crayons. More colors than she remembered from her own childhood.

At first Becca didn't seem to know what to do with any of the things until Daisy showed her how to lick the stickers. During the few minutes she had her back turned slicing peppers and onions for the jambalaya, Becca stuck scratch-and-sniff stickers all over the table and fridge. They smelled ghastly, worse when mixed with the scent of onion. It was enough to make Daisy's eyes water.

She finished what she was doing, then soaked the stickers off. They were stubborn little buggers, too. But she triumphed, and settled Becca at the table with a pirate's coloring book next. Returning again to her cooking, Daisy had barely set the cast-iron pot on a back burner to simmer when she spied Becca munching on a purple crayon. From the colored rings around the kid's mouth, she'd already sampled a green one.

"Oh, no, baby!" Daisy snatched the box and read the fine print to see if the crayons were toxic. Hadn't she read about red and yellow dye? As Daisy pried what was left of the purple crayon from Becca's viselike grip, the girl began to kick and scream. Who'd have thought a five-year-old could be so tenacious? Or that she'd throw such a fit? Lord, but the neighbors would think she was killing someone.

Daisy's heart was already beating like a buoy bell in a high wind when Temple strode through the door and demanded to know why Rebecca was screaming and banging her head on the wall.

Daisy looked stricken. "She ate a crayon. Maybe more than one. I'm so sorry. If you stay here, I'll run and call Dr. Rankin."

Temple laughed. "All kids eat crayons."

"They do?" Daisy pulled her fingers from between Becca's lips and swept a lock of hair out of her own eyes.

"Well, I mean they do at first," he qualified. "It surprises me about Rebecca, though. From the time she was two, she'd sit quietly and color. She kept inside the lines, too," he said proudly. "At least she used to," he muttered as he paused to examine the outline of a pirate ship slashed through with purple, green and orange stripes. Something akin to sorrow flickered across his face and shadowed his eyes.

Every time she saw that look in Temple Wyatt's sky blue eyes, Daisy wanted to assure him that his daughter's present state was temporary. She said nothing, however, because Dr. Rankin's team hadn't given any guarantees that it was.

"You probably think all parents claim their kids are precocious," Temple said when he saw what appeared to be doubt etched on Daisy's face.

"I'm afraid I don't have many preconceived notions about kids." She dampened a washcloth and set to work scrubbing Becca's face clean of its rainbow hues. "I never baby-sat as a kid, and I rarely see my nieces and nephews."

"That's too bad." Temple flashed her a sympathetic glance. "Although, I didn't feel the same about my friends' kids as I do about my own. There's something humbling about the process of childbirth, especially when it's your child." He thrust his hands into his back pockets and gazed out the kitchen window at the brackish water lapping at the dock a short distance away.

Daisy lifted Becca to her hip long enough to stir the mixture on the stove. Was what he said true? Daisy had never thought Violet or Jasmine seemed particularly moved by the birth of their children—other than to dress their newborns like little dolls to show off. But then, look at the example they'd had to follow. Their mother hadn't been humbled by anything. Without remorse she'd walked away from her daughters. Just as Becca's birth mother had done.

Daisy slapped the lid on the pot and turned the gas flame to its lowest. "If motherhood is so great, why do so many moms just take off?"

Temple whirled from the window, surprised by her vehemence. "Are you asking why my marriage failed?"

"No." Daisy's breath caught. The raw pain was back in his eyes. Not wanting him to misunderstand, she blurted, "I...my own mother flew the coop. I always wondered how she could up and leave her kids like that." Her shrug was offhand—meant to hide how deep the hurt went.

Temple wasn't fooled. "Maybe it wasn't about you," he said quietly.

Daisy's temper flared. "My father, you mean? He was a wonderful gentle man. *She* wanted fancy clothes, a better house, a newer car. So she went out and found someone willing to give her those things. And she never looked back. At least not until my father had us raised."

His eyes narrowed. "So weren't you better off living with your dad?"

"You're darned tootin'. Only... he and my sisters forgave her." Daisy's eyes glistened unexpectedly with tears, and she spun away so he couldn't see.

Temple heard a decade of hurt in her last sentence. He wished he had the power and the knowledge to ease her pain, but he didn't. He'd been on both ends himself. Hurting and being hurt. "Forgiveness doesn't come easy," he said slowly, feeling the truth of it coil like a tight knot in his stomach.

Daisy turned back, her eyes clear again. "I wouldn't have figured you for a philosopher, Wyatt."

He massaged the back of his neck. "I spent the last hour on the phone with Miranda's parents. They asked a million questions I couldn't answer. Not that they'd listen. They've got a blind spot where their daughter's concerned."

"Oh, Lordy."

"Yeah. They want me to hire a boat and take a run out to Rum Row." He gazed into the distance again, looking troubled.

A shiver snaked up Daisy's spine as she recalled the speedboat that had seemed to vanish into thin air. She hugged Becca tight. "There's nothing out there but endless miles of white caps. The Coast Guard didn't turn up any identifiable debris. In those crosscurrents, it probably all washed out to sea. What do her folks think you'll find?"

He closed his eyes and dragged thumb and finger across both eyelids. "A miracle maybe. The kind I prayed for every night during the months she had Rebecca. I just wish I hadn't said such terrible things about Miranda. It's hard not to feel this . . . this superstitious fear that my thoughts might have killed her. That they cost Dwight and Ila their daughter."

On the spur of the moment, Daisy placed her free hand on his arm. His eyes flew open and their gazes clung for several seconds before she said lightly, "In some circles you might be that big a cheese, Wyatt. Not around here, though. The sea sort of lives by her own rules. Mere man doesn't have a whole lot of clout. So don't go beating yourself up. Okay?"

Temple couldn't help smiling. Daisy Sloan was trying to make him feel better—she was the last person he'd have expected to do that. Strangely enough, her back-handed attempt did lighten his mood. "Okay," he said, covering her hand with his larger one. Again he was shocked by uncommonly soft cool skin. He fought an impulse to carry those same fingers to his chest for warmth. The awkwardness of his feelings compelled him to switch subjects. "Whatever you're cooking is making me hungry. When's dinner?"

"Supper. We call the evening meal supper." She quickly withdrew her hand from beneath his and in a re-flex action wiped it down her shorts, hoping to rid her-self of the strange tingle. "And tonight its pretty plain," she said. "Jambalaya and French bread. Anything fan-cier, and you'll have to take a run uptown."

"It'll be fine, Daisy. What time?"

They were both surprised at how easily her first name rolled off his tongue. Temple recovered first. "Calling you Miss Sloan does seem ridiculous, given our present living arrangement. For Rebecca's sake, let's bury the hatchet. Will you call me Temple?''

She cleared a throat suddenly gone dry.

''Or stick with Wyatt,'' he said as he watched the red stain of embarrassment creep up her neck.

''Temple.'' She tried it out. ''It's an unusual name.''

His lips curved in a smile. ''It beats Taj Mahal. I was conceived there, so I'm told. Actually Taj is my legal name. Use it at your own risk. It caused me many a bloody playground fistfight, until my mother recognized the error of her hippie ways and finally began using Temple on school documents.''

She shook her head. ''Taj Mahal, huh? Isn't that a mausoleum? However do you suppose your parents...? I mean, can you imagine...?''

He coughed discreetly and her face erupted in flames.

''Forget what I said,'' she mumbled. ''This discussion has gone far afield from Becca eating crayons.''

''*Rebecca*. You have no idea how hard I argued to get my daughter a normal name. Miranda wanted something unpronounceable. 'Something transcendental.'''

Daisy bent her head and brushed her nose across the child's pugged one. ''Pardon me for saying so, but it doesn't sound as if you two were well suited.''

''I, uh, was ready to settle down. Mutual friends introduced us. Miranda was very beautiful. And very seductive.''

The blush crept higher on Daisy's neck. He'd made no mention of love. Obviously she was out of her league here. ''So, getting back to names, I suppose it's a good thing she didn't end up being named Moon River or something.''

''You mean Moon Unit? Not a chance. I wasn't the hippie. My parents were. Actually they weren't,'' he corrected. "They were upper middle class and they fell in with a trend during the early hippie days. Flower children dropping out and all that. My grandmother called it a phase, and she was right." He smiled ironically. "Mother would die if she dreamed I knew about this."

"I doubt we'll ever meet, so I sure won't tell. And Rebecca still won't like her name, you know. Her friends will have names like Jordan and Whitney, and she'll think Rebecca's old-fashioned." On failing to coax a reaction from the girl with that bit of wisdom, Daisy turned and rolled her eyes at the father.

Temple laughed. Then he sobered and gazed longingly at his daughter. "I'd give anything to see Rebecca complain about her name or anything else. I want her the way she was. Bright. Happy. Talkative. Perpetual motion of the mouth."

He shifted and looked away from the silent girl who had her head buried beneath Daisy's chin, her right thumb in her mouth. "It's almost as if she's a different child," he said, voice strained. "Rebecca never sucked her thumb. Not even as a baby. I couldn't sleep last night for wondering if she'd ever be the same again." His voice broke. "Will she ever be all right?"

Daisy's heart went out to him. How difficult it must be to see his daughter like this, so far beyond his reach. Lordy, he must feel helpless.

"Did you discuss those things with Dr. Rankin?" she asked suddenly, bending to show the child in her arms the black cat, Troublemaker, that had just sauntered in.

"No." A futile gesture followed Temple's admission. "Guess I was too busy being angry. I need to go talk with him again. Really talk."

"That'd be a good idea. The doc's a nice guy. Social Services wanted to put her in foster care, you know. Dr. Rankin fought them."

"I didn't know that." The pressure of the past few days closed in on Temple. He rotated his shoulders to ease the tightness there. "Sounds like I owe him for more than her medical care."

"Around here we don't keep score."

"I see." But he didn't. He honestly didn't know why she'd taken umbrage at his well-meant words. "Then why did you invite me to dinner in exchange for the breakfast I fixed? And why did you throw a fit about the rewiring?"

Visibly flustered, Daisy went to the stove and made a show of stirring the mixture, which had begun to thicken. "It's just different, that's all. It's because…you're a man and I'm a woman."

"Do tell." Temple hid a wry smile. "You strike me as a woman who believes in equality between the sexes."

"I do," she snapped. "Fixing dinner for breakfast is a fair trade."

"Ah. But if our positions were reversed, you wouldn't give me money to rewire my house."

"I would so!" she flared.

He watched her square her shoulders and angle her chin, and he decided to let well enough alone, instead of probing further. "Well, I'm glad we had this enlightening talk. What time is supper, did you say?"

"I didn't." After a brief silence, she shrugged. "Seven. Sharp."

"Yes, ma'am," he said, managing to sound humble. When he reached the door, he stopped and turned. "That's not seven bells or anything, is it? With all these ship's clocks around here, I want to be sure we're both working off Greenwich mean and not some weird nautical time."

Daisy rolled her eyes. "Go by your diamond-studded brass works, bucko. Seven o'clock, central time."

He glanced at the Rolex on his wrist. "A college-graduation gift from my mother," he muttered. "I did mention she'd reverted to type, didn't I?"

He tossed off a wave and ducked out. Daisy listened to his tread on the stairs. It did her heart good to glimpse another crack in his facade. Wiping a smug grin from her face, Daisy set Becca in a chair at the kitchen table and gave her a picture book.

Not long after that, she heard Temple come downstairs again. A moment later, the front door slammed. In the alley, an engine roared. Daisy hopped up and pulled the window curtain aside. She was in time to see him drive off.

"Hmm." She frowned. Of course he didn't owe her any explanations about where he was going or how he spent his days. On the other hand, she *was* the person looking after his child. What if something happened to Becca, er, Rebecca while he was out? Besides that, he was new in town. He didn't know the people or the places. Other than the hospital or Dr. Rankin. Maybe that was where he'd gone?

In the second or two it took her to drop the curtain, Daisy's irritation dissipated. It was a small island, and he was a big boy. Goodness, the man owned his own plane and jet-setted all over the world. Anyway, it was nothing to do with her if he skipped off to Timbuktu for a day.

Technically she was his landlady. Period. And even that was even more than she'd bargained for when she'd impulsively gone to bat for Rebecca.

Easy to say that his whereabouts were none of her business, but when seven o'clock rolled around and he hadn't yet returned, Daisy began to worry in earnest. Nothing in this town stayed open past six except bars and restaurants. She stared at the table she'd set so nicely for three. Surely he wouldn't go elsewhere to eat without giving her a call. Then again, she really didn't know him.

That was evident when she'd rummaged through Rebecca's suitcase earlier and found nothing but dresses with matching hats, purses and even shoes. Not one pair of shorts or jeans or long pants of any sort. Had it been an oversight, or did he expect his daughter to be a fashion plate twenty-four hours a day?

As if that wasn't annoying enough, her jambalaya was done to perfection. "Damn you, Temple Wyatt. Five more minutes and we're going to eat without you. Aren't we, kid?" There was no response from Becca.

Before even the first minute had passed, though, a car pulled up outside. Almost immediately sneakered feet pounded up her back steps.

Temple burst through the door. "Sorry," he breathed. "The time got away from me."

"No problem." Daisy rose and coolly walked across to the stove. "I haven't even put the French bread in the oven. Go wash up."

"Thanks. I'll be right back." He smiled at his daughter who was seated on the floor petting the cat. Her response was to bellow and scamper away to hide behind Daisy's legs. Temple sighed, his shoulders slumped as he backed away.

"Careful, sweetie," Daisy murmured to the girl, "I'm working with hot stuff here."

Becca ignored the plea and held up her arms, wanting to be picked up.

"I'll leave," Temple said. "I just wish she'd..." He swallowed hard, let the sentence hang and strode from the room.

Daisy picked Becca up and set her on the edge of the sink. "Come on, kiddo. We've gotta wash cat off your hands." When she said "cat," Daisy could have sworn the girl looked right at Troublemaker and then opened and closed her hand as if she wanted to touch the animal again. Her breath caught. Where was Temple? Was Rebecca's small act significant? She would've liked some corroboration on that and several other things that had happened today.

The minute Temple returned and they sat down to eat, she blurted, "I think Becca's aware of animals. This morning she seemed to react to the koala you brought. Just a minute ago I'd swear she responded to Troublemaker. That's my cat," she said when Temple looked blank. "I should have said something before you went to see Dr. Rankin. I, uh, assume that's where you spent the afternoon?"

"No. But I'll make it a point tomorrow. Are you positive? What did she do?"

Daisy slipped an ice cube into Becca's bowl of jambalaya to cool it more quickly. Where *had* he been for three hours if not with Dr. Rankin? Not that she cared personally, she reminded herself. It was general curiosity.

She frowned. "I'm not positive they're conscious reactions," she said as she ladled the shrimp stew into Temple's bowl. "Maybe it's only my wishful thinking."

"Mine, too. I'll call first thing to see if Dr. Rankin has time to talk. Until then, if you'd jot down what you saw in that journal you're keeping, it'll be easier to tell him exactly."

"Writing isn't as easy for me as telling, but sure, I'll try. Good heavens, look—her bowl is empty. She seems to like jambalaya." Daisy tipped it so he could see.

Temple stared. He'd barely taken a bite. "It's spicy enough to light up my nose. I know I said Rebecca liked flaming things, but I try to put out the fire first. Are you sure she didn't dump it on the floor?"

"You're not tied to the chair," Daisy said, her hackles rising as she ripped the foil off the loaf of garlic bread. "No one's forcing you to eat. Correct me if I'm wrong, but the way I remember it, you invited yourself to supper."

"I'm only teasing you." Temple might have said more, but he was interrupted by someone banging on the kitchen door. "Could it be lover boy?" Temple smirked. "Can't you picture his reaction when he sees us sharing a meal?" He calmly helped himself to two slices of bread.

Daisy rolled her eyes and called, "Come in." Then she lowered her voice. "Daniel isn't a violent man. It's just...you have to act that way on the docks or get drummed out of the fleet."

As it turned out, the visitor wasn't Daniel Coletti. A younger, more wiry version of the man they'd been discussing poked his head through the opening.

"Yo, Daisy." He stepped inside and closed the door. "I wanna talk about leasin' your boat. Oops! Sorry. Didn't know you'd be eating. I can stop back later." Large almost black eyes made a sweeping assessment of Daisy's guests before the young man's straight brows came to a V over his hawkish nose, and he grasped the doorknob to leave.

"Stay," Daisy ordered. "Come. Join us. I fixed jambalaya."

"You've got company. I don't want to horn in." That last sounded a little sullen.

"He's not . . ." She was going to say, "company," but in the time it took her to choose her words, Temple yanked out a chair and said smoothly, "I live here. And you are . . . ?"

"Sal Coletti." Scowling, he drew a hand through his thick black hair. "You're the Californian, right? Dan'l mentioned you."

Temple's eyes twinkled. "I'll bet he did. You must be the little brother. Grab a bowl out of the cupboard, sport. No need to run off on my account. Although, if you want any hide left on your tongue," he confided, "you'll sneak out and grab a burger."

Daisy sniffed indignantly. "Don't listen to him, Salvatore. This is really quite mild." She glared at Temple and dug out another place setting.

Sal's puppy-dog gaze followed her a moment, then he deliberately wedged the remaining chair between Daisy and Temple, obliging Temple to move against the wall.

"You sure you want to lease the *Lazy Daisy*, Sal?" Daisy asked as she filled his bowl. She appeared blissfully unaware of the undercurrents between the two men as she went on, "I don't want there to be trouble between you and Daniel because of me."

Sal fingered the pack of cigarettes rolled in the sleeve of his navy T-shirt. "In case you haven't noticed, Daisy, I'm all grown up. Daniel still acts like a mother hen."

Daisy passed him the bowl, looking stern as she broke off a piece of bread and slapped it on his plate. "Who took care of you and put food on the table and clothes on your back after your dad died and your mother crawled into the bottle, Sal?"

His eyes flashed a moment, then he lowered his gaze. "How long do I hafta pay for being the youngest kid? I've hauled nets for him since I got out of high school. He wouldn't let me drop out of school, or I'd have my own boat by now."

Daisy nipped at her bottom lip. "I don't think Daniel considers it a debt. He wants a better life for you both."

"That's just it. We don't see eye to eye. I don't happen to think there *is* a better life. I love what I do."

"But, Sal . . ." She glanced at Temple, who sat quietly eating. Unconsciously her eyes begged for his support.

What the hell, Temple thought. He'd throw in his two cents' worth. "You're fighting a losing battle, Daisy. What Sal's saying now—isn't that almost verbatim what you told Daniel last night?"

"Yes. But I was mad at him. Later I started thinking about the flip side. About those years when the pickin's are slim and I barely make ends meet. Equipment costs are on the rise. It's darned tough getting reliable help. And sometimes the weather's terrible all year."

Temple reached for his water glass. "I run into the same problems building resorts. Land prices skyrocket. Unions are always on my back. Weather forces delays. That's business."

Sal ignored Temple. His gaze remained fixed on Daisy. "I'm reliable," he said. "Give me a chance." Reaching over, he grasped her hand. "Plenty of guys support families shrimping. You know *I* could."

Daisy stared disconsolately into his dark eager eyes. Why hadn't she seen before that he had a crush on her, like Daniel said? "It'll only be until Becca gets well. Rebecca," she corrected, tugging her hand from Sal's as she darted a glance of apology in Temple's direction.

He saw that she'd sidestepped the real issue—*that Sal wanted more from her than a boat*—and conveyed it with his eyes over the rim of his glass.

Pretending she didn't know what the look meant, she fixed Becca another slice of bread. "The boat's ready any time you are, Sal."

He punched a fist in the air. "All right! I promise you won't regret this. I'll even report in every night."

"Well, now that's settled," Daisy said briskly, "let's eat. Later we can draw up some kind of a contract."

"I have a broad-based lease upstairs in my briefcase that would probably work." Temple made the offer against his better judgment.

"Really?" Daisy eyed him dubiously.

"Yes, really. I'm always looking to lease or buy new property. In fact, I ran across a likely spot today."

"Here? In Galveston?" Daisy blanched.

He anchored her with a cool gaze. "I build quality resorts. I'm not proposing anything sleazy, for goodness sake. I don't flout local ordinances and I don't ask for special concessions."

"Hmm." She picked up her fork and stabbed a plump shrimp. "Then what do those high-priced lawyers of yours do to earn their keep?"

Temple's laughter bubbled up from his belly.

Sal's sidelong glance skipped from one to the other. Clearly their byplay eluded him, and he resented it.

Temple found the young man's resentment sobering. Last night Daniel had declared his kid brother half in love with Daisy. Not true. Sal Coletti was full-blown head-over-heels in love with her. Temple doubted she knew how serious this kid's feelings really were.

He should probably warn his naive landlady. But just as he opened his mouth to suggest that Daisy might want to give the situation and the lease more thought, he caught her disapproving stare. It struck Temple that if she hadn't been willing to accept the truth from Daniel last night, no way in hell would she listen to a newcomer like himself. Lowering his gaze, he went back to eating the now cold, but still spicy-hot jambalaya.

"Outsiders are always waltzing in here, buying up our land, positive they can make a killing," Sal blustered. "My advice, Yank, is to check out their lousy track records before you throw your money away."

Temple paused, spoon halfway to his mouth. He wanted to laugh again. Imagine, the kid warning him off. He'd bet his last white shirt that Sal Coletti's remark had nothing to do with business. He was being cautioned to stay away from Daisy Sloan.

"Is that your way of saying Yankee, go home?" Temple ate an entire spoonful. Damn, but this dose was really loaded with cayenne pepper. It nearly burned a hole through his palate. His eyes watered.

Daisy smiled and touched a napkin to her lips. Tempting though it was, she wouldn't tease him about his low tolerance for spicy food in front of Sal. Tension was already thick between those two. Couldn't Temple see that Sal was just trying to be protective? Brotherly, even. Daisy thought it was a sweet gesture and said as much.

"Sweet!" Temple choked on his disbelief. "Excuse me, please," he said, folding his napkin and rising. "I'll leave you two to your mutual-admiration society. I have work to do. Coletti." Temple dipped his head curtly. "We'll meet again, I'm sure."

"Don't bank on it." Sal made no pretext of friendship.

"Salvatore! You've got no call to be rude. Apologize." Daisy met and matched the young man's scowl.

"Too late, he's gone," Sal said, brightening.

She turned and saw it was true. Temple had left the room. "What is it with you and Daniel both treating one of my boarders so badly? Have you two gone loco?"

He pushed his bowl aside and stood. "Maybe it's you who's gone loco. Who is this guy, and what do you know about him?"

She drew back stiffly. "He's a man who offered us a blank lease to fill out on the *Lazy Daisy*. That's assuming you and I can strike a deal."

His bravado slipped a notch. "Aw, Daisy, you wouldn't renege. I already told all my friends. Loren Bonner said he was willing to keep the same schedule he had with you. I thought we were set, Daisy."

"Me, too, Sal. But I don't need added stress." She indicated Becca who had gobbled up her second bowl of jambalaya and was nodding off in her chair. "If you'd like to trade problems with Temple Wyatt about now, I'm sure he'd be willing."

"I get your point," he mumbled. "Me and Dan'l—we just don't understand why the kid latched on to you."

Daisy sighed. "It's all very complicated. According to Dr. Rankin, it was because I was the last person she saw before the yacht blew up and she went into shock."

"That's something else. This whole thing has the guys in the fleet spooked."

"My mistake was in not sticking with the fleet," she told him. "Then again, if I had, Becca wouldn't have survived."

He nodded. "Yeah. She's a cute kid. But we'd all feel better if the Coast Guard had found that speedboat. Just as well you got your feet grounded in sand for a while."

She gave his arm a punch, happy to get the conversation back on a more even keel. "Spoken like a man who wants my boat,'' she teased. ''Hey, I'll clear the table if you go ask Wyatt nicely for one of his lease forms.''

''Done.'' Sal swaggered toward the door leading to the stairs. '''Cept I won't promise nicely. I save that for babes like you and old ladies.''

''Listen, tough guy,'' she called, ''I don't fit either of those categories, and if you call me a babe again, the lease is automatically terminated. Got that?''

She waited, but there was a suspicious silence from the hallway. Mouthy kid. He'd learn she meant business.

Much later, after the deed was done, the lease signed and her kitchen spotless, Daisy slipped into a mild case of the blues. For some years she'd been in control of everything to do with the *Lazy Daisy,* and every aspect of her own life. With her signature on that form, she suffered a vague discomfort that this was somehow the beginning of the end. The end of what, she couldn't say, but it was an unsettling reaction. So unsettling that she didn't want to go upstairs. Instead, she gathered up the sleeping Becca and went outside to watch the sun go down.

THE MOON WAS OUT, full and bright when the silence in the house drove Temple downstairs to see what had become of Daisy and Rebecca. He found them on the front porch, idly rocking in the creaky old porch swing.

''Ah, there you are,'' he said. ''It's a nice night for moon-watching. Mind if I join you?''

The magnolia-scented night remained silent except for the rhythmic squeak of the wooden swing.

Temple labored to see through the shadowy darkness; The porch was screened. Rebecca's eyes were closed. She looked content on Daisy's lap, cuddled in a quilt he vaguely recognized as being from her room at home. A wave of nostalgia swamped him, along with disappointment. He shifted the two thin books he held from one hand to the other. Obviously once again he was too late to read Rebecca a bedtime story.

Moonlight reflected off the shiny surface of the top book, and Daisy felt a stab of sadness. Toying with one of the girl's blond ringlets, she whispered, "Poor kid conked out the second she finished dinner. I'm afraid I'll wake her getting her upstairs."

"I'll carry her. Are you ready to go now?"

"No, not yet."

He picked up on the listlessness in her tone. "Are you all right?"

Again, silence.

"Did Rebecca get into mischief? I meant to come down earlier, but I wanted to wait until your new partner left. Maybe I expected to hear a champagne cork hit the ceiling or something. So, did the form work?" Temple went fishing without apology.

Daisy slowed the swing. "No mischief. No champagne. And the form was almost too easy. Is that all there is to forming a partnership?"

"Ah." There was a world of understanding in his one-word reply. He leaned against the porch rail, making sure he didn't put the full weight of his back on the upper screen, and waited for her to elaborate. It wasn't like her not to spit out what was on her mind.

When she went back to swinging and staring at the moon, Temple wondered if he'd been right about the things that were bothering her. "Business partnerships can be a lot like marriages," he ventured a bit cynically. "Some work well and last forever. Some fail and end in divorce. In either case, it helps to know a partner intimately first. How well do you know Coletti?"

A faint smile tugged at the corners of her lips. "It's none of your business of course—but not *that* well, Wyatt. And we're talking a partnership of a few months, tops. Not forever."

Temple couldn't say why he felt relieved. He just did. Until he recalled how blissfully ignorant he'd been of women's wiles when he'd charged headlong into marriage with Miranda. "I'm probably not the best person to give advice on partnerships," he said, straightening away from the rail. "It's a big leap of faith any way you look at it. Maybe you'd like to be alone to think things out. What time do you want to take Rebecca up? I'll come back for her—say, at 9:30."

"There's coffee in the pot," she said, hoping to prolong his stay. "I wouldn't mind company." She held her breath. Could he tell how disturbed she felt by his presence—yet how much she craved it?

Temple hesitated. In the moonlight, her eyes were large. Dark like velvet. Soft. Needy. Not for the quick release provided by a lover but the comfort of a friend. He didn't know if he could offer it, if he could be a friend. Frankly that kind of relationship required a whole lot more from a man than being a lover did. And he'd vowed after Miranda had drained him dry of honest emotions that needy women were strictly off-limits.

He'd meant it, too. Still did. But everything changed when Rebecca started out of a sound sleep with a heart-wrenching sob, and Daisy Sloan focused all her attention on his child. The vulnerability left her eyes to be replaced immediately by a generous dose of tenderness. Even someone as jaded as Temple recognized love when he saw it.

As his daughter relaxed again and curled into Daisy's slender arms, he felt himself giving in.

"Coffee. Two cups coming right up," he said in a gravelly voice that barely disguised how deeply he'd been shaken.

CHAPTER SEVEN

"SHE'S DOZED OFF AGAIN," Daisy murmured as Temple returned with two steaming mugs. "Let me slide her off my lap onto the swing seat. I don't want to risk spilling hot coffee on her."

He smiled, passed Daisy a mug, then set the one he carried for himself on the porch rail. "Would it be all right if I held her? It's not as if I need the added caffeine before I turn in."

"It's decaff," she said, starting to rise. "But sure. Go ahead. She's your daughter."

"Stay." Temple placed a hand on Daisy's shoulder. "There's plenty of room, and I'll need you if she spooks again."

A sensation of heat stole into her body from beneath his palm, trapping Daisy where she hovered. Her mind scrambled to find a valid excuse to leave. After a moment's tug-of-war within, she sank back with a sigh.

Temple picked up the quilted bundle with care. He grew still when the swing creaked. But when Rebecca didn't stir, he eased back, although he continued to hold his breath. When all remained silent except for the occasional chirp of a cricket, he released it. "I wish I could understand what's going on with her." He shrugged, careful not to disturb his sleeping daughter. "I stopped by the medical-school library today after visiting the police and the Coast Guard. The librarian found some articles explaining shock."

"What a good idea." Daisy sipped her coffee and waited for him to say what he'd discovered. She felt an unaccountable easing of her mood; this explained, at least, how he'd spent the afternoon.

"You think so?" His tone sounded gloomy. "If anything, I'm more confused. With shock, so much is wait-and-see. And no two cases are the same. As far as I could tell, one that involved a boating accident off the coast of Southern Cal in the late eighties bore some similarity to Rebecca's. The child, a boy of three, spent several hours in the sea. Eventually he was diagnosed with retrograde amnesia. Only three, and he'd lost his past!"

He looked so distressed that Daisy reached over and took his hand in hers. "Don't," she chided gently. "Dr. Rankin didn't call it amnesia." She balked at telling him that Becca's team had bandied about terms like retrograde amnesia, aphasia, and Broca's amnesia. But why add to a father's worry when the doctors couldn't agree? "Dr. Rankin called it a temporary disorder brought on by trauma," she said firmly.

"She doesn't remember anything. What's that if not amnesia?"

Daisy pursed her lips. "*Temporary*. Concentrate on that word."

"You're right. Thanks," he mumbled. "No sense looking for trouble. Tomorrow morning I'll sit down and talk with Dr. Rankin. Meanwhile, let's find another subject to pass the time, shall we?"

She nodded and released his hand to curl in the corner of the swing. Setting her mug aside, she took a tube of lotion out of her shorts pocket. "Well," she said as she uncapped the tube and squeezed a generous portion onto her palm, "we could discuss the resort you want to build on Galveston."

Temple breathed in the provocative scent of magnolias. At least now he knew why the air surrounding her always smelled like a courtyard in the French Quarter. At first it seemed a small thing to watch her smooth the lotion onto each finger. But when Temple suddenly experienced a not-so-subtle tightening below his belt, the trivial act took on new significance.

"No? Well, what then?" Extending a bare foot, she nudged his thigh.

The tightness increased. "I . . . uh . . ." he stammered. "Uh, tell me about those old Victorian homes on Broadway," he blurted, feeling his words tumble out too fast. "I might go with that style." Shifting Rebecca so he faced Daisy, Temple said in a more deliberate tone, "Are they open for tours?"

His gaze strayed to her toes, which rested by his leg. Why hadn't he noticed before that she wore polish on her toenails? When he first met Miranda, she'd painted hers, too. A habit she'd quit during pregnancy. That made him remember how much she'd hated being pregnant. She'd hated the time he spent on business, too. Maybe he should have worked harder on his marriage. But that was past. Too late and best forgotten.

Now if he could stop thinking about Daisy's toes... He moved abruptly on the bench seat and made the old swing shudder. Bare feet were not the topic under discussion. What was it Daisy had said about those old homes?

"Are you listening to me?" she demanded, pausing to recap the tube of lotion. "I said you should make time to tour Moody Mansion and Ashton Villa while you're here. Those are the homes you drove by. The Bishop's Palace is on Broadway, too. Its architect was quite famous. Nicholas Clayton.''

"No kidding? I've seen his work." Temple welcomed the new focus for his attention. "Say, if you're a connoisseur of Victorian-style architecture, you'd love my resorts in Charlotte Amalie and St. Croix." Temple stopped speaking as Daisy's rich laughter spread over him.

"The farthest I've been from home is New Orleans. I'm quite sure I'd like *any* of the architecture in Charlotte Amalie and St. Croix." She took another sip of coffee. Leaning back, she said in an amused tone, "Too bad you and Daniel didn't hit it off. He'd love to hear about your resorts. He subscribes to three tour magazines, and he's read everything in our library about exotic destinations." She smiled. "He's so sure he has to leave Galveston to see anything worth seeing. Would you mind telling him we have noteworthy old buildings here?''

Temple frowned. "I didn't get the feeling yesterday that you were trying to talk him into staying. Guess I was wrong.''

She got slowly to her feet, stifling a yawn. "It's not my place to influence him either way. You know, I'd love to spend some time badgering you about your plans for the Island, but you did say Jeb Matthews is bringing in a crew of electricians early tomorrow morning. And I'm too tired to argue about that anymore. I'll just deduct the baby-sitting like we discussed and pay you back the rest when I can." She yawned and covered her mouth with one hand. "Would you mind taking Becca upstairs now? Rebecca," she hastened to correct.

Temple didn't want to rehash the wiring issue, either, but he was disappointed to see the evening end so soon.

Not that he couldn't have gone to the health club he'd joined yesterday. But that wouldn't have answered a need for quiet conversation. It occurred to him, not for the first time, that men did not tend to sit around and talk. They were content to grunt in unison.

Tonight was different. Enjoyable. Surely it wasn't female companionship he craved. That idea shocked him. From the outset of his marriage, he and Miranda had done little in the time they had together but argue. It left bitter memories and kept him from going out of his way to date after his divorce.

When he'd first met Daisy Sloan, Temple hadn't even liked her. Liked her less when she stood between him and Rebecca. He certainly hadn't expected his feelings to change when he moved in here, he thought as he awkwardly gathered up his daughter.

Daisy touched his arm and shook her head when he would have tried to juggle his coffee mug. Smiling, she collected both cups and indicated by a nod that she'd take them to the kitchen. Her smile and her gesture left him with an odd feeling of intimacy.

He nodded brusquely. Lord, where was his good sense? Hadn't he screwed up one relationship big time? He didn't want to try for two. Besides, Daisy Sloan was a homebody, and by virtue of his business, he was anything but. What could the two of them possibly have in common?

She brushed past him, telegraphing a second major jolt to Temple's groin, and he was awfully afraid he knew what they had in common. Physical attraction. And not all one-sided, either. He knew it with certainty when he saw her slop coffee. Great. Just what he needed. More complications in his life.

Upstairs Temple waited impatiently outside Daisy's bedroom door while she shut off the lights below. The best thing he could do now would be to tuck Rebecca in fast and get the hell away from Daisy Sloan. Maybe this was just some phase of the moon or something. Maybe by tomorrow things would return to normal between them.

Temple's chest constricted as he watched her bound up the winding stairs. *Please, Lord, let me get back to normal.*

"Whoee, I'm getting soft!" she exclaimed. Catching her breath, she reached for the doorknob. "I stopped to put the coffeemaker on auto pilot for morning. Look who I found under the kitchen table. Straylia." Daisy waggled the stuffed koala bear under Temple's nose. "Becca must have dropped him when she fell asleep at supper. Goodness, why didn't you go on in? Asleep, that little miss weighs a ton."

"Rebecca," he reminded, almost relieved to see that one bone of contention at least hadn't disappeared. "And have you already forgotten what you said this morning?" He raised one eyebrow. "I'm waiting for permission to go through your room."

She flushed. "Was it only this morning? It seems so long ago." She stepped past him and held open the door, although she refused to meet his eyes. "I imagine you had a good laugh over my little fit. You probably meet much more...worldly women in your line of work."

Temple recalled how Daisy had looked this morning in her white cotton nightie. And how just touching her a moment ago had made his pulse leap almost out of his skin. The last thing on his mind either time had been "worldly" women.

Wisely he said nothing. Instead, he gave his landlady a wide berth as he carried his daughter into the alcove and placed her on the bed. It wouldn't hurt her to sleep in her dress; she'd done it before. Clicking the rail in place, Temple smoothed her blankets. He lingered there until he felt he'd regained control of his hormones.

When he finally left the alcove, Temple was relieved to see Daisy seated at her desk—and still fully clothed. Or, at least, as fully clothed as it was possible for her to be in her seemingly endless supply of shorts.

Bright lights flooded the room and reflected off the brass fittings of the clipper ship on the mantel. Temple felt more at ease among the masculine bric-a-brac in her room than he did standing next to the large four-poster. Skirting it, he walked over to take a closer look at the model.

Daisy glanced up from Becca's journal. "She's a beauty, isn't she? Some say she was the fastest ship in her day. Are you familiar with the *Cutty Sark*?"

"You mean other than knowing it's a damn fine whiskey?" Temple tucked his hands into his back pockets as he turned to face her, laughter lurking in his eyes.

Daisy's chuckle was spontaneous. "Touché. I forget that not everyone cut their teeth on salty tales of the sea like I did."

"I'm sorry I didn't. These models are great. Did someone you know make them?" He hoped the talented craftsman wasn't Daniel Coletti.

"My grandfather built them. That one with the yellow hull is a replica of a colonial merchant schooner. The *Sultana* out of Boston. That sleek mahogany frigate on the pedestal is the USS *Constitution*."

"Old Ironsides?" Temple crossed the room to take a closer look. "Now I see. Wow! I'm afraid I wouldn't have the patience to build one."

"Nor would I. I like the ones in the bottles best, and they take even longer to assemble. Did you see the *Titanic*?" She got up and led the way to a lighted shelf displaying a detailed oceanliner in a glass bottle. "Gramps said this model had over 450 parts."

Temple stared at the ship in admiration.

"The entire Sloan collection was much larger once. A number of valuable pieces were lost in the Great Storm. My great-grandfather had collected an enviable number of original ship figureheads, among other pieces. The only one left is downstairs in the den. From the *Amanda Fenwick*. She's pretty beat up. The best of the ones he managed to save after the hurricane were donated to various museums. According to his log, he sent a museum in Boston several irreplaceable oil paintings by famous ship's artists, as well."

"I'm sorry." Temple said it because she sounded so wistful.

"Don't be. At least they're permanently preserved. So much of Galveston's early history was lost. I'm committed to helping the local historical society hang on to whatever's left."

"Does that mean you're against my building a resort here?" he said casually, taking out his handkerchief and reaching around her to wipe dust from the bottle containing the *Titanic*.

Daisy snatched the square of cotton from his hand and busily polished the bottle herself. "Why would I object to us capturing more tourist dollars?"

"At supper you didn't seem overjoyed by the news. So is it just me personally you don't want around?"

Her hands stilled. She clutched the handkerchief to her breast. He stood so close behind her it was almost overpowering. "No, not at all." But in trying to sound convincing, she couldn't keep her panic from bleeding through.

Temple lightly grasped her arms and turned her to face him. As his body absorbed her involuntary shudder, he realized how much he'd misjudged her. She didn't object to his desire to build on the island. It had been a natural assumption, though, considering that she hadn't defended him against Sal's barbs. Now he looked deep into her eyes and felt her tremble beneath his touch, and an altogether different picture stenciled itself on his brain. Daisy Sloan liked him all right. Maybe too much. And that presented a greater problem.

A problem that faded and dimmed as he bent toward her, drawn by the fullness of her lips and the defiant tilt of her chin.

His kiss, when delivered, came as no surprise to Daisy. And yet, his lips covered hers so softly, with such unexpected tenderness, it was a total shock.

She'd always been stingy with her kisses, even though she'd received her first one at age nine, hanging upside down on the monkey bars. Zeke McTavitt nursed a black eye and split lip for a week. But in fourth grade the word was out: *Don't try stealing kisses from Daisy Sloan.* From that day on, she was very clear about what she liked and what she didn't. And she *did* like being kissed by Temple Wyatt.

His lips were firm, not sloppy wet. He didn't attempt to swallow her whole like some others she'd kissed. He held her delicately, although there was no mistaking the effect her body had on his. His response was all male.

Still, Daisy didn't feel threatened. Of their own accord, her fingers tunneled into the thick hair that didn't quite touch his collar. How many times since they'd met had she watched a shaft of sunlight play across the golden strands and wondered how they'd feel to touch? Well, now she knew. His hair felt soft. Heavenly.

Rarely, if ever, had Temple been tempted to kiss an outdoorsy woman. They weren't his type. Generally he chose his few casual dates from a pool of busy hotel managers. Women who had energy for little more than an occasional dinner out. Women who didn't have time for complicated relationships with single fathers. During the past six months his concern for his missing daughter had precluded even that—which didn't mean, however, that kissing Daisy Sloan just now was the random act of a man too long without a woman. This need to kiss her had been brewing all day. All week. In truth, it had begun that first day in Dr. Rankin's office when she'd been out for blood.

Lord, but he did like a lady with a quick comeback.

Temple paused to catch his breath, and he felt a rush of inner warmth as he gazed down at the woman in his arms. What a contradiction Daisy Sloan was. She had both eyes closed tight like a novice. Yet her lips sought his boldly and without apology.

His teasing smile battled her mouth momentarily for possession of his. Temple lost on purpose. He was impressed by the fact that she traded kisses honestly. There wasn't a shred of coyness in this woman.

Temple liked that, too.

Framing her face with his hands, he kissed her again. This time he fully enjoyed the feel of her firm curves nestled against his chest and thighs. Against his solid erection.

Whoa there, old son! This was a development Temple hadn't been angling for. He eased slowly away from Daisy until only their foreheads touched. Judging by the sheen of sweat they shared, he'd say it was past time they called a halt to this pleasant interlude. Especially as his hands had involuntarily slipped beneath the elastic of her shorts to caress her lower back. But separating proved downright painful. Temple groaned.

Daisy abruptly opened her eyes. She stared at him for a moment, unfocused and wary.

At first rational thought escaped her. Then she jumped back, veiling her sudden guilt with downcast lashes. Immediately she began fussing with the V neck of her T-shirt.

The handkerchief of Temple's that she'd been clutching tightly now lay trampled at their feet. Flustered, Daisy bent to retrieve it. She didn't remember it falling from her hand.

Temple knelt at the same time. Once again their bodies brushed. He would have ignored it had Daisy not flinched. Because she seemed so ill at ease, he placed what he hoped was an impersonal hand beneath her elbow and helped her stand.

"You've been under a lot of stress," he said, sounding quietly matter-of-fact. "Witnessing a terrible accident. Forced confinement. Leasing your boat out was traumatic, to say nothing of having your home invaded." Having run out of logic, Temple carefully weighed his next words. "All that frustration had to go someplace," he whispered, knowing exactly where it had gone.

Daisy didn't think she was the only frustrated one here, and she saw right through his ploy. He, too, exhibited all the signs of someone rattled by a kiss. But since she wasn't prepared to deal with her own part in those kisses, she let it go.

"Leasing my boat *was* hard. And showing you the Sloan collection just now brought back sad memories. All this stuff belonged to my dad. I haven't kept it up like I should've since he died."

"When was that?" Temple asked politely. Any second now, he planned to bolt. He edged toward the door.

Daisy edged in the same direction. "Dad was diagnosed six years ago with arteriosclerotic heart disease. He went downhill fast after he quit shrimping. About five months ago, he just gave up. The hardest part was watching him change. His memory got so bad everyone thought he had Alzheimer's. At one time he was the best shrimper in the fleet. The one everyone went to for advice. But toward the end it was as if I was the parent and he was the child."

Temple stopped short of the door. "Five months ago? Why, you've hardly finished grieving. I remember how long it took when I lost my dad."

"Except that you had no warning. I saw this coming. I should've been able to steel myself."

"I don't know about that. But at least you have siblings to share your sorrow. I imagine they've been a comfort."

She halted at her desk, picked up Rebecca's journal and clutched it to her breast. "My sisters are . . . well, I wouldn't want to call them selfish, but . . ."

Daisy dropped into the chair and opened the book. When she spoke again, her voice held a little catch. "Violet and Jasmine thought I should sell the house and boat and put Dad in a nursing home. I imagine our mother planted that idea." A slight frown marred her brow. "At any rate, none of them were able to get away for the funeral.''

"They made you go through your father's funeral alone?" Temple couldn't think when he'd been angrier at people he didn't even know. She shrugged and waved a hand as if to dispel his concern, or, Temple thought, to indicate that this behavior of theirs was nothing new.

Temple swore to himself then and there that none of her poor excuses for relatives had better show up while he was living in this house. He wouldn't be responsible for what he might say. "After all you went through with your dad, I'm surprised you saddled yourself with Rebecca. Oh, don't misunderstand—I'm sincerely grateful you did."

She shrugged. "I'm not sure you'll believe this, but my decision came about in the blink of an eye. At first I was terribly claustrophobic staying in that hospital room day after day. It's easier now that I'm home. Although I can't say that I'll ever like being cooped up."

"Nor me. So why not take Rebecca out more? Let her soak up some sun?"

"How do you think she'll react to seeing the ocean? So many of Galveston's main attractions have to do with the sea. We're surrounded by water, in case you haven't noticed."

"You've got a point," he said quietly. "Tomorrow I'll ask the doctor his opinion. Better yet, why don't you come with me?"

"I don't want to intrude."

"You wouldn't be. If he gives a green light, maybe we can do something fun with Rebecca on the way home."

"She might enjoy the Railroad Museum. They have a neat excursion train," Daisy told him, warming to the idea.

"But that's not really getting her out to soak up the sun."

"True. Maybe we can do the museum first, then go to the beach. You know," Daisy said wistfully, "when I was her age, I spent endless hours combing the beach for seashells. That, or building sand castles. Have you heard about our annual sand-castle contest? People flock here in droves. It's a pretty big deal."

"Really? I got roped into a sand-castle contest once in Jamaica. Strictly amateur, of course. But our resort staff took first prize. I haven't done anything that silly in years."

"It's not silly, and I'm impressed." Daisy recapped her pen and leaned back in her chair. She'd finally managed to hide all lingering effects of the kisses they'd shared. She might bring them out to savor later when she was alone. For now, though, she appreciated his business-as-usual attitude. "Folks who enter our sand-castle contest sometimes bring their own architects."

"No lie?"

"No lie. Why are you always suspicious of everything I say?"

Temple shrugged. "I don't know where your contest's usually held, but today, while I was out, I saw the perfect place. At the east end of the seawall. Somebody's hauled in tones of fresh sand."

Daisy hooted. "That's our new six-million-dollar restoration project you're recommending we tear up to build sand castles. Listen, bud, that strip of sand is what'll make your resort worth a fortune. Buy your land fast, 'cause the city manager predicts our new beach will draw a half-million more summer tourists when it's done."

"Ah. I see now why the old boys I dickered with today were so firm on their price. They were plenty closed-mouthed, too." Temple pulled a small calculator from his shirt pocket and fed a series of figures into it. "Hmm," he said a moment later. "It might be worth the price they're asking at that."

Well, he *had* been busy today. Even busier than she'd realized. Daisy's heart beat faster at the thought of having Temple stay in Galveston. But would he? Or once his place was built, would he move on to new pastures?

If Temple saw Daisy's sudden frown, he didn't comment. He ran through a second set of figures. "Do you think your old wiring will hold up for me to use my computer and fax machine tonight?"

Her frown deepened. "You're treading on thin ice bringing up that subject. Sorry, I'm afraid you'll have to do without your toys until Jeb's finished."

"That may take weeks. I need to get a prospectus worked up for my bank if I intend to make an offer on that property tomorrow."

"That soon?" Daisy sat straighter. She battled to keep her heartbeat from escalating. "I thought maybe you were joking."

"I never joke about the acquisition of land. I could kick myself that Wyatt Resorts has overlooked such a plum—and one so close to home. Am I missing some obvious pitfall?"

"Hurricanes." Daisy said it tongue in cheek, but it was true. "Living on the island is a gamble," she told him in all honesty.

Temple tucked the calculator back in his pocket. "Living anywhere is a gamble. And don't you get advance warning? Time to clear the beaches and shutter down?"

"I guess." Her reply sounded lackluster even to herself. "As with your quakes, we have doomsayers who sit around predicting the next one will wipe us out."

"Are you by chance trying to scare me off?"

Was that what she was doing? She should encourage him to spend Wyatt Resort money in Galveston. Perhaps her reluctance had to do with the recent kiss that had weakened her knees. If he owned a resort here, he might pop into town with less warning than a hurricane. And the result might be more devastating. What if he got the idea, from the way she'd poured her heart and soul into kissing him, that she'd be available any old time?

All at once, Daisy knew that Temple Wyatt could make her the topic of breakfast conversation all over the Island. The realization was a total shock.

Temple snapped his fingers in front of her eyes. "I can see this is no time to be discussing resorts and hurricanes. You're all but asleep on your feet. I'll leave and let you get ready for bed."

Daisy flushed. How could she have let her mind wander so far astray? "Oh," she began, relieved to change the subject to something practical. "I do have another question. Do you have time to answer?"

"Ask away. I'm not the one who's zoned out."

"Yes, well..." She cleared her throat. "It's about Becca's shorts. Or I should say her lack thereof. If Dr. Rankin says she can go to the beach, she'll either have to be awfully careful or ruin her pretty dresses."

"That's easy. Feel free to whack off her jeans."

"What jeans?"

"I assumed Maddy packed play clothes, as well."

"I don't know who Maddy is, but there's nothing in that suitcase I'd class as play clothes." Daisy pointed to the leather case that still sat open on her bed.

"Maddy's my housekeeper, but she's like family. She takes care of Rebecca when I'm away on trips." Temple covered the distance from the door to the bed in three strides. He sifted through the items in the suitcase, then straightened and rifled a hand through his hair. "I'm sorry. This looks suspiciously like my mother's doing. She came over the minute I told her I'd seen Rebecca on TV."

"You mean she thought Rebecca was performing and needed fancy dresses?"

Temple laughed. "No, but didn't I tell you my mother exchanged her love beads for a platinum credit card? I made the mistake of letting her take Rebecca shopping for school clothes. Mom spent two thousand dollars so fast it would make Cinderella's fairy godmother faint. The result is all these unwearable dresses with matching doodads. I never had the heart to tell her that I took Rebecca out the next day and bought her six pairs of jeans and sweatshirts."

Daisy's lips twitched. "You didn't have the heart or the guts? Are you afraid of your mother, Wyatt?"

"Certainly not! I intended to have her return everything. Then Miranda took off with Rebecca. Things changed—"

"Don't," Daisy interrupted. "It doesn't matter. I know every discount store in town. You'll be able to pick up a few cheap shorts and T-shirts."

Temple bristled. "I'm not insinuating I need to skimp. I can afford to dress my daughter well."

"Excu-use me." Daisy drew back, feeling as if she'd been well and truly put in her place. Her anger simmered. "For a minute there, I forgot I was dealing with *the* Temple Wyatt of Wyatt Resorts."

"I didn't mean..." Temple strode back to her. When he drew close enough to see the shimmer of hurt in her eyes, he also felt the unmistakable urge to take her in his arms again. One small part of his brain kept insisting that would be a bad move. Taking her into his arms would lead to kissing, and kissing very likely wouldn't be enough. Instead of touching her, Temple swore soundly and stalked past her, right on out of the room.

He didn't let the door slam, but he might as well have. The soft click of the latch set Daisy's teeth on edge. For a minute, she could have sworn he'd intended to kiss her again. How could her thinking run so badly amok every time she got within spitting distance of that man?

Spitting mad. That was what she should be. At him and at herself for acting like a foolish teen. Daisy returned to her desk where she logged into Becca's journal every last thing she could remember about the girl's day.

Considering the scowl on Temple's face when he'd left just now, Daisy supposed he'd retract his offer to go with him to see Dr. Rankin tomorrow. And to do something "fun" afterward.

Which was fine by her. Temple Wyatt's idea of fun would probably cost more than she could afford. That was assuming they even *agreed* on what was fun. He said building sand castles was silly. Fun to him was probably sitting stiffly in a five-star restaurant, being served flaming steak by waiters dressed up like penguins.

Daisy pursed her lips and closed the journal with a snap. She put a rubber band around it and set it aside to give Temple in the morning. On second thought, she'd take it to him now. That way there'd be no reason for him to come to her room. She grabbed it up and marched to her bedroom door. She'd just eased it open when she heard his machines humming. Copy machine, fax or computer? Before she could figure it out, his door opened and she saw him carting something down the hall.

Daisy drew back. Was he heading for bed? There was no way she was taking this journal to him in his bedroom. Opening the door wider, she saw that he'd passed his room and was headed for the bath.

Ah. He was carrying towels.

Good Lord! Daisy closed her eyes and drew in a sharp breath. This morning, after Becca's bath, Daisy had rinsed out some underwear. She'd draped the items over the towel bar and the shower stall to dry, and had completely forgotten them.

Neatnick that Temple was... Yes, Daisy heard him cursing. She tiptoed down the hall, going over in her mind what she'd say. But as luck would have it, halfway there she stepped on Troublemaker's tail. He let out a yowl. Darn cat. What was he doing in the middle of the hall?

Temple flung open the bathroom door, clutching a collection of her panties and bras.

"Oops." Daisy's face flamed as she dashed up and snatched them out of his hands. "Sorry." And she was. This was a frivolous side of her she somehow didn't want him to know about—or to judge.

"Nothing I haven't seen before." He gestured toward the bath. "It's the mess I'd like to discuss. Shampoo and conditioner spilled. The bottles uncapped. Damp towels strewn around and powder everywhere. And there's no room in the cabinet for my shaving gear. What *is* all this stuff?" He pointed at a row of shelves overflowing with first-aid supplies. "It looks like a bloody pharmacy."

Daisy wadded her undies into a ball. "I told you all my previous boarders were medical students. Each had his own idea of what belonged in a medicine cabinet. But they mostly showered at the hospital, I think."

Temple crossed his arms. "I shower daily and I plan to do it here. If we're each responsible for cleaning up our own mess, I think it'll work, don't you?"

"Don't get sanctimonious with me," Daisy snapped. "Half of those towels are from your daughter kicking water out of the tub. As are the drying undies, because she soaked me and my last clean set. No doubt Maddy would send *hers* out to be laundered," she said, as she shoved the journal into his hands and turned to leave. "This is my house, Wyatt, and I'll be as messy as I want." Chin angled, she took three steps and landed hard on the cat's tail again. This time Troublemaker's yowl was accompanied by a spit and a hiss, and was promptly joined by Temple's low laughter.

"Maddy's a dear lady," he called, "and a crackerjack housekeeper. But somehow I have a hard time picturing her wearing those hot-pink flowered bikinis you just dropped. She's sixty-five if she's a day."

Bending, Daisy scooped up the bit of brightly colored nylon and her cat, all without breaking stride. She hoped her face wasn't the same brilliant shade of pink as the panties, but she was afraid it was. But that wasn't enough to keep her from smiling the minute she was safe behind her door. Let him spend the night organizing her bathroom. In the space of a few minutes, she had gleaned the answers to at least two of her questions. Temple Wyatt wasn't as immune to her as he wanted to be—and his housekeeper in California was just that. His housekeeper.

CHAPTER EIGHT

DAYLIGHT HAD barely struggled into the sky when two panel trucks filled with workmen arrived at Daisy's home and awakened half the neighborhood. Including Temple, who'd been up until four in the morning working on his proposal for the bank. He already had one leg in yesterday's crumpled jeans when Daisy banged on his bedroom door and yelled, "Rise and shine, Wyatt!"

Hobbling to the door as he yanked the jeans over his hips, Temple almost broke his toe on a box of medical supplies he'd hauled out of the bathroom the night before. He only caught a glimpse of Daisy and Rebecca before they disappeared down the stairs.

"What the hell time is it?" he called, moving to the top of the stairs.

"Coffee time," she called back over a shoulder that was bare except for the thin strap of a lemon yellow sundress. This was the first time he'd seen her in a dress. He nearly swallowed his teeth.

Pausing, she said, "By the way, Mr. Clean, the bathroom looks great. You, however, look worse than something Troublemaker might drag in. Tsk-tsk. You've got ten minutes to shave before Jeb's crew shuts off the electricity."

"Shuts off the..." Temple grabbed the handrail and ran barefoot down the stairs after her. "No. I worked all night on a document I need to fax to my banker in California."

As he closed in on her, Daisy shifted Becca to the opposite hip. A mistake. It put her face-to-face with Temple's bare suntanned chest. Lowering her gaze proved an even bigger error. His jeans, carelessly donned, were unbuttoned.

Daisy revised her earlier assessment. Troublemaker had *never* dragged in anything remotely resembling this. If he had, she'd be buying that darned cat choice cuts of steak. Wyatt's all-too-exposed flesh left her with ideas that had nothing to do with pouring coffee for Jeb's crew.

Temple had suddenly stopped talking about faxing his documents. His gaze focused on his daughter. "Daisy, look," he exclaimed in a low delighted voice. "Rebecca isn't leaping out of your arms to get away from me today."

Daisy glanced away from Temple's smooth muscles long enough to realize that what he said was true. His daughter eyed him warily, but she didn't fight to get away as she'd done before. "What do you suppose it means?" Daisy asked quietly.

Temple's smile lit his entire face. "I'm no doctor, but speaking as her father—it's fantastic! Give me a minute to shave and dress, and I'll come fix strawberry crepes for breakfast. She always loved crepes. I keep thinking it'll only take one small familiar thing to trigger her memory. Who knows? It might be as simple as breakfast."

Daisy found the excitement in his eyes contagious, even though she knew that the minute a breakthrough occurred, both Wyatts would be gone. Just when she'd grown used to having them around. Not only used to it, but if she was honest, she'd admit she *enjoyed* having them around. And she was nothing if not honest.

"You mean you want me to tell Jeb's crew to get lost for an hour or so? Rather costly, isn't it?"

Temple looked out through the living room window at two panel trucks, where at least five men milled around, smoking. He passed a hand over his rough jaw and mentally calculated bodies times the hourly rate, which was a healthy chunk of cash. He glanced back and into Daisy's eyes. "What's a few bucks compared to maybe releasing the one dam in Rebecca's mind that'll make a difference? I'll gladly pay."

Daisy's heart did a funny little skip. Pure unselfish love was a rare and beautiful thing. Present condition excepted, Rebecca Maria Wyatt was a lucky little girl indeed. "I'll go send them away," Daisy said, giving Wyatt her best smile. If he hadn't already wormed his way into her heart last night with the tender loving way he held his daughter, this latest gesture would have cracked open the door and let him in.

"Is there anything I can do to get breakfast started?" she asked, surprising herself. She didn't usually volunteer for kitchen duty. "Anything you need?"

Temple named a few obvious ingredients like flour, sugar and salt. Daisy laughed. "I know we already have that stuff—you bought it yourself." Still grinning, she shooed him back upstairs.

"Mrs. Hargreaves down the street said she'd watch Pipsqueak and Troublemaker today to keep them out of the workmen's hair. Maybe Becca and I will take them over now and stay for a glass of fresh buttermilk. I read somewhere that too many cooks spoil the broth. I'm positive it applies to crepes, too."

Temple smiled and scraped back a lock of hair that had fallen across his brow. "If you're not back in half an hour, I'll eat them all. And at my age, a man can't take too much rich food." He circled a hand over his flat stomach.

Daisy moistened her lips. Who was he kidding? The man was all lean muscle. Lean tanned muscle, except for a teensy strip of white she could see below his open jeans. Hmph. You'd think she hadn't seen lots of nearly naked male bodies out on those shrimp boats. Why, then, did less of Temple Wyatt seem like more? Like too much. Whatever the reason, Daisy elected to beat a hasty retreat. "Half an hour," she said saucily. "And don't overcook them."

"Not to worry. My teacher was a French chef who ran up a bill at my resort in Tahiti that he couldn't pay. The guests liked the way he worked it off so much, I hired him. Now every time I go there, I get free cooking lessons."

"French cuisine won't cut it here, bucko. This is a boardinghouse, not a resort. So, if *you're* planning to run up a bill you can't pay, you'll work it off hauling nets."

"You're a cruel woman, Daisy Sloan. I quite imagine your new partner would feed me to the sharks the first day out." Laughing, Temple retreated up a couple of stairs.

"You obviously don't know how hard it is to get somebody to work nets, Wyatt. Shrimpers have been known to take a sweep of the drunk tanks looking for strong backs."

Temple stopped. "But not you."

"Not me what?"

"You didn't take vagrants out alone on a boat with you dressed like...like..."

"Like what? Spit it out."

Too late, he realized he'd been about to make what would surely be considered a sexist comment. He didn't do that with other women he knew. What was it about Daisy Sloan?

"Like nothing," he growled. "Take every damned degenerate in town out in that leaky tub of yours. End up shark bait, for all I care. It's nothing to me. By the way, that's a nice dress you have on. You should wear dresses more often." He was back up the stairs and his bedroom door slammed shut before she could swallow her surprise.

"Right!" she shouted. "Dresses are so practical for shrimping. For your information, the *Lazy Daisy* is not a leaky tub." She hugged Becca, who seemed alarmed by the loud voices. "Sorry, kiddo, your daddy brings out the worst in me." They'd started for the front door when she decided he'd actually given her a compliment. Even if it *was* a backhanded one.

FIFTEEN MINUTES LATER, showered and shaved, Temple jogged downstairs, whistling. He felt pretty good. More than good. He'd faxed his banker the proposal and had already been faxed back with the go-ahead to buy the land. On the down side, he'd had another phone call from Miranda's parents, asking if he'd found anything. Temple hated telling them that the Coast Guard had nothing and that he hadn't gotten around to hiring a boat to go out and take a look himself. He should do it, if for no other reason than that they were Rebecca's grandparents. His marriage might have been a mistake, Rebecca wasn't. The least he owed them was peace of mind.

Damn. His good mood vanished.

He walked into the kitchen and smack into Sal and Daniel Coletti. His mood deteriorated even further.

"Where's Daisy?" demanded Daniel, punching the air with Daisy's coffeepot. Sal glared with equal fervor over the rim of a cup he held to his lips.

"Help yourself to coffee, men," Temple said sarcastically. "I'm making strawberry crepes for breakfast. Should I plan on serving two more?"

Sal Coletti's lip curled. "Look, Mr. Fancy Pants, we just wanna see Daisy."

Temple checked his faded khaki chinos. They were a long way from fancy.

"Yeah, dude," Daniel drawled, draining the pot into his cup. "Don't get smart with us. You're only a big cheese in Cal-ee-forn-i-ay. Not here." He glanced around suspiciously. "Where's Daisy?"

Temple was damned if he would tell them Daisy was two houses down the street. Besides, he was dying for a coffee. Sidestepping Sal, he grabbed the pot from Daniel and dumped the old filter in the trash. What would they do if he casually mentioned having kissed Daisy last night? Rearrange his face? Might be worth the licks he'd get in first. But the lady deserved better than kiss and tell. "Did the shrimp quit running?" Temple asked as he measured water. "Thought you guys went out at daybreak."

"I own the boat, and I go when I want. Where was Daisy last night?" Daniel growled. "I phoned here at ten. Didn't get any answer."

Temple nudged Sal out of the way and took down a cup. Ten was about the time he and Daisy had been out on the front porch. He hadn't heard the phone, but then he hadn't been listening, either. He turned away with a casual lift of his shoulder.

Daniel boxed him against the sink. "We don't like smart asses."

"Really?" Temple shrugged again. "I'm not her keeper, gentlemen," he said, focusing on the sway of Daniel's gold earring.

"Look, pal," the younger Coletti said. "We didn't come to fight with you. Daisy's most always home. Dan'l got to worrying."

Temple understood worry. He'd done enough of it himself over the past six months. He backed off. "Daisy took Rebecca to Mrs. Hargreaves's. If you want to see her, go there. She was home all evening. Sat out on the porch with Rebecca until late."

The two Colettis placed their empty cups in the sink and both made for the back door. "No need to bother her," Daniel said gruffly. "Independent as she is, she probably wouldn't thank us for messing in. Don't need to mention we dropped by. I promised her old man I'd keep an eye out for her, is all. Like to keep my promises. Especially to the dead, if you know what I mean."

Temple guessed that was Daniel's way of saying he had Papa Sloan's blessing. "No problem." Temple studied the coffee that had begun to stream into the pot. "Actually I'd planned to hunt up Sal this afternoon." Temple had a promise of his own to keep. To Miranda's parents.

"Me?" Sal acted surprised.

"Yeah. My ex-in-laws are having a hard time. They don't understand the lack of information regarding the explosion and the wreckage."

Daniel broke in. "They have Daisy's statement."

Temple nodded. "Yes, but they'd like me to nose around and see if anything got missed. I thought if Sal knew anyone who was going to drop nets out there, I'd pay them to tag along for a day."

Sal stroked his chin. "How much?"

Daniel grabbed his brother's arm. "You stay outta the Row, little brother. Daisy didn't have no business being there, and you don't, either."

Sal jerked his arm from Daniel's hold. "I'm my own master, Dan'l. Don't push. And I ain't Daisy. It'll cost ya, dude," he told Temple. "Two hundred bucks, plus you help pull nets. I don't fool around, either. I expect you to pull your weight."

Temple had figured more than twice that amount. And he was no stranger to hard work. Did they think a man got to own world-class resorts without getting his hands dirty? "Tomorrow?" he asked. "I'd go today, but I've got an appointment with my daughter's doctor. Otherwise, the sooner the better."

"Tomorrow it is. Sunup. Pick you up at the curb. Bring your own coffee and lunch. Don't be late. You snooze, you lose. Got that, dude?"

Temple nodded curtly. Spending the day with this turkey wasn't going to be any picnic. He hoped Miranda's folks didn't want him going more than once. If the authorities had found nothing, what could he hope to turn up? He stood for several minutes after the Colettis had left, doing nothing. His stomach felt a little queasy just thinking about going out to where people he knew had died so violently. Where, except for the grace of God and the presence of one woman, he'd have lost Rebecca, too.

Temple roused himself enough to start the crepes just as Daisy and Rebecca walked in the back door. Luckily he'd washed Daniel and Sal's cups, or she would've been even more suspicious about his lack of progress.

"I don't smell breakfast." Daisy wrinkled her nose and sniffed the air. "We're hungry, aren't we, Becca?" She lifted the girl into a chair at the table.

Temple sighed. "I guess I'm never going to get you to call her Rebecca, am I?"

Daisy flushed. "Sorry. I don't know why it's so hard to change. Sometimes I call her my Water Baby." Then she explained why.

Temple nodded. "I know the story." He smiled at the child who regarded him with wide somber eyes. "Well, maybe she'll remember one of the names," he said with a shrug. "I won't mention it again."

"Is something wrong? You look sort of down in the mouth."

"Nothing," he said. "Actually I should be happy. My banker gave me the green light to buy the Galveston property."

Daisy was much more excited about that news than she had any right to be. "Good for Galveston," she said mildly, curbing personal satisfaction as she pretended interest in Temple's batter-measuring techniques. "I guess that's why breakfast isn't ready yet. Why don't I set the table? Jeb's crew will be back soon, and I don't want to have to feed that mob. It'd break the bank. My bank."

Temple chuckled. "The good thing about crepes is that they cook fast. I set the strawberries out to thaw last night. Do you want to pour Rebecca a glass of this milk before I put it back in the fridge?"

"Yeah. Boy, she hated buttermilk. Hasn't she ever had it before?"

"I doubt it. Although I don't know what all Miranda fed her. I thought she might have tried it."

"Apparently not. She spat it out all over Mrs. Hargreaves's new vinyl floor."

"I'm sorry. After breakfast I'll go clean it for her."

"I already did. Found out her new flooring cleans like a dream. And she has six grandkids, so it didn't faze her in the least."

"Then right after breakfast we'll visit Dr. Rankin, if it's okay with you."

She glanced up from setting the table. "I wasn't sure you still wanted me to go."

"Why not?"

"I don't know." She turned back to the table. "We can skip the Railroad Museum if you'd like."

He frowned as he poured the crepe mix onto a hot griddle. "Did I miss something? I thought we decided on the museum and afterward, the beach, if Dr. Rankin had no objections. Oh, and weren't we going to buy Rebecca some shorts?"

"Yes, but I figured since you got the nod on the property, you'd want to go nail it down. Anyway, last night you said building sand castles was silly."

Temple flipped a crepe out on a plate, then covered it with strawberries and sour cream and folded it like a pro. After testing it for warmth, he set it in front of his daughter. He was pleased to see that once again Rebecca made no effort to avoid him.

He lingered at the table for a moment, giving Daisy a sidelong glance. But because he felt he owed her an apology for the way he'd acted last night and because he didn't quite know how to phrase it, he went back to the griddle and flipped out another crepe.

She did nothing to make his apology easy. Finally, as he handed her a plate, he tackled the problem head-on. "Daisy, last night was hormones talking. It had nothing to do with sand castles. I was angry at myself for kissing you when I shouldn't have."

"Why shouldn't you?" Daisy gazed at him over Rebecca's head. Before he could answer, however, the girl pushed her empty plate toward Daisy and mumbled what sounded like "More."

Both adults did a double take. *"Did she speak?"* Temple asked.

"Sounded like it to me. This is what happened yesterday with the cinnamon rolls and the cat. She seemed to say just one word, then nothing more. Rebecca, honey, do you want another crepe?" Daisy leaned over and spoke directly to the child.

Temple held his breath, but only the tick-tock of the clock broke the silence. Rebecca stuck her fingers in her mouth. Temple took the plate away and hurried to fix her another crepe. "She definitely said, 'More.' God, I never thought I'd be so happy over one word. I can't wait to see the doctor. Are you okay with leaving Jeb's crew here alone while we're gone?"

Daisy nodded, wishing he'd go back to her question about why he shouldn't have kissed her. She'd liked the experience, and after thinking about it most of the night, imagined he had, too. But maybe not. Or perhaps he worried that she'd want more than kisses from him—like maybe marriage. He'd be considered a good catch; Daisy knew plenty of women whose fishing expeditions weren't confined to the gulf.

She'd barely tasted the first bite when Temple plopped a second fatter crepe on her plate and roused her from her daydream. Rebecca was already halfway through hers.

"I'm getting full," she protested. "You take this one."

"There's plenty. One won't last you. Better eat while you can."

"I thought maybe while you tell Jeb's men what needs to be done with the wiring, I'd fix a picnic lunch—for the beach,'' she said. ''Unless you'd rather do something else.''

''Railroad Museum first, then the beach. Sounds good to me.''

''Well, we could save building sand castles for tomorrow.''

Temple turned away from her steady gaze. ''I, uh...'' How should he put this without letting her know the Colettis had been checking up on her?

''I didn't mean to imply you had to spend every day with Rebecca and me,'' Daisy rushed, feeling her cheeks heat.

''It's not that,'' he assured her. ''Tomorrow I made plans to go out to Rum Row. Miranda's parents called again. They're really pressuring me.''

Daisy toyed with her strawberry-and-sour-cream sauce. ''I see.'' Her stomach seemed to object to what she'd already eaten. For a moment she saw that yacht again splintered across her wake.

He unplugged the griddle and sat down with his plate of crepes. ''I don't expect to find anything, but maybe by just going, I can help ease their pain.''

''Hey, you don't owe me any explanations. I'll take Becca upstairs to get her cleaned up. Thanks for making breakfast.''

Her prim thanks irritated him. ''Call it fair trade for your picnic lunch. I know you like to keep score.''

''I don't—and I wasn't. It's just that no one's ever cooked for me before. I don't know quite how to act.''

''Your dad never cooked?''

''No.''

''Didn't Daniel invite you over to his place for wine and pasta?''

"Daniel had to fix three squares in his family for so long, in addition to work and school, I don't think he looks at any facet of KP as enjoyable."

"So if his wife works outside the home, she'd have to pull double duty."

Daisy stiffened. "I don't see how that concerns either of us." She stood, carried her plate and Becca's to the sink and put them in to soak. When she finished, she took the child by the hand and led her away.

Damn, Temple thought. He always seemed to put his foot in it where Daniel Coletti was concerned. Why couldn't he just accept what Daisy said—that she didn't intend to marry the guy?

Perhaps because that wasn't the message Daniel seemed to be receiving either.

A GOOD TWO HOURS LATER, after Daisy had dealt with the tantrum Rebecca threw in the hospital parking lot, the three of them sat in Dr. Rankin's office, feeling frazzled.

"This is great news." The doctor looked up from the journal of Rebecca's progress they'd brought in and beamed. "These small snatches of speech tell me you're getting closer to the key that'll unlock her mind."

"I hope bringing her here didn't set her back," Temple said. "She seemed perfectly content in the car, but when we pulled into the parking lot, she went wild."

"That's normal. In a way, it shows a thought process working. She equates this building with the pain of blood tests and such. See how listless she is again? She may do this seeing water, boats and who knows what else." He studied Rebecca for a long minute, then glanced at Daisy. "If you don't mind, I'll have my secretary run a copy of this journal for the other team members. I'll let you know if they concur with me."

Daisy laced her fingers through Becca's damp curls. She didn't know how many such episodes *she* could take—let alone the child. It wasn't so much the tantrum as the terribly blank look that was back in Becca's eyes. "We were going to the beach this afternoon to build sand castles and look for shells. Should we skip it?"

"Did we lose ground?" Temple added. "Or is this a good time to show her there are fun things to do at the beach?"

Dr. Rankin shook his head. "I have to be honest. I just don't know. My experience tells me that even if the ocean causes her a painful flashback, it may also trigger some part of her ability to remember. Frankly I'm glad to see you two attacking this problem together. Everything we've learned about children in shock tells us they need a sense of normalcy. A certain tranquillity, if you will, especially in the adults around them. Sometimes it's hard to achieve, since the parents are also upset."

"How much will she remember about her mother and . . . her mother's friend?"

"Time will tell," the doctor said. "You two may be in for some rough storms. I hope you're both willing to ride them out." He answered Daisy's question, but it was to Temple he looked.

"My daughter is my first priority, Doctor. I've placed a bid on some resort property here, but I can be as involved or uninvolved as Rebecca's situation dictates."

Dr. Rankin closed the journal and got to his feet. "Good, good. That's what I wanted to hear. Let me get this copied, and then you three go enjoy the sun. Remember, I'm available by phone anytime. With luck, we'll see this little lady back on track before school starts."

"I never thought... Will she retain what she's learned?"

"You want answers I can't give. She may or may not have gaps in her past. I'll be just a minute with this."

Once the doctor left the room, Temple stood and began to pace restlessly. Daisy pulled Straylia out of a large jute bag she'd brought. "Aren't you pleased?" she asked Temple. "I thought Dr. Rankin was encouraging."

"Unless you consider that he's guessing about everything."

"Educated guesses," she said doggedly.

He stopped pacing and tugged affectionately on her ponytail. "Remind me to make sure you're always in my corner, Daisy."

Her heart tripped. "Always" had a nice ring. But she was probably reading way too much into an innocent remark. Thank goodness Dr. Rankin whisked back in and dispersed the images that had begun to crowd her mind. Images of the Wyatts bringing love and laughter back to Sloan house... Yet those images lingered even after the doctor handed Temple the journal, even after they said their goodbyes and left the building.

"Where to now?" Temple asked Daisy, watching his daughter unwrap a piece of gum Dr. Rankin had given her. It amazed him that she knew some things instinctively, yet didn't know him.

"To the Strand to get Becca's shorts. From there we can take a trolley to the Railroad Museum and ride the train back. If that goes well, we can try the beach. I know a private spot where there shouldn't be a lot of other kids to bother Rebecca."

Temple's steps slowed. "She used to love being with other kids...."

"And she will again," Daisy said fiercely.

Temple held Daisy's determined gaze captive for a long moment. "In that case, fair lady, I'm putting us totally in your hands."

Daisy felt a sudden need to lighten the mood. "Are you sure you want to give me all that power? I may take you out to the pier and make you walk the plank."

"Not bloody likely. I saw *Hook* five times. I know all the escape routes."

Daisy laughed, then reached down and tickled the little girl, who seemed to have perked up now they'd left the hospital. Becca giggled out loud in the first genuine laugh Daisy recalled having heard from the child. Did she remember the movie? Daisy wondered.

As the three of them climbed into the car, Temple sensed that Rebecca's giggle was another milestone. He rolled down his window and let the morning's tension blow away on the breeze.

This was a treat. He'd rarely taken time off work before his divorce, and none since. They were halfway through their tour of the museum when it occurred to Temple that he and Rebecca should have done more of this sort of thing. And now they couldn't. At least not without Daisy. Thing was—did he *want* to go without Daisy? He found watching those two cavort in the cab of an old steam engine delightful. Pleasure was another feeling he hadn't experienced in far too long.

At the working model train, it was Daisy's turn to stand back and observe. What was there about trains that turned grown men into boys? she wondered wryly when it proved impossible to shake Temple loose. Seconds later she was glad she'd failed. Becca ventured close to her dad and clapped when he blew the train's whistle. The two of them huddled together at the end of a long tunnel. It left a choked feeling in Daisy's throat, seeing those two blond heads so close to each other. His hair streaked by the sun, hers downy as new cotton. Both waiting impatiently for the locomotive to emerge.

Daisy finally wrested them away, only to have them walk her legs off going from display to display. Rebecca fell asleep before they were fifteen minutes into the real train ride that makes a circle tour of Galveston. She'd started out seated on Daisy's lap, her little nose pressed to the window, but soon her eyes drooped and she slid down, her bright curls cradled on Temple's thigh.

"Leave her," he whispered softly when Daisy tried to move her.

Smiling, she sat back. It wasn't long before Daisy decided the other passengers probably took them for a vacationing family. And she felt guilty. Was that because she knew it was a lie? Or because her own family had never done things like this together. Looking back, Daisy realized she'd thought the way they lived was normal. After today, she knew she'd never marry a man who didn't share things like vacations or outings with his family. Things like chores and child care. Of the men she knew well, that narrowed the field to the one seated beside her.

"You're quiet," Temple murmured, reaching over his sleeping child to tweak Daisy's nose. "Why the frown? Aren't you enjoying yourself?"

"Very much," she said, covering a guilty flush with a yawn. "There's something hypnotic about the clackity-clack of train wheels. I'm doing my best not to saddle you with two sleeping bodies."

"That would be a problem if I had to carry you both back to the car," he teased. "To keep awake, why don't you play tour guide—tell me about the landscape and the buildings. Who better than a member of Galveston's historical society?"

Daisy did such a good job she drew an audience. One by one the other sightseers drew nearer, until she was ringed by a cluster of interested listeners.

Temple sat and stroked Rebecca's hair. He enjoyed watching Daisy's animated features almost more than he did learning about Galveston. When the train sped past the waterfront and they were assaulted by the fishy odor hanging over the home of the Mosquito Fleet, Temple found himself speculating as to whether she really liked being a shrimper or if she'd fallen into it because she had idolized her father.

If he hadn't been so hungry, Temple would've suggested they go around again. Luckily he managed to carry Rebecca to the car and get her buckled in before she woke up disoriented. He felt helpless when she began to scream. But Daisy climbed into the back seat and calmed her, and Temple, not for the first time, thanked providence for creating such a strong bond between those two.

"What do you think?" Daisy asked anxiously. "Should we skip the beach? This little kiddo's had a pretty full day already."

"Let's play it by ear. We'll eat, stretch our legs and soak up a little sun. If she seems distressed, we'll leave."

"Good. That's what I hoped you'd say," Daisy told him. "But...I've been looking forward to building sand castles."

"Uh-huh," he grunted. Strangely, though, the idea did hold some appeal.

Daisy directed him to a sheltered strip of sand adjacent to a public park. The park was busy, and by comparison the beach seemed deserted. But the sand was white and fine; thanks to a small trickle from an inlet, it was also damp enough to pack.

"Nice. Not too windy," Temple noted as Daisy gathered up a bucket of oddly-shaped containers, then handed him the picnic basket and a blanket.

"That's another thing I like about this beach," Daisy said. "You know what? I'm starved."

His stomach growled in answer, and they laughed. It didn't take them long to set out and devour the food Daisy had fixed. The problem, as they packed up the remains, was keeping a rein on Rebecca. She'd tugged off her shoes and socks to run in the sand. Leaving Temple to clean up, Daisy dashed off after the girl.

Temple liked listening to his daughter's squeals as Daisy tried to interest her in the bright seashells, rather than running and throwing sand. Both were out of breath and flushed by the time they sauntered back to the blanket to show him their treasures.

"Hey, take it easy," he admonished playfully when Daisy accidentally kicked sand over his socks and shoes.

"Take them off and roll up your pant legs," she instructed, dropping to her knees beside him. "In another month, you'll die out here in long pants. You should've bought yourself some shorts at the Strand today, too."

"I have shorts. But I wouldn't have tromped through the hospital in them."

"Really? Well, then, isn't it fortunate that I saw fit to wear a dress to avoid embarrassing you?" Snatching up the buckets and sifters, she tossed her head and marched toward the inlet.

Rebecca followed, imitating Daisy's flounce so precisely that Temple wanted to laugh. He felt guilty, however, for throwing a damper on the day. After stashing the shells in the picnic basket for safekeeping, he did remove his shoes and socks, rolled up his pant legs and ran after them to make amends.

By then, Daisy had laid the foundation for a very basic castle. Temple hovered over her. "Look, Daisy, I didn't mean that as a dig, at you." He gave a rueful laugh. "You'd understand if you'd seen my shorts. They're old as Noah and twice as holy. I only brought one pair. If you recall, this wasn't intended to be a vacation. I thought I'd be home by now."

His words wounded her—especially the words that suggested he'd rather be home—but she wasn't good at staying mad. "Okay, you're forgiven," she said, handing him a shovel. "I guess you can play with me."

His gaze skipped over her bare feet, swirling skirt and beyond, to her wind-mussed ponytail, then back to her sparkling eyes. His heart started a dull thudding in his chest. He wanted to take her in his arms and kiss her—to sink down on the warm sand with her and make slow delicious love. He took the shovel and grabbed a bucket to keep his hands occupied, realizing belatedly how unsteady they were.

Many things prevented Temple from acting on his desires. Daylight. The park. His daughter, who peered out from behind Daisy's legs apprehensively. And his conscience. This lady was doing him a colossal favor—she'd turned her life inside out for him. Seducing her wasn't the way to repay a debt. Temple abruptly set down the bucket. Turning his back on her, he said gruffly, "You're building that damned thing too close to the inlet. When the tide comes in, all your hard work will be swept out to sea.''

''Spoilsport,'' she called, watching him stalk back to the blanket. Daisy could've sworn he'd really wanted to help. That he'd seemed eager. Vaguely disappointed, she wondered what kept Temple Wyatt from letting down his hair. Whatever it was, she wasn't going to allow him to ruin Rebecca's fun. For the next three hours, she hauled wet sand and made elaborate peaks and turrets. When one wall collapsed and Becca cried, Daisy hugged her and patiently explained that rebuilding was part of the fun.

Temple sat on the blanket, idly sifting handfuls of sand through fingers that itched to cuddle them both. He thought how motherly Daisy looked, consoling his daughter, drawing her into a game about water babies. Moodily, he reflected on Rebecca's mother. What in hell had she been doing in that place they called Rum Row? Anger warred with sorrow as Temple jumped to his feet. ''It's getting late,'' he called. ''Nearly dusk. We'd better go.''

''Come see.'' Daisy beckoned him with a sand-caked hand. Of course, their finished castle was no work of art, but Daisy and Becca thought it was wonderful.

Temple voiced the expected words of admiration.

Daisy thought his delivery lacked the proper enthusiasm and told him so. He snapped back an irritated response. As a result, the three rode home in silence. The sun had set by the time they reached the house. Jeb's crew had gone, but they'd left behind a mess and had shut off the electricity to boot.

''Blast,'' Daisy said. ''We'll have to dig out the lanterns.''

''Does this mean cold food and a cold shower?'' Temple grumbled.

Daisy grinned. "Welcome to Galveston, matey. This is how it is during a hurricane when the storm knocks out our transformers."

"What do you do without electricity?"

"Party hearty, my friend. Party hearty."

Temple couldn't muster a smile to save his life. Watching her play at the beach all afternoon had been pure torture. The kind of party he envisioned probably wasn't what she had in mind.

That cold shower was sounding better all the time.

CHAPTER NINE

"YOU DON'T PARTY. You don't play on the beach." Daisy couldn't believe she'd fallen so hard for this man. A man more suited to her sisters' image of Mr. Right than hers. "What *do* you do for fun, Wyatt?" she asked him.

He refused to be provoked. "Here. Let me carry Rebecca upstairs. Looks like we wore her out. But I think she had a good time today, don't you?"

Daisy heard the thread of underlying doubt in his voice as she took a flashlight from the hall cabinet and led the way upstairs. "It was obvious you were bored senseless," she said. "Becca and I had a great time."

Temple stopped cold. "Why do you do that? Put words in my mouth? I enjoyed myself today."

"You sulked the whole time we were at the beach."

"I did not. Men do not sulk. Where's Rebecca's nightgown?" he demanded, stomping past Daisy into the moon-shadowed bedroom. Not surprisingly, he smacked a shin into her desk and swore. Rebecca shifted in his arms but didn't wake up.

"Stop already, before you kill yourself. I'll change her. Here, take the flashlight and go get the lanterns. You'll find a couple in each bedroom closet and more on the top shelf of the kitchen pantry."

"No, I'll put her down first, if you'll hold the light."

Carefully he made his way into the alcove and placed Rebecca on her bed. "You can't mean to use lanterns every night until they finish the wiring. The foreman said it'd take three or four days. Do you really light those things all over the house during a bad storm? What would you do if they caused a fire? You don't even own a cell phone."

"Amazing, isn't it? I can't imagine how we've lived all these years."

"It's so primitive. Don't you know this is the age of fiber optics and the information highway?"

"Well, Mr. Electronic-Gadget Expert, what would you have us do for light?"

"Go to a hotel."

Daisy laughed. "I beg your pardon?"

"You heard me. I think we should check into a hotel until Jeb's finished. The one where I stayed when I arrived on the island has some nice suites. My attorneys and I had three bedrooms with a living room in the middle. All we'd need are clothes for each of us for a few days. Oh, and my portable computer and the small fax."

"I hope the three of you will be very comfortable," she drawled. "Me, I've lived in this town forever. Can't you hear the buzz if I checked into a hotel with a man? We may not be on your information highway, but gossip here travels with the speed of light."

He looked puzzled as she gently covered Rebecca with the thin blanket and motioned him out. "I guess I don't see the problem," he persisted. "How's staying at the hotel any different from my renting a couple of your rooms?"

"It just is," she maintained stubbornly. "People know this is strictly business. Neighbors, and friends like Daniel and Sal, have seen your room. In a hotel, well, they'd speculate."

Temple ran two fingers along her chin. "You think Daniel and Sal don't already speculate?"

The flashlight Daisy held bobbed erratically. The pupils of her eyes widened, crowding out the color.

Temple heard her breath rasp as she drew it in. He stepped closer and slid both hands around to the back of her head and up, loosening the clip that held her ponytail. A thicket of curls, suddenly freed, brushed his wrists and tumbled over her ears.

"Temple..." she whispered.

"Temple, what? Hold my seashells? Play in my sand castle? We aren't kids, Daisy. Do you have any idea what I wanted to do with you this whole blasted afternoon?"

She lowered her gaze and smoothed her tongue over her bottom lip. When she lifted her head and met his eyes, she supposed his thoughts must have been the same as hers. "You wanted to kiss me," she whispered, and lifted her face to let him do it now. "I guess I knew you wanted to kiss me."

"More," he groaned, crushing her to his chest. "I wanted to do a whole lot more than kiss you, Daisy honey. We're talking get-naked, climb-into-bed, all-out shoot-me-to-the-clouds kind of lovemaking." He lowered his voice. "I still want to."

Daisy shivered. She'd hypothesized plenty about that very thing. Too bad he didn't just act on his impulse, instead of spelling it out. They might already be making beautiful memories—and providing grist for the Island's rumor mill. A minute ago, she would have tumbled into bed with him. Now...well, she couldn't, that was all. Maybe because of the gossip. Or because she couldn't believe in a future for them. Or—and this was the most painful—because she knew it wouldn't mean to him what it would to her.

"Sounds as if you have a lot of experience with this sort of thing," she said solemnly, slipping from his arms.

His first inclination was to laugh. But when she went to stand beside the windows and the rising moon revealed a veiled look in her eyes, he realized she thought he did this kind of thing all the time. In reality, he'd been out of the serious dating loop for years. Ever since Miranda. So now what? His heart still thundered with desire, and he guessed this was where modern couples exchanged blood tests or signed contracts or something. Unsure what to say next, he was relieved when she spoke from the shadows and changed subjects completely.

"Are you hungry? We could order in pizza."

He was hungry, all right. But he didn't need pizza. What he needed was to distance himself from Daisy. Making up his mind, he said, "I think I'll turn in. Remember I said I was going out on the boat with Sal tomorrow? I'm to be outside waiting at dawn."

"Sal? You hadn't said who was taking you. Funny, he didn't tell me. I'm not sure I want the *Lazy Daisy* going into Rum Row again."

"I believe his contract lets him make those kinds of decisions. If you'd wanted to restrict his authority, you should have penned in something."

"How did I know he'd be so foolish?"

"Don't look at me like I twisted his arm. I gave him every opportunity to refer me elsewhere. He set the price. Daniel even tried to talk him out of going."

"Well, then, that's why. Sal's tired of being Daniel's little brother." Ordinarily it wouldn't be any big deal, but Daisy couldn't shake the memory of that yacht. Whenever she thought about it, she felt chilled to the bone. "Don't go," she begged him suddenly. "Your going won't bring Miranda back. Nothing will. You've got no business out there, Temple.''

Daniel had said the same thing, and Temple had more or less ignored it. Now his stomach took a major drop. Was there something she knew that she wasn't telling? "But you went. Twice, according to your report.''

She shivered and hugged herself. ''I didn't give much credence to the stories. You know what they say about the whoppers fishermen tell. But that speedboat was real— and dangerous.''

''Look,'' Temple said. ''I've known DeVaca all my life. If I had to describe him, I'd say he was a true gentleman. He wouldn't be involved in anything... dangerous.'' Temple hunched his shoulders and pressed his lips into a tight line. ''I don't understand this at all.''

''It appears we'll never know what happened,'' Daisy said gently.

''That's just it. Miranda's parents want answers. Hell, *I* want answers.''

''Enough to risk your life?'' Her voice had an edge of panic.

Temple watched how she rubbed at her arms. He saw the lines of worry that bracketed her lips and the fear lurking in her eyes. ''Daisy, I can't think of a single soul who'd want to do me harm. Not one.''

''Yes, well, I don't know.'' She thumped her chest with a closed fist, and the fear in her eyes changed to hardness. ''That boat is my life, Wyatt. If anything happens to her, I'll hold you personally responsible.''

The boat. So this was about money—and some damned smelly boat. ''Fine,'' he said, too loudly, as she brushed past him and left the room. Only it wasn't fine. Moments ago he'd been angling to take her to bed. Now she sounded like . . . Miranda. Temple Wyatt had existed miserably for a year and a half with one woman who cared more for material things than for people, including her husband and child. He wasn't about to make that mistake again.

Hearing his daughter stir in the alcove, Temple cooled his anger and went in to check on her. Undoubtedly their voices had disturbed her sleep. He tiptoed into the alcove, knelt beside her bed and murmured, "When you get well and we go home, puddin', I'm going to spend less time on the road and more time with you, I promise."

She rolled to face him and opened her eyes. Temple held his breath for a moment, expecting her to scream. She didn't. Instead, she gave him the sweetest smile, tightened her arm around Straylia and promptly went back to sleep.

Temple was both shaken and overjoyed, although he doubted she was really awake. Still, what if she subconsciously knew him? With hands that shook, he snugged the sheet up under the dimpled elbow that lay hooked over the koala. Then he stood, smiled down at her and slowly withdrew.

At the door, he ran into Daisy. She handed him one of the three softly glowing lanterns she juggled. "I was just thinking," she said pleasantly, as if they hadn't argued. "Tomorrow, if you don't mind, I may take Becca back to play on the beach."

Temple experienced a sudden gut fear at the thought of his child going off with someone—like she had with Miranda. Just as quickly he got a grip on his emotions. "Realistically I know I have to let go—that I can't smother her. But—" he hesitated before saying earnestly "—you will be careful, won't you, Daisy?"

She gazed at him sadly. "I'm sorry you feel you need to say such a thing to me."

"I'm sorry, too," he said, avoiding contact with her body as he headed for his room. The minute he closed the door, he felt like hell. To take his mind off his troublesome landlady, Temple made phone calls to a few of his hotel managers. It was the first time in a long while, and fortunately none of them had problems for him to solve. Or, perhaps, unfortunately. He still needed something to occupy his thoughts. Oh, well, he had plenty of professional magazines to read. Except that the lantern started to flicker. After half an hour, Temple gave up and went to bed. Sleep evaded him far into the night as Daisy's warning played over and over in his head.

THE MOON WAS STILL OUT when Temple's alarm buzzed. He groaned, shut it off and fumbled for the jeans and shirt he'd laid out the night before. The minute he tied his sneakers he had second thoughts about wearing jeans all day in such heat, and shucked them off, donning, instead, his one pair of disreputable shorts.

He hurried downstairs in the dark, only lighting the lantern after he had the kitchen door firmly shut. No sense in waking the household. It was hard to know what sounded good for breakfast, to say nothing of what a man might want for lunch. After a few false starts, Temple settled on a couple of bagels with cream cheese for breakfast and a cheese sandwich for lunch. To heck with the cholesterol. Recalling the smell that hung over the Mosquito Fleet, Temple wasn't sure he'd be able to eat, anyway. And the prospect of handling those slimy little crustaceans... Temple shuddered.

Thank God Daisy kept a box full of rubber gloves under the kitchen sink. Let Sal rib him, he didn't care.

Contrary to what Daisy believed, shrimping wasn't going to rank up there with one of the great experiences in his life. Too bad these gloves weren't leather. He guessed he should just be thankful they weren't pink.

Temple wished he hadn't thought about Daisy. He felt a vague sense of guilt about the way he'd ended things last night. He'd conveyed the wrong message. Maybe if he left her a note and some cash to take Rebecca to the kiddy rides he'd seen advertised at Moody Gardens, she'd see it as a gesture of trust. Sometime during that long night, he'd realized it wasn't a matter of *not* trusting her. And he was willing to believe she felt some genuine concern about his safety out in Rum Row. Lord, but he worried about her, too. Didn't she have any clue how he felt?

Hoping he was doing the right thing, Temple wrote the note and slipped it under the edge of the coffeepot, along with fifty dollars. Then he gathered up his thermos and his lunch. After extinguishing the light, he made his way out to the curb to wait for Sal.

Daisy let Temple step out the front door before she completed her descent down the dark staircase. Plucking aside the curtain, she watched him saunter to the curb, where he was clearly illuminated by the street lamp. He wore shorts, she saw, and smiled. The man might argue, but he did take advice after he'd chewed on it for a while.

She didn't want him to catch her spying, so she dropped the curtain and wandered into the kitchen to make coffee. That was when she discovered his note. It took her several minutes to recognize that in essence it was a vote of confidence. He *did* trust her. Clutching it, she ran to thank him. But apparently she'd dawdled too long; Sal's Jeep was just rounding the corner at the far end of the street. Daisy was struck by the strongest urge to run after it—to snatch Temple back. She stood, staring into the gray dawn until the paperboy rode by on his bicycle and gave a wolf whistle. The kid couldn't be more than twelve or thirteen. Tossing him a benign wave, she scurried back inside. It was time to feed her animals.

IN THE JEEP, Sal mumbled a greeting of sorts to Temple, then fell silent. Temple wanted to know what shrimping entailed, but on viewing the hulk seated at the wheel, he now wished he'd asked Daisy. Although, considering how she felt about this excursion, she'd probably have told him to go to hell.

"I see you're wearing deck shoes with net over the top of your feet," he said to break the ice. "I only brought these jogging shoes." Temple laughed, hoping to solicit a laugh in response.

Sal cast a quick glance at Temple's shoes. "I hope you're prepared to throw those things away at the end of the day. They'll stink to high heaven."

Temple mentally added eighty bucks to the two hundred he was already paying, then consigned his perfectly good polo shirt the same fate as his shoes. The cost of this jaunt was rising fast. Oh, well, he couldn't look at it in terms of money. Not if it helped Miranda's parents.

"I'm not going straight out to the Row," Sal announced. "It's not the best place to be at daybreak, dusk or after dark."

"You're the captain," Temple told him. "I'm just along for the ride."

"Maybe you're not such a bad sort," Sal admitted grudgingly.

Temple laughed. "I've built resorts in some pretty remote locations. I've developed a healthy respect for local superstitions, voodoo, et cetera."

"Stuff that goes on in the Row isn't voodoo. It's real enough. Drugs and gun-running. Illegals." He tapped his chest. "This hide ain't worth much, but I've grown attached to it."

"Why on earth would Daisy shrimp in such an area, and alone at that?" Temple asked.

"As long as her old man was alive, guys in the fleet didn't mess with her. Now, outside of Dan'l and me and Loren Bonner, she takes a lot of flack for doin' what's considered here to be a man's job. Daisy has a tendency to get off by herself, away from the main fleet. When the shrimp are runnin' good like they've been this year, it's easy to get busy and not worry about your fellow shrimpers until weigh-in. Dan'l said he should've guessed what she was about when she beat him by three hundred pounds of shrimp the day before the explosion. He just didn't add it up."

"Don't get me wrong," Temple said, "I'm not laying blame. I'm very grateful that she was out there that day. I just wondered why she'd take unnecessary chances."

"Money. Why else? Her dad let the house go. She started taking boarders to pay for fixing it up. Plus, he left her with doctor bills. She didn't get a lick of help from those fluff-headed sisters of hers, even though they got an equal split in the will. Didn't come to the old man's funeral, but they called and demanded Daisy sell the house. Took all of her last year's catch money to buy their shares. The only reason she leased me the boat is because she's trying to hang on to the place. It's everything to her."

"Sounds like she's had it rough," Temple said in an abstracted voice as Sal wheeled into the busy parking lot down at the wharf.

"You don't hear her complainin', do ya? Anyway, she's got me and Dan'l lookin' out for her. Daisy's business ain't no never mind of yours."

Temple had just been thinking maybe Sal wasn't so bad. After that speech, he revised his opinion again. "If you and your brother gave a rat's ass for her," he snapped, "you'd have helped rewire that old firetrap. The place has dry rot on the dock side, and come the next rain, the roof over her kitchen sink is gonna leak. You fellows put into port between two and three o'clock. That leaves a lot of daylight to be hoisting a hammer, instead of a beer."

Sal's eyes chilled. "A lot you know, dude. Most afternoons my brother tends bar at the Smuggler's Roost, and I wait tables at Willy G's. Besides, Daisy didn't ask for help," he said sullenly as he hopped out of the Jeep. "She knows all she's gotta do is ask."

Temple wondered if he should apologize for having pegged the two Colettis as lazy louts. But because he didn't like Sal's possessive tone when it came to Daisy, he collected his thermos and lunch in silence. He would, however, judge them less harshly in the future.

"Could you run over what's expected of me?" Temple asked after they'd boarded the trawler. "I've done my share of sailing," he told Sal. "Pleasure boats and power crafts mostly. Although I did do some marlin fishing off Barbados. God, does it always smell this bad?"

Sal grinned. "It ain't lilacs, that's for damn sure. But if you think this is bad, wait 'til the fleet comes back in hundred-degree heat, fully loaded."

"I can hardly wait," Temple muttered as the leanly muscled shrimper showed him where to stow his lunch, then gave him a quick lesson on the winches.

"Here comes Loren." Sal waved to someone on the dock. "We'll shove off now, and give you the two-bit tour en route."

Temple nodded, then turned his attention to the bean-pole youth who'd just boarded the *Lazy Daisy*. Following introductions, Sal and Loren took their stations, one fore and one aft. The boat was soon under way. About midpoint out in the channel, Sal gave two short raucous blasts on a horn. Temple nearly jumped out of his skin and grabbed his ears. Because it was clear Sal enjoyed catching him off guard, Temple braced himself against the rusted railing on the starboard side and vowed he'd be ready for anything the guy might pull.

He thought the first three hours went fairly well. He managed every task either of the seasoned shrimpers doled out. And quite well, even if he did say so himself. As the sun climbed high into a clear blue sky, Temple removed his shirt. Already sweat poured off him in rivulets. He counted himself lucky that Loren kept a variety of baseball caps in one of the foot lockers; after watching Temple wipe off his sunglasses a few times, Loren offered him his pick of them. Since there wasn't one with the San Francisco Giants logo, he selected the Houston Astros. The kid grinned, and Temple wasn't about to tell him it was the cleanest of the lot.

The boat's forward hold was about two-thirds full of smelly wriggly shrimp when Sal announced they'd mosey out toward Rum Row.

"Don't let my dad know," Loren yelled at Sal over the noise of the engines. "He'd skin me alive. Made me promise after that yacht blew up that I wouldn't crew for anyone going out there.''

Sal leveled a thoughtful look at Temple. ''Folks on that yacht, 'cept for the kid, were obviously up to no good,'' he shouted back. ''Ain't nobody got a beef against us. We're just gonna mind our own business. Cast a few nets, maybe take a look around the cove. You ain't yellow, are you, kid?''

Loren shrugged his thin shoulders. ''Rollie Sparks claims he followed a school of shrimp into the Row a couple weeks ago. His boat's a twin to this one. According to Rol, some tough-looking dudes eyeballed him and his crew from the deck of a deep-V powerboat.''

Temple's ears perked up. ''When was this?''

''Thursday, week before last.''

Sal scowled. ''Rollie Sparks is a blowhard. Hear him tell it, he's made it with every dame on the Island. Truth is, the majority wouldn't be caught dead in the sack with him.''

''That's a fact,'' Loren agreed with a chuckle. ''The cute new waitress who worked Saturday nights at Willy G's dumped a pitcher of beer over his head for spreading lies about her. It was great. She said it was worth getting fired over.''

''That happened on my night off. I heard the story, but I didn't realize it was old Rollie. Wait'll I tell Dan'l. No love lost between those two.''

Temple listened to the men's discourse with interest even though he didn't know Rollie Sparks.

They chugged along for maybe twenty minutes before Sal steered them into a secluded cove. Temple had a new appreciation of what it must have been like for Daisy, sailing all the way back to port alone, a terrified child in her care, debris from the explosion in her wake. In spite of the hot day, a shiver shot up his spine. This area was truly isolated. No wonder the boat had gone down without a trace—with no one, except Daisy, to see it. He sighed. Maybe he and Miranda's parents needed to have a memorial service of some kind. Something to create a sense of closure for friends and family.

Temple took a moment now to whisper his goodbyes. He and Miranda couldn't live together and they'd had trouble agreeing on how to raise Rebecca, but he'd never, ever wished her dead. And Domingo. The man had oozed old-world Latin charm. Temple had difficulty believing the courtly hotelier would be involved in anything as ugly as drugs or guns. Sadness stole over him.

"Somethin' the matter, dude?" Sal called. "I've been talkin' to you for five minutes. You seen a ghost, or what?"

Temple straightened away from the rail. "No. No ghosts. Just sorry memories about people I once...cared about."

"You mean the couple who went down with the yacht?" Loren asked.

Temple nodded. He was prevented from speaking by the lump in his throat. "I've read that the sea always gives up her dead."

"Sometimes she's stubborn." Sal shaded his eyes against the glaring sun and cast a glance around the quiet cove. "Looks like we got the place to ourselves today. Why don't we drop a couple nets, then take our lunches in the runabout and go exploring? There's a lot of debris from who knows what caught on those old cypress roots yonder. See, right near the curve?"

Temple looked to where he was pointing. "You're right. Can't say I'm hungry, but the plan suits me." Turning, he deferred to Bonner.

"Yeah, smell kind of turns your stomach at first." Loren lifted his baseball cap and ran a hand through his sweat-dampened hair. "If you don't mind, Sal, I think I'll stay here and crack the calculus books while I eat. I've got a big test next week."

"Okay. Probably just as well not to leave the boat alone. Swells come up without warning in these currents."

The men dropped the nets and anchored the boat in jade green water about a half mile from shore. Temple helped Sal lower the small outboard and waited while he grabbed his lunch sack before following him down the ladder. The tide was coming in. Temple decided that was what had suddenly turned the water a dark murky green—and added the choppiness. He wasn't totally convinced they should be making this run.

Sal started the motor and angled the small boat toward the gnarled cypress. "There's supposed to be pirate caves all along the shore, but you have to know the currents to land. Coast Guard's lost more than one boat trying."

Temple watched Loren and the *Lazy Daisy* grow smaller the closer the runabout came to the shore. He was amazed by the junk caught in the maze of twisted roots reaching out into the brackish water. Soda cans. The top to a woman's two-piece bathing suit, which Sal scooped up and held aloft with a grin. "I'd like to run into this pirate," he joked. "Thirty-eight D if she's an inch." Then he looked sheepish. "Hey, I'm sorry if you think this could've belonged to your ex. I meant no disrespect if she was stacked."

Temple merely shook his head.

"No wonder you dumped her." The swarthy shrimper's rakish grin was back.

"I didn't dump her." Temple flushed and looked away, out to sea. "I guess you'd be closer saying she dumped me."

Sal fidgeted and finally tossed the bathing-suit top back into the underbrush without further comment. "Ah, what have we here?" He cut the motor and let them drift beneath the overhanging limbs. "A chunk of white fiberglass. Looks like maybe the start of call letters."

"And over there..." Temple paddled with his hands, drawing the bow closer to the knotted root. Leaning out, he snagged a larger sliver of fiber. It was free of writing, but paint along the jagged edges bubbled as though singed. Temple held it up for Sal to inspect. "What do you think? Powder burns?"

Sal frowned. "Could be. Coast Guard might've quit lookin' too soon. D'you see any more?"

"No." Temple battled disappointment.

"Might not even be from the yacht. A lot goes on out here. Let's take them, and we'll make one turn around the perimeter while I eat. Then we'll go on back to the *Lazy D* and reel in the nets."

Temple's okay was cut off by the roar of the outboard. He flashed Sal a thumbs-up, instead.

There proved to be nothing else of interest in the cove. Because the tide was sweeping in fast, Sal sped full throttle back to the Boston trawler. Loren helped hoist the runabout aboard. Immediately the three men set to dragging nets. It was a good haul. One that almost filled the aft hold.

"Hot damn." Sal grinned as he shook out the last of the smelly catch.

Temple tried not to gag as Loren shooed sea gulls away and recovered the hold.

"Let's lift anchor and move her about three hundred yards to port," Sal suggested. "We'll fill that foreward hold in short order. Maybe dock in time to crack a beer with Dan'l before we shower and head to our other jobs. That okay with you, dude?" He turned to Temple as he wiped sweat from his brow.

Temple was about to say he'd skip the beer and get home to Daisy, but his words were cut off by the growl of an approaching powerboat. They all turned in surprise. A moment ago there hadn't been any sign of another boat in the area; now this one was closing in fast. All three yelped in a chorus as a row of bullets sprayed the *Lazy Daisy*'s deck, tearing up the old wood.

"Holy shit!" bellowed Sal. "It's that phantom speedboat. Let's get outta here!"

Temple vaulted to the top of the hold. If he could gain a better look, maybe the police would have something to go on. Only he hadn't calculated that the driver—a heavy-set man with dark bushy eyebrows—would make a short turn and roar past them on the starboard side. Too late Temple saw the flash of an automatic weapon in the hands of a tough-looking scar-faced character. A ribbon of fire chewed at Temple's left arm and left it numb. It was a minute before he noticed a steady drip of blood. Detached, he watched it congeal at his feet. Damn! Did he get a good enough look?

The old Boston trawler creaked and strained as Sal hit the throttle with every ounce of pressure the old girl had. He blasted the horn several times to let any approaching craft know they wanted a clear track into the bay.

Loren scrambled on hands and knees over to the ship-to-shore radio. He switched channels to the Coast Guard frequency and sent out the standard SOS. Static drowned out any response. Twice more the deep-V'ed hull screamed past. Twice more the *Lazy Daisy* ate a blast of lead.

Feeling suddenly weak, Temple clung to the cross boom until dizziness forced him to his knees. That was when he realized his blood was staining the weathered deck a ruby red.

Fast as their assailants had sneaked up on them, they disappeared even faster. As though the speedboat had gone up in a puff of smoke.

Temple staggered to his feet. "Where in the hell did it go?"

Loren tugged at his baseball cap and warily scanned the bright blue horizon. "Damned if I know. Was it real?"

Temple clutched his wounded arm with the other and felt his fingers slide through the slippery blood. "Real enough," he managed, his ears beginning to buzz.

His fading voice drew Loren's and Sal's attention. They had barely blinked when Temple tumbled face-down onto the deck—his last conscious thought a prayer for Daisy and his daughter.

NEWS OF THE INCIDENT traveled over the Island like wildfire. Daisy was in Moody Gardens with Becca, eavesdropping on three old codgers, when she heard one of them say that there'd been a shooting out in Rum Row and the Californian, Wyatt, had been hurt. Daisy dropped the fresh blackberry ice-cream cone she'd just purchased. Praying there'd been some mistake, she snatched Becca up in her arms and ran all the way to the car. She'd battled a feeling of impending doom all day.

The drive to the wharf seemed interminable. Traffic refused to cooperate, and all she got were red lights. Her heart thundered in her ears. Her sweating hands had difficulty gripping the steering wheel.

Wyatt hurt? How bad? Her numb brain refused to paint the picture. Sick with fear, she glanced at the sweetly oblivious child. Rebecca licked happily at a cone of Rocky Road. Daisy almost cried.

What if he's dead? Daisy doubted Rebecca Maria Wyatt could ever recover from such a blow. She hadn't known it until now. Or she had, but she'd been denying the truth of how deep her feelings for Temple actually went.

And now maybe it was too late.

CHAPTER TEN

WHEN DAISY REACHED the wharf, she parked and unbuckled both seat belts with hands that shook. Racing down here might have been foolish, she conceded. Even now Temple might be lying in one of the area hospitals—or God forbid—the morgue.

No! Some frantic nurse or admissions clerk was probably trying to call her at home. But why would they? She was nothing to him, had no claim on him. She was his landlady. His baby-sitter. Hired help. She might have been more, but she'd let the moment slide. Now what if she never got the opportunity to tell him she cared? What if she lost him?

Daisy refused to let her mind travel in that direction. "Come on, Becca," she said to the girl. "Let's go see if the *Lazy Daisy* is in port." She clasped Becca's hand and urged her to hurry. *Hurt doesn't mean dead.*

The five-year-old did fine keeping up with Daisy until they reached the slips where the shrimp boats were berthed. There she stopped, wrinkled her nose and refused to go a step farther.

On the one hand, the action frustrated Daisy. On the other, she was encouraged. Becca obviously didn't like the unpleasant odor. Her behavior was an honest-to-goodness normal reaction. Daisy could hardly wait to tell Temple. As she stood there wondering where he might be, an aid car and two police vehicles pulled out from the docks and screamed past. The lights and sirens frightened Becca so badly that she dropped what remained of her ice-cream cone and promptly started to cry.

In a quandary, Daisy didn't know whether to hop in the car and try chasing the emergency vehicles or to calm Becca and then seek answers among the crowd she saw gathered at the pier. Good sense won out. She knelt and murmured soothingly to the child. "Shh. Don't cry, sweetheart. Your cone was almost gone. Let's go get a cloth from the car and clean your face. We'll pick up Straylia while we're there. I'll bet he's never seen so many boats."

Becca pulled free of Daisy's arms and ran toward the car as if she'd understood. Daisy's mood took an upswing. Temple would be overjoyed at the news—*provided he was in any shape to receive it.* She opened the trunk and quickly found a damp washcloth in the beach bag, refusing to let her happiness be dimmed.

It wasn't until Sal Coletti charged through the parking lot at a dead run that Daisy realized she'd parked in the row of cars across from his Jeep.

"Daisy," he said blankly. "What are you doing here? Did the police call you?"

"Police?" Her heart did a double flip and felt as if it landed upside down. "I came because I heard Temple's been injured."

Wiping a grimy hand across his pinched lips, he rolled his shoulders forward. "I gotta go. Wyatt was hit twice in the left arm. Nicked a big vein. The police told me to meet them at the hospital to give a statement. I left Loren to unload and weigh in." He dug car keys out of his bloody jeans pocket and turned to leave.

"Stop." Daisy grabbed his arm. "Nicked. How do you mean, nicked?"

"I thought you knew. Bullets. That son of a bitch in the powerboat showed up again. You've got a helluva boat, Daisy. None of us would be here if she hadn't carried us into patrolled waters before those dudes did us in."

When Becca squirmed, Daisy realized that she'd almost washed the skin off the kid's face. Snatching the koala bear from the bag with hands that were far from steady, Daisy asked in an undertone, "How bad was Temple hurt?"

Sal's eyes narrowed marginally. "You didn't ask about the *Lazy D*'s damage."

She helped Becca into the front seat. "The boat's nothing, Sal. She can be replaced. Now tell me about Temple."

The young shrimper colored. "So *that's* the way it is? I told Dan'l you were sweet on the city dude. He said you'd never be taken in by some California bimboy."

"Bimboy?" Daisy turned from buckling Becca's seat belt. "Temple Wyatt a bimboy? That Daniel can be such a jerk. Not to mention obtuse." She took a deep breath. "Look, Sal. This isn't the time to be petty. Do you see that child?" she hissed as she shut the door. "She's already lost one parent. What do you think will happen if she loses the other? Now tell me where I can find her father."

His flush darkened. "Trauma Center. Where do you think?"

"I should've known. I almost went there first."

"God, I stink," he said suddenly. "I hope the police know what they're in for, havin' me give a statement before takin' a shower."

"I rather think they're more concerned with getting a description of those characters than they are in how ripe you smell," she said, yanking open her door.

"They don't need me for that. Wyatt's the only one who got a good look. Me and Loren were too busy makin' tracks outta the cove."

"So you're saying Temple's in good enough shape to talk?"

"Hell, yes. He was squawkin' about having to see a doc. The dude doesn't have a lick of sense. He was bleedin' like a stuck pig and thought he could get in the Coast Guard boat and lead them back out to the Row."

"I should think not," Daisy said with an indignant huff. But the icy fist that had squeezed her heart from the moment Sal said Temple had been shot began to ease. She thought she could at least drive to the hospital without getting in an accident.

"Lead on, McDuff." She made a feeble attempt to tease Sal. But once Daisy climbed into the driver's seat, she was surprised to find that her hands still weren't steady enough to turn the key. After three tries, she succeeded. But only because she paused and gave herself a stern talking to.

The hospital wasn't far. However, getting there seemed to take forever. Tired from the kiddy rides at Moody Gardens, Rebecca dozed off before they'd gone a block. She was fast asleep by the time they reached the hospital. Sal, who'd taken a shortcut and was already there noticed the trouble Daisy was having trying to manipulate the limp child from her car.

"I'd offer to help," he called from his Jeep, "but then you'd have to burn her clothes when you get home. And they look pretty new."

"They are. I'll manage. I just have to position her right. There, see?" Daisy finally got Becca's legs straddled around her waist. It was awkward because the girl wouldn't let go of Straylia.

Sal dashed up two flights of stairs to the emergency room and waited impatiently while Daisy puffed her way to the top. Amazing how quickly one got out of shape, she thought. It'd only been a month or so since she'd hauled in her last shrimp net.

Inside, Sal hung back, away from a line of people waiting at the counter.

Daisy had learned enough about the hospital's bureaucracy during Becca's stay that she bustled past reception in search of someone with greater authority.

A few feet into the room, Daisy heard Temple's angry voice spewing from one of the examination cubicles. "No pain medication!" he roared. "You patched me up. Now go, and let me talk to the police."

A knot untied in Daisy's stomach. If he felt well enough to dish out orders like that, he must not be badly off at all.

"May I help you?" A dark-haired nurse in stained and faded scrubs appeared out of nowhere to block Daisy's access to the room. Although she spoke to Daisy, the woman centered her attention on the blood-encrusted Sal.

"You got a couple of policemen in there?" Sal pointed to the room Daisy had been about to enter. "I'm meeting them."

"Yes, but..." The nurse looked him over, obviously trying not to react to the smell permeating the air around him. Eventually she lost the battle. "Phew! If you're not in need of treatment, there's a men's room down the hall where you can wash up. You—" she turned to Daisy "—be seated. You can't just barge in on a patient."

Daisy dredged up her best smile. "We're Mr. Wyatt's family." She indicated the sleeping child with a jerk of her chin. Rebecca *was* family. Before the woman could demand proof, a red-faced nurse rushed out of the room carrying a metal tray that still bore a full syringe. *Saved from pretending I'm his wife,* Daisy thought as she deftly exchanged places with the nurse Temple had succeeded in evicting.

He looked up with a scowl as she entered, obviously prepared to go round two with the woman. When he saw that it was Daisy, his eyes lit up and his features rearranged themselves into a welcoming smile. Momentarily dismissing the policeman holding the clipboard, Temple held out his good hand to her.

She took it, noticing that his left shoulder was heavily bandaged to the elbow. Two spots of blood had seeped through the gauze. Her eyes widened, and she squeezed his fingers tightly.

"Looks worse than it is," he growled, his voice soft out of deference to his sleeping daughter. He slipped his hand from Daisy's grip long enough to smooth Rebecca's sleep-flushed cheek. "Let me finish giving my statement, then I'll fill in the blanks for you," he told Daisy. "This time I want the police to catch those bastards. They got too cocky for their own good today. I managed a decent look at the driver." Turning to the policeman, he said, "I'm pretty sure he works at DeVaca's Rio resort. At least he did a year ago."

Daisy gasped and dropped heavily into the chair beside Temple's bed. "Are you sure? Why would one of Mr. DeVaca's employees do such terrible things?"

Temple shook his head slowly. "Don't ask me. Unless he and Domingo had a falling out. Disgruntled ex-employees have been known to get vicious. Your description of the power boat was right, Daisy."

The policemen hadn't adjusted to Daisy's sudden intrusion. Glancing quickly at Temple, the younger one said, "I'm not sure I buy that theory, Mr. Wyatt. Why would a disgruntled employee hang around after he blew his target away?"

"Beats me. You're the ones who've studied the criminal mind."

The older of the two officers doffed his hat and massaged his close-cropped silvery hair. "The chief thinks our perp believes somebody on that Boston trawler can identify him. If the doctor releases you today, Wyatt, we'll want you to come down to the station and look at mug shots of known South American drug dealers. Between you and our artist, maybe we can come up with a workable likeness."

"Brazilian authorities," the second officer chimed in, "think the demolition experts who took out that yacht might have been running high-grade cocaine. And you're right, Mr. Wyatt. They've gotten bolder. Border patrol is afraid it might mean there's a big drug deal in the offing. If those scraps of fiberglass you found match De-Vaca's yacht, you might be at even greater risk. The chief wants a watch on your house tonight."

Temple shifted on the bed. He placed a broad hand on Daisy's shoulder. "I don't have a house," he told the men. "I'll bunk at a local hotel until this is over. Which one do you recommend for security?"

Again the older policeman—named Vic—smoothed a hand over his crewcut. "No hotel is safe, son. Too open and too many entrances to guard."

"What do you mean?" Daisy asked, reaching up to cover Temple's hand with hers. "Why would you move from my place?"

The younger officer, Al, glanced at her with interest. "Sloan is your last name, right?" He flipped through his pad when Daisy nodded. "Don't you own the trawler?"

"This doesn't involve her," Temple said. "She's leased the boat to Sal Coletti. Where is he, anyhow?"

Al scribbled furiously. "That the guy you said clamped off your vein and saved your life, Mr. Wyatt?"

"Really?" Daisy exclaimed. "Sal saved your life? He didn't mention anything of the sort to me." She clung to Temple. "I followed Sal here. He went to wash up."

"Tell you what. You look a little peaked," the cop said to Daisy. "Why don't you and the kid wait out in the reception area?" Al slipped a beefy hand under Daisy's elbow and hustled her and her sleeping charge to the door. "Trade you," he joked to a nurse who met them with Sal in tow. "Miss Sloan for Mr. Coletti."

The nurse nodded and beckoned to Daisy.

"Look, it's my boat." Daisy planted her feet. "I'm the only witness to the first incident," she told the policeman. "And this child is the one survivor from the yacht. I'd say we have a vested interest in what goes on here." She met his eyes. He glanced over at the older officer, still standing next to Temple's bed.

Before any decision was made about her staying, however, Daniel Coletti burst through the double doors at the far end of the corridor. He shook off the nurse who tried to stop him and thundered like a wild man to the doorway of Temple's room, where Daisy and his brother stood talking with the police.

"I just pulled in to dump my load and heard about the shooting," Daniel said as he grabbed Sal's arm. "I warned you to stay away from the Row! Do you think next time you might listen to me, little brother? And you," he said, jabbing a finger at the man lying on the hospital bed. "I told Daisy and Sal you were trouble with a capital *T.* This is all your fault, Wyatt. If you weren't already hurt, I'd work you over myself."

"Who the hell are you?" Al stepped forward, brandishing his clipboard. His disapproving gaze rested on Daniel's stubbled chin and swinging gold earring.

Becca woke up, looked around and started to scream.

"This place is a damned zoo," declared Vic, the veteran officer. "All we want to do is find out how this man got shot." He indicated Temple with a jerk of his thumb, only to discover the patient climbing out of bed. "Where in blazes do you think you're going?"

"To the police station," said Temple through gritted teeth. "Sal will drive me there. Daisy is going to take Rebecca home. And Daniel's going somewhere to chill out with a beer." Reeling, he steadied himself on the metal footboard.

For a full minute, no one moved, including the child who'd succeeded in getting a stranglehold on Daisy's neck. That is, no one moved until the nurse bore down on their cubicle with a rickety wheelchair. Motioning Temple into the chair, she issued virtually the same orders he'd given, only with more authority. "Mr. Wyatt," she said disdainfully as she handed him his insurance card and his bill, "you are free to leave us. The doctor says go home and rest." She shoved him into the chair and wheeled him toward the door, raising her voice. "Please take the rest of this motley crew with you. Any sign of infection in those wounds, go see your family doctor. Otherwise, the venal sutures will dissolve on their own. Oh, and next time you get shot, try to do it among better-smelling companions.'' She all but dumped him at the curb, sniffed at his followers, then swished back inside.

Temple was first to laugh, even though it hurt his arm.

Daisy was next to join in. ''Brother,'' she gasped, bouncing Becca on her hip, ''I guess she wouldn't like it if you paid your bill with fifty pounds of shrimp, would she?''

''Stop.'' Temple laughed harder. ''The doctor looked like he smelled something bad the whole time he worked on me. Now I know why I got such quick service. It had nothing to do with the seriousness of my condition.''

The cops grinned, too. ''Then I guess you won't be offended if we do let you ride to the station with your friend here,'' said one, pointing to Sal.

''I'll run home and get Temple some fresh clothes,'' Daisy offered. ''Then I'll stop at Daniel's and pick up stuff for Sal. You have a shower at the precinct, I presume.''

Both policemen nodded. Daisy put Becca down, then hand in hand they dashed to her car before either Temple or Sal had time to object. She let Daniel's grumbling go in one ear and out the other.

She completed the circuit in record time, even though at the Colettis', she got a ten-minute lecture from Daniel about not getting involved. He had to tend bar within the hour, or he'd ''by damn go in her place,'' he said.

Later, when Daisy parked outside the police station, she handed Becca the bag with the men's clothes to carry. The girl hummed as she skipped up the steps. It amazed Daisy how normal she seemed. In fact, she appeared better adjusted in most settings these past couple of days. Was that significant? Was she slowly awakening from whatever terrors held her captive? Granted, she had cried at the hospital today. But she'd been asleep; when she awakened, there'd been a lot of strange faces to deal with. And she calmed down quickly. Not like the way she'd acted even just a week ago.

Certain that each of these new achievements built toward ultimate success, Daisy walked into the station with a lighter heart. "We're here to bring Temple Wyatt and Sal Coletti some clean clothes," she told the sergeant at the desk.

"Thank goodness!" he exclaimed. "Captain Riggs has called down here twice to see if you'd arrived. Said he has all the windows in his office open and it still smells like a cannery. You want to give me the bag?"

"No," Daisy returned, sweetly but firmly. "They're expecting me, too. Could you direct me?"

At first he seemed taken aback. Then he did as she asked without calling ahead, for which Daisy was grateful. If they were overtaxing Temple, she intended to see that he left and got his prescribed rest.

Temple glanced up to check out the sudden low rumble of voices, and saw Daisy and Rebecca enter the room. Heads swiveled as Daisy ambled toward him through two rows of desks, and Temple realized she'd abandoned the frayed jeans she'd worn earlier. Her short red skirt brushed her tanned legs. A red-checked sleeveless jacket, a vest really, skimmed her slender waist. Most of the men in the room followed her progress.

Temple quashed a smile. As usual she was oblivious to the stir she created. And as usual, her springy curls escaped their ribbon clip. These past couple of days in the sun had highlighted the gold in her hair. Temple saw envy flash across the pale faces of the women officers, who were tied to uniforms and desks.

Daisy stopped several feet away from where Temple sat in a straight-backed metal chair, working with the composite artist who faced him. She bent to whisper in Rebecca's ear. A moment later, the child sidled shyly toward him and held out the large grocery bag she carried. Temple's heart went into a tailspin. Speechless, he reached out with his good arm to accept the bag. Tears sprang to his eyes, impairing his vision.

Father and daughter stared at one another for a poignant stretch of time. He, with misty eyes and a joyous smile. She, without expression of any kind. Still, Temple considered this small achievement a major breakthrough. Rebecca had approached him with minimal urging from Daisy. The child hadn't screamed in terror, hadn't run the other way. *Hallelujah!*

"Well, hello, sweetheart," the artist said, turning with a broad smile when he looked up from his work and noticed the child. "Aren't you Miss Cutie Pie? Where did you come from, darlin'?" Swiveling, the artist got his first glimpse of Daisy. He let out a long low whistle that sent Rebecca scrambling back to hide behind Daisy's legs.

"The little one is my daughter," Temple murmured in a voice that betrayed his emotion. "Remember the child who was thrown from the yacht?"

"Oh, yeah. Say, man, I'm real sorry. I didn't mean to scare her." The artist set his pencil aside and picked up the bag that Rebecca had dropped. He passed it to Temple. "At least now you and Coletti can go shower and rejoin the human race. I'll be happy to keep these two nice ladies entertained while you're gone." His dark eyes made another clean sweep of Daisy.

She ignored the artist's brash flirting as she threaded her fingers through Becca's curls. She could see that the picture on his board was only half-finished. For that reason, she would have offered to leave and come back later—if Temple had moved less stiffly. Or if she hadn't seen that his face was pale with repressed pain. As it was, she decided to try her hand at shaking him loose now.

"We came to give you a lift home," she said lightly.

"I can't leave yet, Daisy. We're finally making headway. No need for you to hang around, though. I don't want you involved. I'll take a cab to a hotel when I'm done. If and when I think it's safe, I'll send somebody to pick up more of my clothes."

He might as well have not spoken. "I don't think that's what the doctor had in mind when he wrote orders stating you should go home and rest," Daisy said in mild rebuke. "Those guys in the speedboat have been skulking around Rum Row for over a month. I doubt they're going to run off tonight. Their kind never does. And you're not going to any old hotel. Who'll look after you?"

Temple shifted. With some difficulty, he finally stood. Whatever he'd been about to say was interrupted by the police chief, who stuck his head into the room. "That the woman who brought you fresh clothes? What are you standing around jawing for? Hit the showers. And take Coletti."

Looking sheepish, Sal stepped out around the tall rawboned chief of police. He took care not to let so much as their shirtsleeves touch. "Hey, Daisy." Sal lifted a hand in greeting. "Why didn't you holler? It's gettin' kinda rank in here."

Shrugging, Daisy turned back to Temple. "Can you shower without getting your bandage wet? I don't suppose they have any Saran Wrap to put around that arm."

The artist chuckled. "Nurse or sister?" he asked of Temple. "Or both rolled into one?" His tone teased, thinly disguising his interest. "Or..."

"Neither," Temple growled. "She's a friend." But his liquid gaze caressed her in a manner that spoke of a lot more than friendship.

"Yeah. Sure." The young artist's brow arched.

"Do I have T-bone written on me someplace?" Daisy demanded, settling her hands on her hips. "You're acting like a couple of dogs scrabbling over a bone."

Sal, who'd just reached them, gave her the once-over and frowned. "It's that outfit. It's a wonder the smoke alarms didn't go off when you walked in. Why don't you run on home? We don't wanna give Galveston's finest heart attacks, do we?"

By now smoke was all but coming out Daisy's ears. "I believe I'm capable of deciding when to leave," she said in her iciest voice. "I *had* planned to run down the street and pick up hamburgers for everyone."

"Sounds good to me," the artist said, digging in his pocket for a five-dollar bill. "If there's anything I like, it's a lady who knows her own mind."

Neither Temple nor Sal acted too pleased. But Daisy wouldn't be swayed. She began taking food orders. So they gave theirs before going to the locker room.

There were a few times after the hamburgers had been consumed that Daisy regretted her decision to stay. The chairs allotted to visitors were hard, and she'd forgotten to grab the book, *The Water Babies*, that she'd been reading to Rebecca. Fortunately the hamburger place gave out balloons and toys with their kiddie meals, and Daisy played chase-the-balloon in the hallway until she was worn out. As they played, Becca said four words— "Give it to me." Daisy wanted to tell Temple at once. Except that he was looking more fatigued by the minute, so she thought it best to let him finish the composite.

At last she heard someone say the pictures of the two suspects were completed. She stood, determined to see that the police, who seemed to have limitless energy, didn't claim any more of Temple's flagging supply.

"All done?" she asked cheerfully, coming up behind the artist.

He turned, a smile on his face. "Yes, ma'am. Mr. Wyatt's satisfied we've got a good likeness of two of the men. We're faxing copies to the Rio police and Mr. DeVaca's hotel. To see if we can come up with any names."

"Tonight?" Daisy sounded aghast.

Temple shifted the sling supporting his injured arm. Daisy could tell it hurt like hell, but he said stoically, "I swear this is the very last thing I'm going to do tonight, Daisy. If we can get a positive ID out of Domingo's staff, it's bound to have a favorable impact on their APB."

She threw up her hands. "It's rubbing off. Less than a day, and you're beginning to talk like a cop."

The artist laughed, then stood and stretched. "Thanks to TV, we cops have no mystique left."

Daisy found herself laughing with him. "Okay. I give up. Scram, you two. Send that to South America on your handy-dandy info highway. Becca—Rebecca—and I will wait in the car. Come on, my water baby," she said, grasping Becca's hand.

"Don't go outside alone." Temple grabbed her arm, which in turn hurt his own, and it showed in his grimace.

Daisy turned. *"Et tu, Brute?"*

"These are hardened criminals, Daisy," Temple explained, lips pinched. "Not Sunday-school teachers. They've hung around just waiting for the *Lazy Daisy* to show up again. Last week they stalked a boat a lot like

her. We got lucky today. Now we have their backs to the
wall, and they'll get braver.''

Daisy's brow wrinkled. ''In what way? Surely they
could have found me anytime.''

An officer seated a few feet away spoke up. ''They
could have. But they'd be doubling their risk pulling
something in town. They knew from news stories that
you were out of commission, which meant they could
afford to sit and wait. Today they thought you'd gone
back to work. But since you leased the boat, all they've
done is increase the number of witnesses. Not a good
position for scum like that. The chief wants a man on
your house tonight, and one on Coletti's.''

The fine hair on Daisy's neck rose. Her grip tightened
on Becca's hand. Plain as day, the girl said, *''Ouch!''*

Both Daisy and Temple exhibited shock, then delight.
''There's more,'' she told him excitedly. ''Earlier she
asked me for the balloon. I think she's slowly coming
around, Temple. Will having a policeman watching the
house stifle her progress?''

He raked a hand raggedly through his sun-streaked
hair. ''I don't know. Maybe I'd better go to your house,
after all.''

Sal swaggered up in the middle of their conversation.
''You got Daisy into this mess, dude. Why don't you take
the kid and go back to California where you belong?''

Temple flinched, but Daisy bristled. ''Sal Coletti,
what's gotten into you? You know perfectly well that I'm
to blame, if blame's the word. No one made me shrimp
in Rum Row. I'm sorry I let you lease my boat and get
involved. I guess the best any of us can do now is see this
through. Go ahead, Temple, send your fax. Then let's all
go home and cool off.''

Sal's angry glare blazed between Daisy and the man she'd chosen to defend. He stuffed both hands in the pockets of his cutoffs and jingled his loose change. "It's pretty plain where your allegiance lies, Daisy-girl. If you come to your senses, you know where to find Dan'l and me. Not even you are worth getting shot at. As of now, I'm going back to pulling nets for my brother."

She gaped, hurt, as he walked away. Finally the sandy-haired officer who had delivered the warning a moment ago called to Sal and took off after him. "Wait, Mr. Coletti. I'll tag along, since I'm staking out your place."

Sal snarled a blistering epitaph.

Temple brushed a finger over Daisy's rigid jaw. "I'm sorry," he whispered softly. "Maybe when Sal calms down..."

She shrugged. "It's his choice. I didn't twist his arm in the first place. Besides, I'd never forgive myself if anything worse happened on my boat."

"Last night you said I'd be held accountable if something went wrong. I will be," he vowed. "Tomorrow we'll get someone to assess the damage. I don't expect you to believe me, Daisy, but I never dreamed in a million years that anything would happen."

"I do believe you." She reached up and cupped his face, using her thumbs to lightly smooth away the tense lines bracketing his lips. Pain lines, she thought. "Go do your faxing. Becca and I will wait right here." She raised up on her toes and kissed his cheek.

His good hand automatically flew to his face.

The artist ripped the two sketches off his pad and handed them to Temple. "Lucky dog," he muttered. "I should've known you two are an item." He clapped Temple on his uninjured arm. "Take care of her, buddy.

I hope you don't need my professional services again."
He turned off his desk lamp, smiled at Daisy and left.

She stared after him, openmouthed. "No," she protested feebly, "we're not an item." But Temple strode off
and left her talking to herself.

"I hear you," said a young policewoman from a
nearby desk. "I don't believe you, but I hear you." She
slanted Daisy a knowing grin, hefted her handbag and
sauntered off in the direction of the outer door.

"Well, Becca," Daisy murmured as she sat down and
pulled the tired child onto her lap, "am I that transparent?" The girl tucked her head against Daisy's shoulder
and trustingly closed her eyes.

A good hour later, just when Daisy had begun to yawn,
Temple returned. "Did you get an ID?" she asked after
gently waking Becca so they could follow the police officer who'd been assigned to watch her house.

"On one of them," Temple told her. "Halsey Shaw,
alias Harold Shaw and Hal Shoemaker, not to mention
a few more. According to DeVaca's night manager, he
has references on file—probably forged. Domingo fired
Shaw about eight months ago for tapping the till. The
manager also said they'd had some guests' jewelry disappear."

"Doesn't look good for Mr. Shaw," Daisy mused as
she unlocked the car. "Do the employees know Mr.
DeVaca is presumed dead?" she asked when they were
under way.

"Yes." He closed his eyes, rather than watch her ne-
gotiate traffic. "The manager mentioned things are
messy. It seems Domingo has two children and three ex-
wives ready to fight over his estate."

"Ouch," Daisy said as she pulled up in front of her
house.

Becca awoke and sat up. She held out the finger Daisy had squeezed earlier and in all seriousness repeated, "Ouch."

Daisy and Temple fell together laughing. "Invite our watchdog in for coffee, why don't you," she suggested, "while I scoot this little miss to bed. Unless you're too tired to stay up for coffee," she added, suddenly solicitous of Temple's condition.

"No, it sounds like a good idea. And it'll give our guy a chance to take a turn around the house."

Neither knew what a good idea it was until they stepped through the door—and discovered the house had been trashed. Apparently quite recently. As they entered by the front door, they heard footsteps running out the back. By the time their police escort had tripped his way through the pots and pans tossed around Daisy's dark kitchen, a speedy runabout was making its way down the inlet past her neighbor's dock, Even though it looked hopeless, the corporal gave chase out the back door.

"That does it," Temple said to Daisy. "I'm sending you and Rebecca to stay with my mother where you'll be safe."

"Safe? Where this whole thing started? Anyway, I'm not yours to *send*."

But the dark fires that smoldered in his eyes said differently.

CHAPTER ELEVEN

"I'M NOT TRYING to flex muscle, Daisy. I'm worried about you and Rebecca. We can't even see to clean up the mess those scavengers made until daylight. Please, humor me just this once. Let's go to a hotel for tonight."

Daisy studied his drawn features in the light of the flashlight beam. She saw the concern he'd voiced. Not the macho I'm-right-because-I'm-a-man reasoning so freely employed by the men who worked the docks. Real consideration.

"All right," she said, shocking him. "Let me go upstairs and pack a few things for each of us." She hitched Becca higher on her hip and started up the stairs.

"Daisy, wait. Will I offend you if I ask you to let Corporal Phillips give the upper floor a once-over first?"

She glanced toward the dark landing above. "I'm independent, Wyatt. Not stupid. Where is he, do you suppose? Not only that, where're Pipsqueak and Troublemaker? I left them inside this morning. They always come running to be fed when I get home this late."

"You're right. I haven't seen or heard them since we walked in." Temple tried not to look alarmed.

Corporal Randy Phillips burst in through the front door, startling everyone who'd seen him leave by the back. Sheathing his weapon, he said grimly, "Saw two goons in a speedboat. Decided chasing 'em was no use, and I'd be smarter to come back and radio the Coast

Guard. They suggest you folks stay someplace else tonight.''

"We were just discussing that." Temple straightened his sling. Unconsciously he massaged his aching elbow. "Daisy's going to gather some things from upstairs. Would you go with her? I'll take another turn around outside. Her pets haven't shown up. They may be hiding in the bushes."

The officer frowned. "I rattled the bushes, looking for lingerers. Didn't see so much as a mouse." He turned to Daisy. "Why don't you leave the little girl on the couch down here? She must be getting heavy."

Daisy shook her head. "We're fine." She smiled into Rebecca's sleep-slack face. "I like to keep her close in case she wakes up. Kids need to feel secure."

Temple felt his heart leap. Again he marveled at Daisy's protective attitude toward his child. She'd once said she didn't have much experience with kids, when in fact she was a natural. He could imagine her with a whole flock of her own children. *Their* children. It was a cozy picture. Far from the reality of their lives. He heaved a sigh. Maybe things were coming to a head, and that reality would change.

She bobbed the flashlight beam toward his face. "Are you okay, Temple? Why don't you sit? I'll check outside after I throw some clothes in a bag."

"No." There wasn't a heartbeat between her words and his reply. His feelings for her still gripped him. Feelings so strong that he snapped when he didn't mean to. "You just don't get it, do you, Daisy? This isn't some storybook lark. These guys are playing for keeps."

"I never thought it was a lark," she said quietly. Too quietly. She spun on her heel and marched up the stairs. On the landing, she turned and picked him out with her flashlight beam. "I didn't get shot like you did, Temple. My flesh didn't bleed. But I saw that yacht. I see it and your daughter's terror in my dreams five nights out of seven. Don't you ever suggest again that I take any of this lightly. *Never.* Do you understand?"

"God, Daisy, I'm sorry." Temple raised his good hand beseechingly. It was too late, however. She'd turned away again and melted into the darkness above. "Go with her, Corporal," he begged.

"Okay, sir," returned the young officer. "It's funny— these are the times we think women need a soft touch, yet they're the tough ones and men draw into themselves. I see it all the time." Leaving Temple with that bit of wisdom, he, too, was swallowed by the yawning blackness above.

Temple digested the corporal's words. He hated that a kid nearly half his age had to point out something so obvious. Uttering a sharp oath, Temple stalked outside, determined to find Daisy's animals.

As the corporal said, the bushes revealed nothing. Farther afield, Temple at last saw the glow of a pair of small eyes peering out from beneath Daisy's neighbor's beached rowboat. "Here, kitty kitty," he called softly, not wanting to get shot again should he be mistaken for a burglar. But the black cat didn't seem to care about Temple's situation. Belly to the ground, the rascal slunk out from beneath the boat, raced a few feet along the fence, then disappeared beneath it. "Dammit, Troublemaker," Temple muttered. Beyond in the velvety night there was a *whish* and a *thunk*. Suddenly the cat blinked complacently at him from atop the neighbor's porch railing. Temple swore again and eased open the wrought-iron gate. The squeak was so loud it gave him pause. He was certain that any minute lights would pop on all over the house and he'd be facing doddering old Mr. Jessup's unsteady shotgun.

Would wonders never cease? His luck held long enough for him to creep up on the cat. Then, one-handed as he was, Temple faced the problem of what to do with his flashlight. Heartened by the fact that the animal had started to purr, Temple doused the beam, tucked the flashlight into his sling and then lunged. "Gotcha," he whispered triumphantly as he grabbed the cat by the scruff of the neck. The surprised animal let out a yowl and a hiss, but Temple didn't care. He lost no time skedaddling from Jessup's yard. Once he made it safely back inside Daisy's yard, he didn't know if he had energy even for her to repeat this exercise with her dog. In spite of the sling, his injured arm was beginning to throb fiercely.

Lucky for him, Daisy had found Pipsqueak upstairs. "They locked the poor little guy in my closet," she told Temple when once again everyone met in the littered kitchen. "Which was why we didn't hear him bark. This house has good insulation."

Temple placed the cat in front of his water bowl, knelt and scratched him idly behind the ears. "What are we going to do with them tonight? Although I don't think our hoodlums will make another pass through here, do you, Corporal?"

The policeman turned from lighting the second of two lanterns he'd salvaged from among the debris. "Even if they do, I'll be here. And I'll look out for the pets. You two go get some rest. Looks to me like you've got a full day of cleanup around here tomorrow."

"Upstairs, too?" Temple stood and leveled a questioning glance at Daisy.

Still holding Rebecca, Daisy shifted. She didn't want to tell him. "We brought your laptop computer downstairs, Temple. I'm afraid they ruined your PC and fax."

"Those bastards." Temple dragged a shaking hand through his already rumpled hair. "I'd like to meet up with them in a dark alley."

"Don't even joke about it," Daisy said, lips pursed. "Ruffians like that have no conscience."

"You should see what they did to her room," the young policeman murmured in an aside to Temple. "Senseless wanton destruction."

"Daisy, no! Not your grandfather's ship models." Temple crooked a finger and lifted her chin so that he could look her in the eye. "What did they wreck?"

Her chin trembled. Tears clouded her whiskey-colored irises. "Things," she said bravely, although her voice broke. "Could we go now?" She pulled away. "I don't want to think about it anymore tonight. I'm sure it won't look half so bad in daylight."

Humbled, because he knew how much she loved those ships, and angry, because their destruction was so pointless, Temple vowed to make the unknown assailants pay. "I'll call the hotel," he said, "if Corporal Phillips will help you load our bags in the car." The officer agreed, and also radioed for another police car to drop by and follow them to the hotel. Soon, Temple, Daisy and Rebecca were on their way to a quiet beach hotel. If they needed any reminder that they weren't headed on a fun outing, they only had to look behind them at their police escort.

As if Daisy's day hadn't already gone from bad to worse, it turned out she was acquainted with the night manager and both desk clerks. One of them, Doreen Yarnell, was a former high school classmate. The worst gossip in town, next to Jana Jefferies. And now Doreen showed an inordinate amount of interest in the fact that Daisy was checking in late at night with a man. A gorgeous man.

Doreen fairly simpered when she informed Temple the three-bedroom suite he'd requested—the one he'd rented with his attorneys—was occupied. The only suite they had left was smaller. Two bedrooms.

"Daisy?" Turning, Temple gave her the option to stay or go.

She saw the tired lines around his eyes that probably meant he was running on reserve. "I'll bunk with Becca," she stated firmly, though she doubted if even that proclamation would deter Doreen's wagging tongue.

Nodding, Temple turned back and picked up the pen. It wasn't easy digging out his wallet and credit card one-handed.

Doreen remarked at least three times on his bloody bandage as she waited for the computer to spit out its approvals and verifications.

The snoop was hoping for juicy news to spread, Daisy thought sourly. She was extremely glad that Temple didn't offer even a shred. Let Doreen and her colleagues theorize. Daisy felt all eyes boring into her back as she fell in behind the bellboy, whose surreptitious glances and little smirks did not escape Daisy's notice.

Temple excused himself for a moment to go tell their police escort what room they'd be in. Daisy thought she was the only one who noticed the bellboy's attitude, but right after Temple had tipped the man and closed him out of the suite, she knew better.

"Tongues are wagging already. I'm sorry, Daisy," he said, poking his head briefly into the two side bedrooms, "You called it right. I'm afraid we're about to be served up over-easy for tomorrow's breakfast all around town. If they were my employees, they'd be replaced."

She shook her head. "In order of importance—what with you getting shot and those goons trashing my house—Doreen's twitty little scandalmongering is the least of my worries." She paused in the center of the room and looked around with interest. "Wow, these are nice digs. I had no idea. You know, I've never stayed in a hotel before."

"Never?" Temple turned from his cursory inspection of one of the bedrooms.

Daisy shrugged. "It's no big deal. Which bedroom do I get?"

"I should give you the bigger one. It has the better view, I'm sure. But it also has double doors leading out to a balcony. Not that our police buddies aren't attentive, but they said themselves that hotels aren't the most secure places in the world."

She gazed at him a moment, appreciating that, tired as he was, his first thought had been for her safety. "What's an ocean view? I see it every day of my life. What I'd really rather do is order something from room service. I've always imagined doing that. Except I sort of thought I'd be on my honeymoon—all dressed in flowing chiffon." She blushed then. "I mean, I never expected that during my big hotel debut, I'd be sleeping with a restless five-year-old." She laughed then and went to claim the small bedroom, unaware that Temple stood, his eyes making a somber survey of her back. He just couldn't picture her in yards of chiffon. Form-fitting satin with little straps maybe. Some hot shocking color would suit her—and him.

"Both beds are queens," he muttered as she turned, caught his gaze making a leisure stroll up her body and gave him a quizzical look.

"On second thought," he said, "you take the bigger room. We're twenty floors up. Those guys would have to be related to Spiderman to scale the walls."

"This room will do fine. Don't think you have to treat me special, Wyatt, just because this is my first time in a ritzy hotel."

"You *are* special, Daisy," Temple said gravely. "Don't ever let anyone tell you different."

Their eyes locked for several gentle moments. Then Daisy grew uncomfortable and cleared her throat. "I, um, Becca's getting heavy. I think I'll put her down."

"By all means." Temple sounded flustered, too, as he reached around her and snapped on the light in the smaller room. A bright peachy glow bathed the bed. Daisy hurried past him with a quiet thanks.

"I'll call room service," he offered. "What sounds good?"

She glanced up from smoothing a hand through Becca's tangled ringlets. "You won't laugh?"

Temple shook his head, laughter the last thing on his mind.

"I have a yen for breakfast," she said. "Something simple. Is that possible?"

"This is a five-star hotel. Anything is possible. Or at least it would be in a Wyatt hotel."

"Maybe I'll visit one of your resorts someday," she said lightly.

"Anytime. Tomorrow." His tone wasn't casual even though he leaned casually against her doorframe. "I'm dead serious about sending you and Rebecca to San Francisco until the police smoke out our shooters. I suggested you stay at Mother's because San Francisco can be overwhelming to someone who's never been there. But you could as easily stay at my penthouse.''

The whole time he spoke, Daisy eased Becca into a frilly nightgown. She also shook her head repeatedly. "A penthouse with a housekeeper. Me? Temple, I wouldn't know how to act. I've never even flown in an airplane before. The farthest I've been from Galveston is the time my sister had a baby and I drove to New Orleans to help out around the house—as *her* housekeeper. Get the picture?''

Temple didn't like the tone of their conversation. She seemed to be pointing out their differences to distance herself from him. "It's nothing we have to decide tonight, Daisy." He switched gears. "Now what about French toast? Eggs? If I recall, the chef here makes a good Spanish omelet.''

"Anything," she said. "And order Becca a pancake sandwich, why don't you? She barely took two bites of her burger earlier at the police station. She likes pancakes and eggs, and I don't mind waking her to eat, do you?''

"Did you hear me ask Dr. Rankin why she sleeps so much?''

"Yes. I understood him to say we should force her to keep regular hours.''

Temple's troubled gaze lingered on his daughter's face. "He said sleep is another avenue of escape. Yet, when I think how frightened she must have been, I'm not sure I want her remembering.''

Daisy reached over and turned the lamp down to a soft glow. "Of course you want her to remember, Temple," she chided. "She has to remember to get well. And she *will* get well." Daisy stood. She met him at the door, the certainty of her words written in the stubborn set of her jaw.

"You're right. As usual." Straightening away from the casing, Temple brushed his knuckles across Daisy's determined chin. "What makes you so wise?"

A slight flush stole deliciously along her neck. Her eyes, no longer serious, softened and centered on Temple's lips.

He first leaned toward her, then drew back. From the moment he realized those thugs were after the *Lazy Daisy,* he'd wanted to gather her close and keep her safe from any and all who'd bring her harm. But she'd been so prickly about coming to a hotel with him he didn't want her to think he was trying to take advantage. "I'll make that call to room service. What would you like to drink?"

A mischievous chuckle followed him to the phone. "I'd *like* champagne to round out my honeymoon illusion," she said, slipping around him to walk over and flop tiredly on the flowered couch. "But I'll settle for tea. Bergamot, if they've got it."

Her request swirled around inside Temple's head. He wouldn't have guessed she'd be the champagne type. Or had he lost touch with the romantic gestures that pleased a woman? Perhaps it had simply been too long since he'd found any woman he wanted to please.

Temple suddenly knew he wanted to please Daisy Sloan. "If it's champagne you want, madam, it's champagne you shall have." He punched the button on the phone with a flourish and ordered before she could tell him no—which she did.

"I was kidding," Daisy sputtered throughout his brief conversation. "Can't you just imagine? Doreen'll take out a billboard uptown if she finds out they've delivered champagne to me. To us. Bro-ther!''

"Relax. She won't know. I ordered a carafe of mimosas, instead.''

"What's that?'' she asked.

"Champagne mixed with orange juice. It goes well with breakfast. And it fools nosy people like Doreen. Not that you should live your life worrying about the Doreens of the world.''

She stared at him a moment, all manner of wonderfully illicit visions running through her head. "You're absolutely right. Now who's wise?'' She laughed, scooting over as he lowered himself beside her on the couch.

"But I hope you'll pardon my saying I can't figure you out. In some ways you thumb your nose at convention while in other ways you're almost Victorian.''

She shrugged a shoulder. "It's the same with Galveston, you know.''

"So it is. And definitely part of its charm.''

Daisy sprang from the couch, made uneasy by the way his eyes roamed over her. "If it'll be a while till our food's delivered, I think I'll freshen up.''

"Go ahead.'' Leaning back, he closed his eyes.

To keep from reaching down and stroking his stubbled jaw, Daisy made good her escape.

Fifteen minutes later, when she returned from the bathroom feeling much restored, someone was pounding on the door. Temple had stretched out on the couch and appeared to be fast asleep. Daisy hated to wake him, but she had no idea if he intended to put the food against the bill or pay cash. And should she offer to pay half? She wasn't even sure how much food cost in a place like this. Did she have enough money on her? By the time she reached the door, having decided to sign Temple's name to the ticket and settle up with him later, he jolted awake.

"Don't open that door without asking who it is!" he yelled, scrambling to his feet. Wavering for a moment, he soon recovered his bearings and strode past her to demand a name from their visitor. Even though a masculine voice proclaimed room service, Temple only cracked open the door the length of the chain.

Daisy thought his precautions silly. But she wasn't the one who'd been shot at. Six weeks ago, she'd naively felt safe in Galveston. Those jerks in the powerboat had changed everything.

The aroma of food wafting through the door was heavenly. When Temple released the chain and rolled the cart into the room, Daisy padded after him like a hungry puppy. She chuckled as Temple parked it beside two cane chairs. "I must look a lot like Pipsqueak does when I go to fill his doggy bowl. You'd think I hadn't eaten all day."

Temple smiled. "Well, come and dig in."

But in spite of her own hunger, Daisy remembered her plan to wake Rebecca. Excusing herself, she hurried off to the bedroom. Careful as she was to keep her voice low, Becca sat up with a start. "Daddy," the girl whimpered. Daisy heard her say it plain as day. In the midst of thrashing about on the bed, she called for her father again—louder this time.

Temple came running, his face as white as the bandage around his upper arm. The minute he stepped close, Rebecca seemed to grow confused. She barreled into Daisy's waiting arms and hid her face.

"Was I hearing things?" He was visibly shaken.

"I heard it, too. Only I don't think she was fully awake. But it's a good sign. Let's go eat—we'll try to act normal.'' Daisy set Temple's daughter on her own two feet and led her from the room.

At first Rebecca didn't show any interest in eating. She prowled, touching first the couch, then the chairs. Daisy sat down, picked up her fork and launched a one-sided conversation with the girl. She explained that they were on a sort of mini-vacation at the hotel. After a few minutes, Temple got up and went into the bedroom, returning a moment later with Straylia. To the surprise of both adults, Rebecca ran up to him and snatched the koala from his hands.

''Straylia's hungry,'' she announced, and promptly sat in Temple's chair. In the coy way girls often had of wrapping their dads around their little fingers, Rebecca refused to look directly at him. She kept tabs on his every move from beneath her lashes. And she didn't object when he placed a chair from the desk next to hers.

There was an even more surprising development. As if someone had flipped a switch, she began chattering incessantly between swallowing bites of her pancake sandwich. Not about the accident or anything that had happened before that. And she didn't seem to recognize the adults. But she recounted most of what she and Daisy had done that day. They'd gone to the beach first and built a big sand castle, she said—presumably to Temple—but before they'd left the beach it had washed away. Then they'd gone to another place where they went on rides, and....

Neither Temple nor Daisy interrupted. Communicating with their eyes, they tacitly agreed to let Rebecca ramble. She talked in fits and spurts, glossing over the trip to the hospital, yet describing in great detail the toys that had come with her hamburger at the police station.

When she seemed to run down, Temple filled two champagne glasses with the mimosa mixture from the carafe. Beaming, he clinked his glass with Daisy's. "To a new beginning."

Daisy's breath hitched. However, she was spared the chance to place her own interpretations on his words when Rebecca raised her glass of milk and joined in the toast. Temple's hand shook, but his pleasure in the moment shone in his eyes.

Daisy realized that, despite all the previous times she'd been dizzied by Temple Wyatt's fleeting smiles, not one had really compared to this. It was something about his eyes. Before tonight, his eyes had never quite lost their distant edge. Except maybe that one time in her bedroom when they'd shared a kiss. Even then, his eyes had betrayed a different kind of heat beneath their normally guarded surface.

Desire, she supposed she'd have to call it. For certainly it wasn't love. Frowning, Daisy held out her glass for a refill. Love wasn't so hard to recognize. She saw it in Temple's expression when he looked at his daughter. She felt slightly flushed just being in its aura—and oh-so-tempted to pretend his love was aimed at her, as well. Now that she knew for sure how love looked shimmering from a man's eyes, she was positive she'd never settle for less.

What if she never met a man who felt that way about her?

"Story?" Becca piped up hopefully as she set her empty milk glass down. Staring straight at Daisy, the little girl batted her incredibly long dark lashes.

Temple nudged Daisy's arm. "A book. Did you pack any?"

"I brought *The Water Babies*," Daisy murmured, coming out from under her fog. "We're on chapter five. Why don't you read to her?" she urged Temple in an undertone as he continued to study her expectantly. "It's in the pink duffel." Resting her chin in her hand, Daisy returned his steady gaze.

At first he seemed reluctant, as if leaving the room meant the magic of his daughter's speech would be lost. Then with a barely audible sigh, he clambered to his feet, went into Daisy's bedroom and came back with the well-read volume. Taking a seat on the couch nearest the lamp, he opened the book to the marker and started to read aloud, although Rebecca hadn't moved from her chair.

In a soft voice Daisy reminded Rebecca how much she liked the story. Soon the child crawled down. Eventually she crab-walked over to the far end of the couch, where she stayed well out of Temple's reach.

Pleased, Daisy finished her drink and poured herself another. It wasn't long before Rebecca placed Straylia on the center cushion next to Temple and eased closer to see the colorful pictures. Daisy knew she'd carry that image in her heart forever.

Temple had a wonderfully deep reading voice. Almost hypnotic. He didn't seem to trip over the long sentences the way she did. Daisy felt more than one tug on her heart as he read about the underwater sprites she'd teasingly described to Rebecca that day in the cove. So much had happened to all of them since then. Daisy felt bad about the tragic circumstances that caused their lives to intertwine, but not about the fact that they had.

Rebecca patted the picture and laughed musically when Temple read the lecture on ethics given by Mrs. Bedonebyasyoudid.

Daisy's mind skipped from the story to their situation. What had any of *them* done to deserve being shot at and chased by thugs? But, of course, even in the book there were innocent victims caught up in mischief not of their own making.

Sighing, Daisy wondered if the mimosa wasn't making her a little too relaxed. She quickly set the glass aside.

Temple heard her sigh from across the room. He glanced up, lost his place and stumbled over the words. There was a floor lamp behind Daisy that shone through her red-gold curls—a bright nimbus around her delicate oval face. From this distance he couldn't see the gold flecks in her dark eyes, but he knew how they normally sparkled. Tonight her eyes seemed unusually soft and dreamy. A flame of passion curled in his stomach and spiraled downward.

"The water dogs. You didn't read the part about the water dogs," a little voice prompted.

Temple tore his gaze away from the woman across the room and gaped in surprise at the child who had, sometime in the past few minutes, slipped under his good arm and now pressed tightly against his side. It took him another moment to digest what had happened. There was no question how he felt about this child of his, he thought, as his heart filled with overwhelming tenderness. And not long ago, he wouldn't have believed there'd be room there for anyone else. But Daisy Sloan had sneaked in when he wasn't looking.

All senses on alert now, he began reading again. But the words of the story flowed more haltingly and with an occasional rough catch.

As recently as last week, Temple wouldn't have believed his body could be so torn between the joy of having Rebecca's soft curls lightly brush his chin and wishing her safely asleep in the next room so that he could kiss Daisy. Kiss her, touch her hair and go on to explore every inch of her body.

Good Lord, what kind of father did that make him? Temple paused and smiled mistily down on the mop of blond ringlets that burrowed against his shirt. It made him a father who felt fully alive for the first time in a long, long while. For an unguarded moment, he savored each of the separate passions. To Temple's profound joy, he found it made him feel like a whole man again. And a damned lucky one.

As his daughter's small body sagged with tiredness, he watched the blue eyes so like his own fight to stay awake, and he picked up the pace of his reading. He didn't, however, skip any words, even though his eyes kept straying to the woman across the room.

Moments after the strange fairy came on the scene and sang her strange song, Rebecca lost the battle to sleep. Her blue-veined eyelids closed. Dark lashes fluttered softly, then lay still atop sun-kissed cheeks. Temple finished reading the last few lines of the chapter before he shut the book. "I don't think I've ever read this. A few adults I know could benefit from its lessons," he said, smiling at Daisy.

"It's fairy tale cover to cover, but it made life easier for me when my grandfather's boat went down in a bad squall. I prefer to think he's frolicking with the water babies."

"He was never found?"

Daisy shook her head.

Temple cleared his throat. "Does that happen a lot?"

"Not so much now with the advances we've made in weather forecasting. Plus, the boats are better equipped.

But, yes, if you live by the sea, you know you might die by her.''

Temple rubbed his arm absently and shuddered. ''I've never given much thought to dying.''

''I don't dwell on it. Anyway, we were discussing the merits of the book. When Rebecca remembers the accident, maybe she'll recall this fairy tale. It always made me feel better to envision a mythical world at the bottom of the sea.

''God, Daisy. Can't you get a nice desk job in town?''

''That's an odd question.''

Temple ran his fingers through Rebecca's curls. ''Don't you want to get married and have a family?''

''Isn't it a little late to be playing twenty questions? Would you like some help getting little Miss Sleepyhead to bed?'' she asked, deliberately changing the subject.

Temple glanced at his watch. It was nearly midnight. No wonder he felt as if he was running on empty. Well, he was and he wasn't. He felt so tired he could barely move, and every muscle in his body hurt like hell. His blood was a different story. It heated and sang in awareness of the woman who rose and walked breezily toward him. Nor did the awareness abate after they'd put Rebecca to bed.

It did take a small detour, though, when Daisy pointed to fresh blood on his bandage. She stepped close and offered to rewrap it.

''With what?'' he murmured, reveling in the scent of magnolia that swirled around her.

''Sit. I threw some stuff in my bag. Don't you remember? My bathroom's stocked with every emergency supply known to medical students.''

''Okay.'' He capitulated when she fetched the bag. ''But be careful.''

"It's pretty swollen," she said after removing the sling and uncovering the ragged wound. "How does it feel?" She ran her fingers lightly over the flesh above his stitches. "Your deltoid muscles are bunched," she told him.

"Ah…" Words tangled around Temple's tongue as he gazed at her full lips.

She withdrew her hand, eyes darkening in sympathy. "I didn't mean to hurt you."

"No… you didn't. Those muscles are in a knot," he rasped. "So are the ones here." He pointed to his shoulder blade.

She nodded. "The trapezius." She massaged a circle with three fingers. "It's tight all right."

"How do you know so much about muscles?" he growled, suddenly fighting tightness elsewhere.

Her smile was slightly smug. "I used to coach my med-school boarders before their tests. You'd be surprised how much rubbed off."

Temple closed his eyes and let the lingering cloud of her perfume envelop him.

Once the knots were eased, Daisy assembled the new bandages. Then she helped him off with his torn shirt and redressed his arm. She thought he'd dozed off as she worked, but when she leaned over to tape the back, he reached up with his good arm and pulled her down.

Her protest was swallowed by his kiss. She tasted of orange juice and champagne. Much sweeter than the drink he'd sampled firsthand. Temple smoothed his fingers over her jaw, her ear, her springy hair, and he forgot all about his good intentions and his physical limitations as his heart began to gallop wildly.

At first Daisy shied away from his naked chest. She didn't want to hurt him. But soon she couldn't think straight. He didn't act like a man who was hurting. His skin was warm, ropey with muscles. He smelled faintly of the soap they'd given him to shower with at the police station.

Temple wanted to caress her breasts, but his good arm had become trapped against the back of the couch. He kissed her long and hard, and in the midst of his frustration, he gave himself completely to the flow of feelings. "We need more room," he murmured, leaving them both unsteady from his last kiss. "There's a roomy bed next door."

"Rebecca—"

"—has been sleeping through the night," he finished in a husky voice, warm with promise. He kissed the soft skin beside her eye and the cleft of her chin, then nibbled gently on her earlobe.

Daisy couldn't think why she shouldn't join him in that big bed. Or should she? He hadn't exactly spoken words of love. She'd been so certain of his feelings before, certain that what he felt for her had more to do with sex, with physical attraction. But now love shone from his eyes. And it was centered on her. It pulsed around her. His last kiss was full, urgent on her mouth, and ended with a delicious melding of tongues. Her last thread of resistance snapped as she rose and led the way to his room.

CHAPTER TWELVE

DECISION MADE, they didn't tarry. Nothing about their relationship had been in half measures. They'd sparred with gloves off from the first, and now they headed into lovemaking the same way. Just inside the room, Temple caught her in an embrace that left no doubt as to his need for her.

Flames licked at Daisy from the inside out, and she wondered if it was possible to disintegrate from the heat. The large three-quarter moon that shone brightly through the uncurtained balcony doors seemed cool by comparison.

Temple, so long in control of every aspect of his feelings, felt almost giddy. Daisy's firm warm body, the glow of a tropical moon, made him feel young again, carefree. He waltzed her to the bed and he bent down to strip away the spread with his good hand. He wondered if she was as dizzy with anticipation as he, then straightened slowly, needing to catch his breath.

"What's wrong?" she whispered, her heart beginning to pound.

"Nothing," he whispered back, tuning out the pulsing ache in his arm. "Absolutely nothing," he repeated on a groan as his hand dropped to her breast, sending her heart and his into frantic confusion. By the time he captured her lips beneath his, the ache had made a subtle shift to a much lower region. But everything he needed to make all his aches go away he held in his arms.

Caught in an undertow of sensations, Daisy struggled to keep her head above water. She wanted to savor each experience as it came.

Temple tried to free her hair from its confines, but impatience made him clumsy. She took a moment to trace his face and his lips with trembling fingers. Then, showing more patience than he, she unclipped the bow and let it fall. Touching him had almost been her undoing. His skin, smooth and hot, stoked the inner fires she'd purposely banked. She sank to the bed, one leg drawn beneath her. He did a smoother job of unbuttoning her sleeveless red-checked jacket and then laid a trail of kisses from her ear to the hollow of her throat.

Breathless, Daisy stood, kicked off her sandals and, before her nerve left her, shed the rest of the outfit that had been such a hit at the precinct. Wearing only the briefest red bikini panties and a shy smile, she returned to Temple's arms.

Temple suddenly lost all ability to reason. His remaining clothes seemed an insurmountable barrier.

But he needn't have worried. Daisy helped to untie and discard his sneakers, and after a series of kisses, she was the one to drag the jeans down off his hips. "Wait," he gasped, when things were almost out of hand. "In my back pocket...in my wallet, there's..." He let the words dangle, cradling his throbbing arm.

She did as he asked, and after she opened the section he indicated, an array of colorful foil wrappers spilled across the pale yellow sheet, and it was Daisy's turn to gasp. She turned to him with accusing eyes. "My God, so many kinds! What are you, a sex maniac?"

"No." Temple laughed sheepishly and felt the laughter echo inside his head. "I don't lay in a supply for travel, if that's what you mean."

"You can't mean you bought them on the Island!" she yelped. "That news will be the talk of the town."

"Daisy, calm down. I didn't buy them at all. Medical supplies weren't all your medical students hoarded. So, do you have a preference?" he asked, nuzzling her ear.

"I, ah, no." She followed him back to the pillow as he reached into the stack and handed her one. "What if I can't do this?" she whispered against his lips.

"You have to or we stop right here."

Fingers shaking, Daisy ripped the packet open and followed his equally shaky instructions. And the rest was easy once Temple set his sights on pleasing her. For Daisy Sloan made love the way she did everything else, to the utmost and without inhibition.

She abandoned herself to the rasp of his tongue on her flesh and eagerly returned the favor.

He loved the way her pulse skittered under his lips, and the way her eyes grew wide, dark and meltingly soft when he stroked her. Temple kissed and caressed, intending to pleasure her for hours. An instant later, however, she erupted like a geyser and the pace skidded out of his control. It had been a long time since his need had been so great. In desperation and in spite of his wound, Temple tried to hold back, wanting a good experience for her.

Mistakenly he assumed he could harness the desire that lapped at his blood and pushed his urgency over the edge. And he misjudged Daisy's determination to have it all— to reach the highest pinnacle hard and fast. He rolled her on top, ignoring the blinding pain that shot up his arm.

Her hips drove against him until he was irrational with need—until he arched high off the bed and his mouth made a foray up her rib cage. When he reached her lips, he moaned with both pain and pleasure. They went around the last curve together and tumbled, together, into an ecstatic release. "I love you," she whispered.

Had she really said those words? Dazed and out of breath, Temple toppled sideways onto the love-damp sheets, uncaring at the moment that he landed hard, sending yet another stab of pain up his arm. His good arm cradled Daisy's shuddering body close until he felt the series of aftershocks recede. They lay in silence for so long that he feared, among other things, that he'd hurt her. When his heart finally slowed its breakneck gallop, he spoke her name.

"Daisy?" His voice seemed to reverberate in the quiet room as though through a loudspeaker. It made her body buck.

Assuming he was in pain, she scrambled to her knees and rolled him gently onto his back. "Oh, Temple!" she exclaimed. "Did I hurt you?"

He moved his good arm, which had flopped across his face. He opened one lazy eye and searched hers. "Isn't that my line?" he asked huskily, watching moonlight spill over her shoulder, illuminating the golden freckles that dusted her nose. God help him, but he wanted her again. He wouldn't have thought it possible. But however willing the spirit might be, the flesh was weak. It was as if a hundred devils poked pitchforks into his arm.

Daisy held still for his intense inspection just so long. She wasn't nearly as comfortable with her nakedness in the aftermath as Temple apparently was. Although she'd gladly repeat the experience ... It'd been like riding a fifty-foot swell and diving into the eye of a hurricane. But now—well, why was he staring at her like that? Daisy groped blindly among the tangled sheets and came up with her vest. Temple's jaw worked as if he was tense. She felt miraculously free; obviously he hadn't been as pleased.

There was no love in his eyes now, Daisy saw. They were dark, troubled. Shadowed by pain—or regret? Was it because she'd said she loved him? If only he'd say something. But the joy was patently one-sided. Quietly she gathered the rest of her clothing. His silence spelled remorse. Daisy could take anything over remorse.

Temple clawed his way through a hazy cloud of pain in time to see Daisy—two Daisies—striding toward the door. He struggled to sit up, but black spots danced in front of his eyes. A crushing weight down one side seemed to hold him prisoner. He fell back to keep from passing out. "Daisy, I'm sorry," he managed to whisper. And he was, wholly so; he didn't know why one of the most beautiful experiences in his life was ending all wrong. But the door had already closed on his words.

By the light spilling in from the sitting room, Daisy had seen the quiver of his hand. She'd heard the vibration in his voice as she went out and slammed the door. Her steps slowed a moment. Was he all right? He'd been shot; he'd spent hours in the emergency room. But, no, there'd been nothing wrong with his vital organs. The rat. She laughed hysterically, then burst into tears.

Temple absorbed the noise of the door slamming. The day's events came crowding back as he heaved himself up. It was as if he was still aboard the *Lazy Daisy,* the boat rocking under his feet. He found his pants and got first one leg in and then the other. He gave up trying to zip them. Tenderness for Daisy warred in his heart with fear for her and Rebecca. A pressing fear that something terrible was going to happen.

He stumbled toward the door and bumped into the wall. Why had Daisy left his bed so abruptly? They should still be lying there, curled into one another. A desperate need to see her, to see that she was all right, hammered at him. By the time he found the door and braced himself with his good hand, she'd disappeared. The door to her room was not only closed, it was locked, he discovered a moment later.

"Daisy," he croaked.

She didn't answer.

Hell! He'd have to sort things out with her tomorrow. Today, he revised, remembering it was well after midnight as he set a wobbly course for his bed. Feeling the bandage constrict, he tried to adjust it and noticed that his hand came away bloody.

"Holy hell!" Had he broken stitches during their wild dance across the sheets? he wondered, paying attention to the fingers of heat that snaked up his arm.

The room seemed to pulse around him, forcing him to close his eyes. Sleep. That was what he needed. Later, it was late... He couldn't seem to focus his eyes well enough to read the bedside clock.

"To hell with sleep," he muttered. It was his responsibility to figure out a way to get Daisy and Rebecca away from those crazies. But he needed to open the balcony doors first. It had grown fiery hot. Or was it cold? Freezing. His teeth started to chatter. What had he done with that bedspread? In his attempt to get up and find it, Temple fought against a swirling black vortex that tried to drag him down. He teetered a moment, lost his balance and toppled over.

Daisy had just stepped out of a shower that hadn't done a thing to cool her passion. She was in the midst of toweling her hair when she heard a noise. A thump. Had

Temple thrown something across the room? Maybe a shoe? Relieved when Rebecca didn't so much as stir, Daisy tiptoed over to the common wall. She felt foolish after standing with her ear flattened there for five minutes. Or perhaps furious was more like it. He was probably sleeping like a baby. *He'd* awake rested, and she'd look like something the cat dragged in.

Stalking back to the bed, Daisy whacked her pillow to plump it. Why on earth should she think he'd give her feelings a second thought? He'd gotten what he wanted. Just because *she'd* been blinded by love. Why hadn't she listened to Daniel and Sal? They'd tried to tell her he was just a big-city dude on the prowl. Well, she wouldn't have to worry about Mr. Taj Mahal Wyatt much longer—if he'd even told the truth about his name. With the progress Rebecca had exhibited earlier, he'd probably take off tomorrow. Back to their fancy penthouse and designer labels. With that thought came enough tears to soak her pillow. Enough tears to send her into a troubled sleep.

DAISY FOUGHT HER WAY up through the fog as something soft nudged her face. "Go away, Pipsqueak," she muttered, gently batting at the dog, who thought it was his sworn duty to get her up at the break of dawn. The sound of a childish giggle had Daisy's eyes popping open. Nothing familiar came into focus. "Ugh," she groaned, causing another spate of giggles to her right.

Turning, Daisy came face-to-face with Straylia. Becca, fully dressed in clean clothes, knelt in the middle of the bed, her cherubic face wreathed in smiles. She tapped Daisy's face rhythmically with the stuffed bear. "Who're you?" the child twittered without a trace of fear. "Straylia says you're Goldilocks. I told him that's silly. Goldilocks isn't real." The blue eyes inspected every inch of Daisy. "Since we're at a hotel, I figured you're some kind of nanny. My daddy hires them to stay with me while he works." She sighed. "I wish you *were* Goldilocks."

"Why?" Daisy's voice was croaky with sleep. She bolted upright, her brain jumbled with the possibilities Dr. Rankin had outlined. Regression was one of them. Had Rebecca recovered her memory, some of it, and lost the recent past? "Why do you wish I was Goldilocks?" she asked, wishing Temple was here to deal with this latest development.

"'Cause I hate waiting around Daddy's hotels. It's boring."

"Well, my sweet water baby, you're in luck today. It's not one of daddy's hotels, but he's snoring away next door." She pointed in the direction of his room.

"Really?" The bright blue eyes rounded with pleasure. "Daddy's here and he's not working? Come on, Straylia, let's you and me go see."

"Wait, sweetie." Daisy suddenly had a vivid flashback as to how Temple Wyatt had looked sprawled on that bed. In the buff. And those little foil packets strewn across the covers—not that Rebecca would understand them. Her words of caution came too late, however; the child's nimble fingers unlocked the door, and she was out before Daisy managed to untangle her legs from the sheets.

Moving fast brought out soreness in places that taunted Daisy with a clear reminder of the activities that had taken place in Temple's bed last night—along with their abrupt end. Daisy ran a hand through her hair and slowed her steps.

How could she have overslept? She'd fully intended to get up early, call a cab and walk out of here. After all, she had her own problems at home, problems that needed attention. She could still grab her things and leave if she got to Rebecca in time. Something of a dull ache lodged in Daisy's chest as she thought about not seeing the child again. She knew that once she stepped through the suite door, she would sever all personal ties to the Wyatts, father and daughter. Of course, she'd owe him money for the wiring forever. But maybe the bank would lend her some against the *Lazy Daisy*. That reminded her of yesterday's damage to the trawler, and she groaned in hopelessness.

Out the bedroom door, Daisy turned and nearly ran over Rebecca.

"Daddy's sleeping on the floor," the girl announced.

"On the floor?"

Rebecca nodded. "His face feels all hot and sweaty. I tried to get him to wake up and talk, but he only makes funny gurgling noises."

"Oh, no!" Daisy remembered the loud thump she'd heard. That had been . . . what time? She looked at her watch. Three hours ago at least. He'd taken that room because he'd been worried about a visit by the men from the powerboat. Had it happened? With shaking hands, she set the child aside and dashed into Temple's room.

He was indeed on the floor—and hot, as Rebecca had said. Thank heaven he wasn't dead. But something was wrong. He was mumbling. Crazy talk. Daisy threw open the curtains over the side window to let in more light, then knelt to check his pulse. Irregular. There was blood on his bandage, too. Not enough to worry about, she thought, but then, she wasn't a nurse. Daisy glanced up to see Rebecca hovering in the doorway. Tears streaked the girl's pale cheeks.

"Is my daddy gonna die?" she asked plaintively.

Daisy wished she could give an unequivocal no. "We're going to get him some help. You be brave, you hear?" As she reached for the bedside phone, Daisy wondered if this had triggered Rebecca's memory of the other accident—the one involving her mother.

Someone with a Midwest twang answered on the third ring. Daisy explained to the clerk that Mr. Wyatt had been taken ill. She requested an ambulance. Thank goodness she didn't have to deal with that nosy Doreen.

After Daisy had covered Temple with the bedspread, discreetly as possible picking up all the foil packets and shoving them in the pocket of the jeans she'd quickly pulled on, she gathered Rebecca into her arms for a generous hug. "Why don't you go out and sit in the big blue chair? Call me the minute someone knocks. You can watch TV if you like. Only don't turn it up so loud that we can't hear the door. You know how to work the television?" Daisy asked.

Becca rolled her eyes. "Silly," she said. "Everyone knows how to work a TV."

Daisy frowned. Up until yesterday Rebecca Maria Wyatt hadn't remembered how to color. Just like that, she'd become a normal kid. Which was what Dr. Rankin had said might happen. But if Becca had recovered her memory, she hadn't said a word about events leading up to the accident.

"Darn. What's taking that ambulance so long?" Daisy muttered as Temple moaned and flung the spread off his injured arm. That was when Daisy got a good look at the series of angry red streaks running down the inside of the badly swollen arm. "Blood poisoning," she whispered aloud. She'd changed his dressing shortly after midnight. The streaks hadn't been there then. Daisy wondered if she'd done something horribly wrong; at the same moment, Rebecca called to say there was someone at the door.

Daisy had never been so glad to see anyone in her life. A policeman walked in on the heels of a young man with long hair, who said he was the medic. "I replaced last night's escort," the officer informed Daisy. He removed his hat and stepped inside the bedroom where she'd led the man with the medical equipment.

"I overheard the clerk giving the medic your room number and came to see what was going on. You should've called me first, you know."

"I forgot all about you," Daisy said honestly. She jerked her head toward Temple's prone form. "I think the gunshot wound he got yesterday is infected."

Rebecca ran over and tugged on Daisy's blouse. "Was that why my daddy saw the doctor yesterday? He got shot?" Her eyes brimmed with tears. "People *die* when they gets shot."

The policeman, whose name tag said he was Sergeant Chap Denton, issued a low whistle. "She talks," he whispered. "Can she give us a make on either of our shooters?"

Daisy put both arms around the child, gathering her close. She glared at the man in the blue uniform. "Last time I looked she was still a minor. Don't you need permission from her father to question her?"

Smirking, he bent to pick up a foil packet. "Afraid our questions might lose you the goose that lays the golden eggs?"

Daisy's breath hissed in between her teeth. Fortunately the medic got to his feet just then, asking the sergeant to call down and have his partner bring a stretcher. "Classic case of septicemia," he said. "I've administered antibiotics, but the doctor may want to keep him in hospital overnight. Mr. Wyatt's coming around, but he's still in shock.''

"He had a shot of antibiotics yesterday,'' Daisy said defensively.

"Maybe not strong enough. Blood poisoning sets in fast. Did he forget to take his penicillin last night?''

"I don't think he even got the prescription filled. It's probably still in his shirt pocket.''

The medic gave her an assessing look. "This is what happens when you don't follow instructions. Oh, good. Here's the stretcher. You can trail in your car, Mrs. Wyatt. We can't let a kid ride in the ambulance.''

Daisy blushed. "I'm not Mrs. Wyatt. I'm his child's sitter. Where are you taking him?'' she asked, refusing to retreat from the medic's once-over of her sleep-rumpled appearance.

He named the hospital where they'd been yesterday. Daisy nodded briskly.

"So you'll be there to help check him in?'' the medic persisted. "Mr. Wyatt isn't making much sense, and it sounds as if he's worried about his daughter. Is this her?'' He smiled at Rebecca.

"Tell him to relax,'' Daisy instructed their go-between. She couldn't bring herself to face Temple. Not yet. Not until she sorted out what was going on.

Yet as they wheeled him out, fear swelled in her heart. Temple's normally tan skin blended too well with the stark white of the sheet. Should she have seen this coming? Had it been made worse by their romp?

Sergeant Denton broke into her thoughts, saying he'd wait downstairs and follow her to the hospital. The dolt didn't even have the courtesy to apologize for his un-called-for rude remark.

Feeling suddenly tired, she forced herself to start packing their bags. Did anyone care that she wasn't the same woman who'd entered this room last night? A lot of momentous things had happened since she'd gone through their trashed bedrooms and packed a change of clothing for each of them.

Daisy felt grungy, in spite of the quick shower she'd taken last night. She'd like another, but she had Becca to consider. The girl was talking a blue streak about nothing in particular. Daisy recognized it as the kind of meaningless chatter that went with nerves. She'd talked Daniel's ear off a few times herself during her dad's illness.

With a last sweep of the room, Daisy gently shooed Becca toward the door.

"Where am I going?" Becca hung back as Daisy stepped into the hall.

"To the hospital to make sure your dad's okay and they have everything they need to admit him. Overnight," she added. "It'll be all right, Rebecca."

"Then where am I going?" The girl dragged her heels now.

Daisy had grown weary of answering the same question. However, she sensed the girl's distress. "Where do you want to go, Becca?"

The little lips pursed. "My name is Rebecca Maria Wyatt. Not Becca."

Surprised, Daisy thought back to the day in court when Temple had made the same declaration. Remembering how he'd looked brought a lump to her throat. "All right," she said around it. "I'll call you Rebecca and you may call me Daisy. Would you like to stay at my house until your daddy gets well? I have a dog and a cat," she tossed out as extra enticement.

"And a pony? I want a pony. My grandmother says city girls can't have ponies. And Daddy's hotels won't let anyone have animals." She gave Daisy a pretty dimpled smile. "I'll go with you, but only till Daddy gets well—unless he can come, too. He gets lonesome without me, you know."

Daisy's heart wrenched. Had Rebecca said those same words to her mother? And did Miranda promise her a pony to get her to leave? Daisy's stomach knotted. Come to think of it, Rebecca had now mentioned everyone in her family *except* Miranda. Was that significant? While they were at the hospital, she just might drop by Dr. Rankin's office to see what she could find out.

The opportunity to ask came sooner than Daisy expected. At the hospital's front door. The chief of staff was hurrying out as Daisy and Rebecca reached the entrance. Daisy had been trying to lose Sergeant Denton. She quit the chase and stopped to return Dr. Rankin's greeting. "Were you coming to see me?" he asked. "I'm just on my way to speak at a Rotary luncheon." He smiled at Rebecca, who gazed at him openly without any of her former anxiety.

They were standing near the gift shop. Daisy quickly pulled twenty dollars out of her purse and handed it to Rebecca. "Why don't you go in there and buy your daddy flowers?" she suggested. "Show the lady at the counter how much you have to spend."

"I know," Rebecca said, puffing out her chest with pride. "I can't spend the whole twenty 'cause there's tax." With that she bounded off.

"Well, well." Dr. Rankin lifted a brow in surprise. It stayed elevated while Daisy quickly outlined the events of yesterday—minus the lovemaking of course.

"Very interesting," he murmured. "Would you tell her father that I'd like the team to examine Rebecca again?" The doctor checked his watch. "If I don't get going, I'm going to be late."

"Is something wrong, Dr. Rankin? Temple will ask why you want to see her. I...he doesn't know yet that she mentioned her grandparents—but not her mother."

"There's no rush," the doctor said. "Events may come back to her slowly. Seeing the ocean or a yacht might trigger a memory of her mother and the accident. Or—" he nibbled at his lower lip "—she may have lacunar amnesia."

"What's that?"

"The inability to remember isolated events. She may block out that particular incident forever. It would help if our psychiatrists could do some tests."

Daisy glanced toward the happy little girl who was skipping out of the shop holding a bright bouquet of...daisies. Her heart soared.

"I'll tell him," Daisy promised, a catch in her voice. "I won't guarantee he'll make an appointment, though. I believe he'll return to San Francisco soon."

The policeman's ears perked up, and he stepped closer at that bit of news.

"Really?" Dr. Rankin stroked his chin. "I have to admit when the two of you came to see me the other day, I thought I detected something developing between you. Too bad it didn't work out."

"Yes, it is," Daisy murmured almost inaudibly as he pointed to his watch, shrugged and, after a quick salute, trotted off. Her life would be pretty empty when Temple left, she realized. But he *was* going, surely as the tide had swept away the sand castles she and Becca had built. And there wasn't anything she could do about it. For the first time Daisy understood the futility her father must have felt at her mother's leaving.

For the first time she understood what he'd meant when he said that love wasn't always enough to bind a person to you.

CHAPTER THIRTEEN

AN ELEVATOR and two wrong turns later, Daisy arrived at the correct ward. Rebecca skipped merrily at her side, and Sergeant Chap Denton walked two paces behind, which set her teeth on edge. People watched them out of the corners of their eyes and whispered as they passed. Then they were stopped at the door to Temple's room by a no-nonsense sign: Visitor Restriction.

"Wait here," Daisy instructed Rebecca. "I'll go ask what this is about."

"Infectious contaminants," the nurse at the desk said tiredly. "Are you his wife?"

Daisy was getting plenty peeved about being mistakenly thrust in that role. "No," she said shortly. "I've brought his daughter to see him."

The nurse closed a chart she'd been writing in. "Child or adult?"

"Child," Daisy said. "She's five."

"No can do, then. Too risky." The nurse shook her head as she pulled out another chart. "The doctor ordered cultures. Mr. Wyatt's visitor-restricted until we see if it's a staph infection."

"That's potentially serious, isn't it?"

"You'll have to speak with his doctor. Who did you say you were?" The nurse stopped what she was doing and took in Daisy's disheveled appearance.

"I didn't. His daughter brought flowers. May we leave them with you?"

"By all means. I have nothing better to do with my time than deliver flowers."

Daisy checked her watch. It wasn't even ten o'clock yet. Poor woman must have had a rough morning. "We'll call Temple's room and let him know they're here," Daisy murmured.

Back at the door to his room, she relayed the news to her companions. The sergeant suggested he walk Rebecca to the desk with the flowers. He said he wanted to use the phone there to call the chief and ask what to do about security.

Daisy waited until they turned the corner out of sight before she pushed open the door to Temple's room. She wouldn't go right in, of course, but she had to see for herself that he was all right.

He lay on the bed, eyes closed, an IV drip connected to his good arm. Was it her imagination, or did his face have a bit more color? Even at that, he lay so still. She suddenly recalled that last year, a young robust shrimper she knew had cut his hand on a fish-boning knife. He'd developed blood poisoning and in two days was dead. Daisy's hand flew to her mouth to stifle a cry of fear. To keep from disturbing him, she backed out and closed the door.

She adjusted her shoulder bag and stiffened her spine and discreetly wiped her eyes. At least she appeared in control now. She stepped briskly away from the door to wait for the others.

As Rebecca and Denton came toward her down the hall, Daisy saw the smile on the sergeant's face. "Good news," he announced the minute he was within earshot. "Chief says they picked up two suspects trying to sneak aboard your boat shortly after dawn today. One matches the composite your friend Wyatt put together yesterday, though the second man doesn't quite match number two. I'll see the pair of you home, then pick up the mug shots and bring 'em here. Soon as the doc gives the okay, we'll see if Wyatt can pick those two out of a lineup. Otherwise, there's not much to hold 'em on.''

''But if they were sneaking aboard the *Lazy Daisy*...''

''Too soft. They claim they'd been hired on to pull nets for someone named Duffy and must have stumbled onto the wrong boat by accident.''

''Probably Michael Duffy. He runs four shrimp boats. But he doesn't own a Boston trawler. Maybe Sal or Loren can identify them.''

''Nope.'' He shook his head. ''Wyatt's the only one who got a good look.''

Daisy darted a nervous glance over her shoulder at Temple's door as she reached for Rebecca's hand. ''In that case, Sergeant, don't you think it'd be wiser to stay and guard him, rather than follow me across town?''

''I'm following orders, Miss Sloan.''

''Oh, for crying out loud.'' Daisy glared at him.

His eyes narrowed. ''We've learned that DeVaca's yacht did go down in Rum Row. Got a positive ID from the lab on the fiberglass scraps Coletti hauled in. Seems the yacht had just been painted and the paint's unique.''

As they headed downstairs, Daisy looked quickly to see if the Brazilian's name had any effect on Rebecca. But the little girl skipped along ahead, paying no heed to the adults' conversation. Once outside, she concentrated on not stepping on any cracks. That brought a smile to Daisy's face, who wasn't so old that she couldn't remember doing that a few times all the way down the Strand. Her dad had been ready to throttle her.

"You find something amusing about that lab report, Miss Sloan?" Chap Denton scowled at her.

She stopped beside her car and tucked a windblown strand of hair behind her ear. "Sergeant, I had the bad luck to drop anchor near the yacht in Rum Row on the best shrimping day of the year. Unfortunately I'll probably see that explosion in my sleep for the rest of my life. If those men are responsible, I personally hope you get enough evidence to lock them up permanently and throw away the key. Which won't happen, I might add, if you're busy bird-dogging me." She wrenched open the passenger door and helped Rebecca.

The sergeant held his retort until after Daisy had finished buckling Rebecca's seat belt and had shut the door. "I guess you're so testy because your meal ticket's being shipped back to Frisco."

Daisy stopped on her way around to the driver's side. "Should that cryptic message hold some significance for me?" she snapped, brushing past him to unlock her door.

He settled his hat on his head and smirked. "According to the nurse, Wyatt insisted on calling Grandmama right after they got him settled. 'Course she only heard one side of the conversation, but she said it sounded like Wyatt's sending the kid home ASAP."

Daisy felt as if she'd been blindsided by a loose boom. It had happened once on Daniel's pleasure ketch. For a month she'd nursed a goose egg on her forehead the size of Plymouth Rock. Maybe this blow wouldn't leave a scar, but Daisy'd be hanged before she'd let Denton see how much it had hurt.

Marshalling every scrap of restraint she possessed, Daisy said coolly, "It's always been Temple's intent to take Rebecca home as soon as she'd regained her memory. Now, if you don't mind, Sergeant, I believe I have a mess to clean up at my house. I'd like to get at it.''

He'd been blocking her door and seemed disappointed by her lack of concern at his news flash. He stepped aside to give her space. She slammed the door, had the car started and was almost across the parking lot by the time Denton rallied and jumped in his cruiser. Which was quite all right with Daisy. She would've hated to have him witness the tears suddenly spilling down her cheeks.

Rebecca saw them though. "I don't like that man," she said. "He hurt your feelings. I'm gonna tell my daddy. He'll make that meanie say he's sorry, Daisy."

Rebecca's words made Daisy laugh—and cry all the harder. When did Temple plan to tell her she was being relieved of his daughter's care? It was the final crushing blow to her ego. No matter what he'd said in that note about trusting her, he obviously *didn't* trust her to keep Rebecca safe.

Her tears dried of their own accord. To her, death of trust was like the end of hope. She was a woman who lived by simple rules. By and large, all the islanders did. They were the basic rules of survival handed down through the generations, beginning with those who'd lived through the great hurricane. Compared to that, she told herself, today was strawberry cheesecake.

Until Daisy Sloan met Temple Wyatt, her attitude had been more or less "when the going gets tough, the tough find a way to have fun."

"Say, Rebecca Maria Wyatt," Daisy said bravely, taking one last swipe at her eyes, "what do you say we ditch your meanie and go build us a giant sand castle?" This was more like something the old Daisy Sloan would propose.

The girl clapped her hands. Her eyes sparkled. "A big one? Big enough for a real princess?"

"You got it, kid." Daisy felt excitement sing through her blood as she abruptly made a right turn, then another, and headed back the way they'd come. She glanced in the rearview mirror. Sergeant Denton hadn't expected her to bolt. He got caught at the light. Daisy grinned and jogged three streets over and cruised down an alley. She was cooking now. He'd think she vanished. "Poof!" She laughed and, without knowing the real joke, Rebecca laughed with her.

Daisy parked in a small lot off Avenue Q–and a half— another of the unique things about Galveston that made her love the city. They gathered their buckets, shovels and sifters and walked straight down to the seawall. Daisy chose a spot where the sand was damp and where they'd blend in with everyone else. Because her fuchsia blouse was rather distinctive, she'd donned the navy windbreaker she always kept in the trunk of her car for emergency squalls.

As the base of the sand castle took shape, the morning sun warmed their backs, and Daisy felt her cares slip away. She discovered Rebecca had both the creativity and the patience for an ambitious project. The clever patterns she made around the doors and windows with shells soon drew a crowd of onlookers. By the time they had the construction waist-high and had added two turrets, bystanders began to say it resembled Bishop's Palace downtown.

"It does not," insisted the girl a bit petulantly. "It's a castle."

Daisy nudged her with a sandy elbow. "Let people think what they want," she whispered. "We know the truth, don't we?"

Suddenly she shivered, feeling a chill. Someone had blocked the sun at her back. She twisted around, more than half expecting to see an angry Chap Denton. To her surprise, a man with smoldering dark eyes stood just behind her, staring at them. Or rather, at Rebecca. In spite of the fact that he looked vaguely familiar, Daisy's protective instincts kicked in. Possibly because there was nothing warm or friendly in his gaze.

Keeping a firm hold on the bucket of sand, Daisy placed herself squarely between the man and the child. He didn't turn away; instead Daisy found herself looking down the barrel of the small gun he'd suddenly whipped out from under his short gray jacket.

Reacting—in what she would claim later was strictly a reflex—Daisy sprang forward on the balls of her feet and swung the heavy bucket of sand. Aided by a gust of wind, the bucket not only whacked the man upside the head, but it tilted and dumped wet sand into his eyes, nose and mouth.

His weapon flew into the crowd, where luckily it was retrieved by one of two stalwart joggers, who then came to assist Daisy.

Amid screams and a scramble of bodies trying to get away, the huskiest of the joggers wrestled the assailant to the ground. Much to Rebecca's delight, Daisy yanked the shoelaces out of her sneakers and tied the bad guy's hands behind his back. Borrowing someone else's shoelaces, she repeated the process with his ankles until he was trussed up like a turkey.

"Goody, goody, you got him!" Rebecca chortled, jumping up and down. "I can't wait to tell Grandmother Wyatt. She doesn't think I should wear sneakers. *Ladies* shouldn't, she says." Rebecca screwed up her face.

Daisy was saved from disagreeing with the wisdom of Rebecca's grandmother by the arrival of a policeman. Apparently a quick-thinking tourist saw what was happening and called the police from her car phone. By the time three more carloads of armed officers descended on the beach, the incident—which was so short it hardly qualified as an incident—was over. Except that Daisy and Rebecca's sand castle had, sadly, been trampled into the ground.

A police officer she'd seen yesterday at the station replaced Daisy's shoelaces with handcuffs and handed her laces back to her as if they'd been dipped in something unpleasant. After he returned the other pair to their owner, he looked at her and drawled, "Miss Sloan, Galveston was a relatively quiet community until you sailed into Rum Row a few weeks ago. Just this morning, the chief suggested taking up a collection so that you could move to Houston. After he gets this report, he may suggest Siberia."

"Me?" Daisy's eyes widened in innocence.

The officer sighed. Then as his buddy led the assailant away, he began taking statements from the witnesses, who all wanted to talk at once. Each lauded Daisy for her bravery.

She quietly gathered up the buckets, shovels and sifters, keeping a worried eye on Rebecca.

The child tugged on her windbreaker. "Aren't we going to build another castle?"

Daisy didn't want to frighten the girl, but her own fear had begun belatedly to set in. She stuffed her shaking hands deep into the pockets of her scruffy jeans so that no one would see how near she was to falling apart.

A young law officer, a man barely old enough to shave, approached Daisy gingerly. "Miss Sloan." He doffed his hat. "Could you please follow us to the station?" He nodded toward the cruiser where the assailant sat, the object of gawkers. "Chief thinks he's another of the men who shot at Mr. Wyatt."

"Of course." Daisy shuddered. "That's why he looked familiar. He's the man in the second composite. Probably one of the two who trashed my house. I should be home now cleaning it up," she babbled, crossing her arms and running damp palms nervously over her elbows.

"Yes, ma'am. But it's really important. We can hold him on the weapons charge, but we'd have a stronger case if we tie him to the two men we already have in custody."

Daisy nodded. She wanted that, too—a stronger case so that the whole thing could be wrapped up. Even though it meant seeing the last of the Wyatts. In fact, if at this moment Temple asked her again to accompany Rebecca to San Francisco, she might just go. But he wouldn't. Especially not now. Lord, if anything had happened to Rebecca today...

Daisy's knees threatened to buckle even as she reached for the child's hand and trudged slowly after the officer.

It was approaching noon by the time they were finished at the police station. The gunman did indeed know the two who'd been caught sneaking onto the *Lazy Daisy*. They greeted him, but he snarled at them to shut up—which they did, like clams. None of the three let out another peep. The only information available was what came up on the computer following fingerprinting. Each of the three had a string of aliases. The one who'd pointed the handgun at Rebecca was the elusive Halsey Shaw, Domingo DeVaca's former employee.

Maybe now they'd finally get some answers, Daisy thought, as she walked from the building with Rebecca, their young police escort right behind.

"I'm hungry," the little girl announced as they neared the car.

"I'm not surprised," Daisy returned. "It's been hours since we ate breakfast. Do you remember the pancake sandwich you had at the hotel last night?"

"Pancake sandwich." Rebecca wrinkled her nose scornfully.

"It was good," Daisy said. "And you snarfed it up, young lady. So what are you hungry for now?"

Rebecca appeared to consider this question while she snapped her seat belt—by herself this time, Daisy noticed proudly. She told their police escort what they planned. Back at the car, she buckled in and had the car running when Rebecca smiled and said, "Know what sounds yummy? Kiwifruit and banana salad."

Daisy remembered the day Temple had reeled off the list of foods his daughter liked. It'd been the morning after he'd blown the lights with his electronic arsenal. Daisy thought he'd been putting her on. She laughed. Apparently he hadn't been. "Honey, I hate to admit to a kid that I don't have a clue how to fix kiwi salad, but I don't. Could you pick something else?"

The blue eyes rounded seriously. "We aren't dressed to go someplace fancy like my daddy takes me. Maybe you should pick, Daisy."

"Gee, thanks. Are you saying I know slobby places to eat?"

"Sorry," chirped the girl. "I didn't mean to hurt your feelings."

"You didn't." Daisy chucked her under the chin. "Hey, no long faces. I know this neat little fish place down by the water. We can eat out on the deck and watch the waves roll in."

"Fish and chips." The blue eyes brightened. "Yum." She patted her tummy.

Daisy was struck suddenly by a similarity in Temple's and his daughter's smiles. Though slightly crooked, their smiles wreathed their faces, prompting an answering smile in anyone nearby. Daisy's heart gave a little lurch. There wasn't any future in torturing herself with such thoughts. Maybe with this mess finally winding down, her life would get back to normal. She tried to work up enthusiasm for "normal." Try as she might, only a strange sadness surrounded her.

Fortunately Rebecca didn't seem to notice the change in Daisy. Having found her voice at last, the girl talked a blue streak while they sipped root beer out of fruit jars and waited for their fish. She talked about school and her teacher as if she'd attended yesterday. She told Daisy all about the doorman at the condominium in San Francisco, confiding that he gave her bubblegum, which annoyed Grandmother Wyatt no end.

Daisy didn't realize it, but she had formed some not-altogether-flavorable opinions of Temple's mother.

"What about your other grandparents?" Daisy blurted without thinking.

The girl stared out over the ocean, a faint scowl marring her smooth brow.

For a minute Daisy thought she wasn't going to answer. The gap in their conversation widened. Thankfully, Daisy saw the waitress wending her way across the deck toward them. She had just served the officer who sat in a corner trying to be unobtrusive. Just before the harried woman reached their table, Rebecca murmured, "Daddy says I make them nervous. Granny Ila isn't well, and Granddad Dwight can't take care of her *and* me. I think they don't want me there 'cause I'll see they're sort of poor. So they send me presents on my birthday and at Christmas. Not the kind you play with. Glass things to sit on the shelf or dolls that're just to look at. You know the kind I mean?''

Daisy nodded. Her heart went out to Temple's daughter. Among that crowd, she didn't get to be a kid at all. Did Temple know how lonely Rebecca was? How astute? She thought not. There was a big lump in Daisy's throat when she accepted their plates from the waitress.

Both woman and girl ate every last morsel and giggled together about being too stuffed to walk. Daisy paid the bill, reluctant to leave this relaxing spot. She envisioned what it would be like to have a daughter like Rebecca to take shopping, to the movies, out to eat occasionally. There'd be Girl Scouts, dance lessons and trips to the library. They were buckled in the car and nearly home before Daisy called a halt to her daydreaming. What made her think she had what it took to be a mother? Mothers had to deal with bad times, as well as good. Tears, as well as laughter. No one gave lessons in motherhood. But still, Daisy thought she had what it took. Love and understanding.

She'd no sooner pulled into her driveway than Corporal Randy Phillips dashed out of her house, Temple's cellular phone clutched in his hand. "Holy moley, am I glad to see you two!" he shouted. "Talk to Mr. Wyatt." The young police officer thrust the phone at Daisy through her open window. "He's heard rumors about a run-in on the beach and he's driving me nuts."

She accepted it gingerly. "Temple. Hello. You must be feeling better. What's up?"

"What the devil's going on?" he roared. Daisy winced. Without waiting for an answer, he outlined in detail everything Daisy already knew about the little incident at the beach—how foolish she'd been to ditch her escort. What risks she'd taken. Et cetera, et cetera.

"It's over and we're both fine," she said. "Things were tense for a minute, but everything came out all right. The man's in jail with the others. Don't worry. You just get well," she advised brightly.

Officer Phillips arched an eyebrow when Daisy glossed over what had happened. "Do you like the flowers?" she added, glancing obliquely at the child who'd just unsnapped her seat belt. "Rebecca chose them herself. Here, why don't you thank her?"

That suggestion had the desired effect. Temple's useless sputters smoothed to a low rumble as Daisy turned the phone over to Rebecca and climbed wearily from the automobile. Then she went around and helped the child out and led her up the porch steps and into the house. All the while Rebecca kept up a running dialogue with her father. In the kitchen Daisy stopped short. What had been wall-to-wall food and pots and utensils when she left—was it really only last night?—now looked spic and span.

Surprised, she spun and pinned the corporal with a questioning glance.

He shrugged. "I got bored," he whispered so as not to interrupt the child who still chatted on the phone.

"Wow! I'll bet your wife loves you," Daisy told him, her voice frankly awed.

"I'm not married," he mumbled. "I come from a big family, and I still live at home. My mom works, and she hands out lists every Sunday night. No distinction between males and females around the Phillips house. I hope you can find all your stuff. I guessed at where it went in the cupboards.''

Daisy laughed, but sobered as she noticed Rebecca had clicked off the phone. ''Uh, didn't he want to speak to me again?'' she asked, trying without success to hide her pique.

''Nope. He said for us both to stay in the house until Grandmother Wyatt gets here. But I left Straylia in the car. I don't want to leave him out there all alone.'' Tears skimmed the big blue eyes.

''Honey, I'll go get Straylia—''

''*No*. Daddy said you hadda stay inside, too.''

Daisy pursed her lips. ''Nonsense. But, Rebecca, what do you mean about your grandmother? You must have misunderstood. Grandmother Wyatt lives a long way away.'' She recalled what Chap Denton had relayed about Temple sending *her meal ticket* home—which still made steam come out her ears—but now it looked as if he'd been right. Daisy just hadn't thought it would happen so fast. ''You're sure he said tonight?'' she asked again. ''It takes time to make reservations and all.''

''Grandmother's gonna be here tonight,'' Rebecca insisted stubbornly.

''I can't believe that,'' Daisy said, snatching up the phone. ''Did Temple give you his number at the hospital?'' she asked Corporal Phillips.

He shook his head and handed her the phone book to look up the hospital's number. ''I'll go out and get her bear. Is there anything else you need brought in?''

Daisy dug in her pocket and came up with the car keys. ''Our bags are in the trunk. And thanks. Won't Chap Denton love this,'' Daisy muttered to herself as she dialed. After she was connected with Temple's room, the phone rang five or six times, then bounced to the unit secretary who informed Daisy that a nurse had taken Mr. Wyatt to the lab. And afterward, he was scheduled for physical therapy.

"But we just spoke with him," Daisy informed her. "Besides, I thought he was on restriction. Please—this is important." To which the secretary replied, "He's been cleared from restriction. And nothing short of a death in the family is that urgent."

Not wanting to worry Temple, Daisy said she'd call back later.

But it slipped her mind after she took the bags up to her room and walked into the mess. Her room seemed worse by daylight. Four model ships were all that had escaped vandalism. The ones in the bottles that she loved best lay among slivers of glass. Desolate, she walked around and picked up a piece here and a piece there. She didn't know where to even begin cleanup.

Randy Phillips hovered in the doorway. "I can either entertain Rebecca downstairs or help you clean up her room so that she can play in there while we sweep up the glass. Oh, by the way—" he snapped his fingers and pulled a piece of paper from his pocket "—the workmen finished with your circuit breakers and wiring this morning. Mr. Matthews did his walk-through and left the bill." Phillips looked away. "I always hate being the bearer of bad tidings."

Daisy reached for the bill, feeling nothing. What was one more blow? She had the money in her account to cover it, thanks to Temple, even though she intended to pay him back every cent. Never mind deducting money for child care; pride—and love—wouldn't allow it. Goodness, but her life had been falling apart lately. She had a boat shot full of holes, no boarder to bring in money and now a humongous wiring debt that would take her into old age to pay back. But it was the loss of her family heirlooms that moved her to tears. "I appreciate your offer of help, Corporal," she sniffed. "But shouldn't you be back on the streets catching crooks—now that they've rounded up the ones who did this?"

"Until they talk, the chief says we can't be sure we've got them all."

"How about bamboo shoots under the fingernails? Just kidding," she said, drying her eyes as she picked her way around the glass to put the itemized bill in her desk drawer. "Rebecca," she called to the little girl, who was sitting quietly on the top step, playing with her koala bear. "How would you like to go downstairs with Officer Phillips and do some coloring? There's a book and crayons in the kitchen drawer beside the sink."

"Okay, but I should change clothes before my grandmother gets here. She doesn't like me to wear pants. Daddy always has me wear a dress when she visits."

"I don't think she'll be here today, hon."

"But Daddy said." The blond curls bobbed wisely.

"It takes time to get a flight from the coast and make all the connections, sweetie. But I'll tell you what. I'll straighten the bathroom first, then your room. When I finish, you can take a bath and put on one of your pretty sundresses."

"Okay. Who made such a mess here?" Rebecca asked. "If I threw stuff around at my house, Maddy'd scold me good."

Daisy was glad Rebecca didn't remember walking in on all the damage last night. "Sometimes people do bad things out of pure meanness, baby. You can tell Maddy all about it when you get home."

"Oh, look—there's your dog. Here, doggie," Rebecca called as she scrambled after Pipsqueak. When she had the wriggling animal caught up in her chubby arms, she turned and beamed at Daisy. "Do I hafta go back home? It's more fun at your house, Daisy. I'm gonna tell my daddy I want to stay here."

Daisy felt as if the air had left her lungs. Just imagine what Temple would have to say to his daughter about *that* suggestion—not to mention the hissy fit his mama would throw. Daisy checked her watch. It had only been ten minutes since she'd last called Temple. Meanwhile, she refused to worry about a meeting that would probably take place tomorrow at the earliest.

She threw herself into cleaning the bathroom. When she finished, Officer Phillips and Rebecca were engrossed in a television program, so Daisy went to put the alcove to rights. After that, while the policeman and Temple's little girl were outside playing ball with Pipsqueak, Daisy got two trash bags from the kitchen and, with a glass of iced tea, trudged back upstairs to start on her room. About midway through salvaging pieces of the ships, she stopped and called the hospital again. This time the doctor was in with Temple. Darn! She'd had no idea he'd be so hard to reach.

Thereafter, calling completely escaped her. By six o'clock, the room looked almost habitable, even though she looked a sight. Dirt streaked her face, and grime covered her clothing. Plus, she was exhausted. Daisy had about decided to call it a day when Corporal Phillips and Rebecca ran upstairs asking if they could barbecue hot dogs out on the grill and eat them down on the dock for the evening meal.

Daisy cast a jaundiced eye at the child. Rebecca had grass stains on both knees of the light pink pants, as well as on the seat. Dirt smudged her nose. Twigs from the bushes decorated her hair. But she had a glow about her

Daisy hadn't seen before. What the heck. If they were going to eat outside, there didn't seem much point in bathing her now. Besides, it was only a couple of hours until bedtime—Temple had tried to keep Rebecca on an eight-o'clock schedule, like the one she'd been used to.

"All right," Daisy agreed slowly. "But I'm too grubby to eat. Let me grab a quick shower and change into clean clothes while you light the briquets, Corporal. Then I'll come down and throw together a salad."

"Yippee!" Rebecca shouted. Daisy smiled as the girl chased Troublemaker back downstairs.

True to her word, Daisy hurried. She discovered, when she went to get dressed, that she needed to find time to do laundry. She had to dig into the pile of things she'd earmarked for the ragbag. At least they were clean, although her chartreuse crop top needed ironing. It might even have shrunk, Daisy thought as she stretched it toward her waist. And tomorrow, she'd have to condition her hair. It was so frizzy from the high humidity, she twisted it into a topknot. However, her hair wasn't quite long enough. Daisy felt the knot slip to the side as she made her way downstairs.

Several tendrils were trailing over her ears before she had the lettuce torn for the salad. But her appearance was the last thing on Daisy's mind when the doorbell rang. Carrying a full bowl of salad greens, she skirted the coloring books on the floor and jerked open the front door. A slender exquisitely dressed woman stood there. A woman whose pearl gray suit, gloves, hat, shoes and purse were perfectly matched. One whose professionally coiffed, champagne blond pageboy didn't move, despite the ever-present gulf breeze. A breeze that was, if anything, growing stronger, judging by the swaying branches and skittering leaves.

The visitor's cool blue gaze started at Daisy's skewed topknot and passed swiftly to her toes. The hand she'd had outstretched when the door opened was withdrawn and now curled tightly around the straps of her leather handbag. "I must have the wrong house," she said around a frozen smile. "I'm visiting—from San Francisco. I'm, er, looking for the Sloan residence. Sorry to bother you."

Daisy now saw something she'd missed earlier. An airport limousine idled in the driveway, its engine running. Again she'd underestimated the Wyatts. Temple's mother—Rebecca's grandmother—had plainly commanded a through flight.

Hell's bells and little fishes! Daisy grabbed for a tighter hold on the salad bowl.

It slipped.

CHAPTER FOURTEEN

THE BOWL HIT THE FLOOR and broke. Glass, lettuce, tomatoes and cucumbers flew as high as Daisy's head. She cried out as a piece of glass struck the top of her foot a slicing blow.

"My dear!" Daisy's visitor spun to see it all. "Mercy, you've hurt yourself. Here, let me help." Snapping open her purse, the woman in the pearl gray suit pulled out a folded linen handkerchief and pressed it to Daisy's wound. Blood oozed through the fine cloth.

"Oh, you shouldn't do that, Mrs. Wyatt. Blood's a bearcat to get out of anything white." Daisy caught the scent of an expensive perfume as her Good Samaritan flapped about.

The woman stopped dabbing at the cut. "You know who I am?" She seemed confused.

"Yes. You have the right house, Mrs. Wyatt. Your granddaughter is out back. We're going to barbecue hot dogs. Please join us. If you'd like, go on through the kitchen, while I clean this up and toss another salad. It won't take a jiffy."

"Hot dogs? Oh, my, no. I haven't eaten one in years. They're filled with nitrates, you understand. But... Rebecca's here?" The blue eyes softened. "Is she really better? I've been so worried. And now this thing with her father. I shudder at the thought of spending a single night in this awful city, but I absolutely could not book a flight out until morning. And there's a huge educational conference in Houston taking up all the better hotels. However, the travel agent assured me that she's booked Rebecca and me into a nice one here. So I'll trouble you for her bags." She glanced about dubiously. "You have staff perhaps?" Straightening, she adjusted her suit jacket, and the chunky silver earring that peeked out from under her hair.

In spite of the ever-widening circle of blood on the cloth and the drops beginning to puddle around her bare toes, Daisy laughed. "You're looking at my staff. That's me. Chief cook, bottle washer, maid and gardener. I'm not a great doctor, though. Do you think this needs stitches?" She knelt to inspect the deep cut.

"Daisy!" Corporal Phillips called from beyond the wall that blocked her from his sight. "The briquets are ready. How are you doing with the salad?"

Mrs. Wyatt skirted Daisy and marched across the living room to the kitchen door. "Young man," she said briskly. "Your wife..." She turned back to Daisy with a puzzled frown. "I'm sure Temple said you were unmarried. Well, it doesn't matter," she said. "The lady of the house needs help. She's bleeding."

His face as white as the ivory walls that flanked him, Corporal Phillips streaked past the woman. His weapon out and ready, he thrust her behind him none too gently.

Mrs. Wyatt screamed. She clutched her throat, her eyes huge. "Mercy, a gun. Oh, Lord, it's all true what the limousine driver said. This place is still a haven for pirates." And she promptly fainted.

The corporal saw her fall, but there was nothing he could do, because by then he'd reached Daisy. "Holy mackerel, what happened? I don't know who to help first." He peeked outside and did a quick check around. "Another intruder?"

Daisy tried to explain. "So you see," she finished, "this is my own clumsy fault. If you'll grab a garbage bag from under the sink, I'll clean up while you look after Rebecca's grandmother. There's so much glass I'm afraid to move very far."

While they were talking, a police car pulled into the driveway behind the limousine, and a uniformed officer climbed out.

"My replacement." Corporal Phillips sounded relieved. "His timing could've been better. Darn. I was looking forward to those hot dogs. They're done to perfection." He kissed the tips of his fingers and made a smacking sound as he turned to kneel beside the older woman.

"Invite him, too." Daisy mopped at the blood, which seemed to be oozing faster. "This isn't my day," she muttered as Rebecca chased Pipsqueak through the house, dog yapping, girl squealing.

"Stop!" Daisy and Corporal Phillips commanded simultaneously.

Rebecca and terrier froze in midstride. Flailing her arms, the child lost her balance and tripped over the woman who blocked the kitchen door. "Grandmother Wyatt?" Rebecca said, aghast. Then she noticed Daisy's bloody foot. "Oh, no! Did the bad man come back? You promised the police would keep him, Daisy."

"They did, honey. I dropped the salad." She sighed. "Please, will someone see to Mrs. Wyatt?" she begged.

Apparently lured by the noise, the limo driver got out and tagged after Corporal Phillips's replacement. "Does the lady in gray know my meter's still running?" the driver demanded. No one answered.

Phillips's replacement wove his way past both of them. His shiny black boots crunched through glass and salad. The instant he saw Officer Phillips kneeling over a body on the floor, his weapon drawn, he, too, whipped out his revolver.

Mrs. Wyatt woke up in the middle of that and promptly swooned again. There was no other word for it, Daisy thought; the woman even fainted elegantly.

"Cut!" Daisy ordered. "Everyone just hold it right there. Corporal Phillips, holster that gun and get me a garbage bag. You—" she pointed to the second man with the badge "—ditto with the firearm. Rebecca, sweetie, you hang on to Pipsqueak and sit down over there on the couch until I get this glass cleaned up. And you... Wesley—" she read the name embroidered on the limo driver's uniform "—cool your heels until the lady who hired you comes to."

"Yes, ma'am," he said meekly. "If you want, I could lend a hand. No extra charge," he added hastily.

"That'd be nice," she said politely as she reached around him and accepted the plastic bag from Phillips. Daisy wanted to laugh at the way everyone had obeyed her. She wished she'd known before how easy it was to take charge. This was more like it. Smooth and orderly.

Experience should have taught her, however, that the calm always comes before the storm. Her idyll ended when the back door crashed open and Sal Coletti bellowed her name, followed by "Hurray for Friday night, doll face. Storm's a comin'. Time to party."

Rolling her eyes, Daisy tossed the garbage bag down and threw up her hands. Not thinking, she stepped forward and landed squarely on a jagged piece of broken glass. Pain shot up her leg. The room and everything in it suddenly blanked from her visual screen.

DAISY AWOKE staring at the spackled ceiling of the emergency room. She'd recognized it when she saw the water mark around the light fixture. It was the same room where Temple had been treated for his gunshot. Groaning at the pain in her foot, Daisy recalled Mrs. Wyatt and the glass.

"Stupid, stupid, stupid." She struck her forehead with her palm. "How could I do something so dumb?" She struggled to a sitting position and blinked at the huge bandage covering her left foot. They even had it propped on a pillow.

"Hey, where is everyone?" No sooner had the question left her lips than a clean-cut man in a suit and tie strolled through the door.

As he came closer, Daisy saw that he wore a small ruby stud in one earlobe.

She almost fell off the bed in surprise. It was Daniel Coletti. Daniel with his hair cut flat on top and short over his ears. Clean-shaven as a banker.

"Who died?" she gasped. Then she caught her breath. The way things had gone lately, someone might well have. But not Temple—they'd taken him off restriction. Hadn't they? He was on the mend. Wasn't he? Her heart tripped up into her throat.

Laughing, Daniel held up his arms and did a slow circular waltz step until he reached her bed. "Whaddaya think, babe—er, Daisy?"

"If no one died, you must be getting married. Tell me it's not Lori Gilbert. You deserve better, Daniel."

"I deserve you, sweet thing, but since you won't have me, I'm going to work for Temple Wyatt at his resort in Lisbon. I leave in two weeks, so I've gotta clean up my act. What you see is the new me."

Nothing could have shocked Daisy more. "Now tell me another one," she teased, trying to sit up and swing her legs off the examining table. At once a pain shot from her heel to her knee. "Ow, ow, ow." She bit back something unladylike and carefully moved her foot back to the pillow. Slumping, she closed her eyes. Maybe they'd given her pain medication, and this was all a hallucination.

"You okay, Daisy?" Daniel said solicitously. "The big man sent me to see. Said he heard a rumor over on the ward. There's more gossip floating around this place than we get on the docks. Hot damn, babe, did you really throw a bowl of salad at old lady Wyatt?"

"I did nothing of the kind, Daniel Coletti," Daisy gasped. "Just what 'big man' is spreading such a lie?"

"Wyatt. But he's not spreading the rumor, doll. He heard it."

"Well, you tell him . . ." She paused, her eyes narrowing. "Oh, for cripe's sake. When did you start being his errand boy? I thought you two couldn't stand each other."

Daniel waved a hand breezily and pulled up a chair. "I been trying to tell you, babe. All that's changed. It started when the police called and asked Sal to meet them this afternoon in Wyatt's hospital room. To take a look at some mug shots. Sal's wheels crapped out again, so bein' a nice guy, I agreed to give him a lift. Well, when we get upstairs to Wyatt's room, the man's on the phone to his resort in Portugal. Somebody'd quit and left him in a bind. When he hangs up, he asks, sort of joking, if either of us wanna go work in Lisbon. Says he needs a boat captain to handle a two-masted sailboat—to take rich dames on shopping trips to towns along the coast. Only Wyatt didn't call 'em dames. I say to myself, Daniel, old boy, if this offer's for real, it's the chance of a lifetime."

He grinned and did his version of a soft shoe. "Here you see it, doll. Shave and a haircut, six bits."

For a few seconds Daisy gaped. Finally it dawned on her that he was telling the truth, and she felt a lump clog her throat. Shrimping wouldn't be the same without Daniel. And this was too many changes to take in all at once. "What about your boat?" she asked when she was able to get the words out around the lump.

"I sold it to Sal." Daniel's voice sounded thick, too. "Who knows? If this gig works out for me, maybe he'll come visit and decide to stick around. According to Wyatt, a guy can make a good living teaching tourists how to bodysurf and stuff. Don't you think Sal would be good with kids and old ladies?"

"Couldn't you do the same thing here?" Daisy asked a little wistfully. "Wyatt's building a resort on the Island, you know."

"I got the fever to travel. Besides, everybody on the docks knows you're in love with Wyatt. It's gettin' hard to keep from punchin' 'em out, if you know what I mean."

Daisy started to object, but swallowed her words because she knew what Daniel said was true. She did love Temple Wyatt. Unfortunately he didn't love her in return. Trying to conceal her emotions, she averted her gaze.

"No denial, huh?" he murmured, picking up her hand. After an uncomfortable silence, Daniel leaned over and dropped a light kiss on her forehead. "You make him treat you right, babe. Else, boss or no boss, I'll take the dude apart from stem to stern. That goes for the old broad, too."

Daisy almost broke down and told him everything. But why spoil things for Daniel? Anyway, before she could sort out her voice from her tears, he straightened his tie, tossed her a careless wave and strolled out in that cocky way he had.

The doctor walked in almost immediately afterward and caught Daisy blotting away tears. "What's this? Pain? That was an ugly sliver of glass embedded in your heel, but your pain medication should've kicked in by now."

"I'm all r-right," she sniffled. "I have so much to do is all, and accidents are just plain senseless."

"That they are, Miss Sloan. But I still want you to stay off that foot for five days. Any streaks up the leg or any undue swelling, go see your family doctor at once."

Daisy felt hysteria rise up. "Believe me, I will." She explained what she'd gone through with Temple's arm. The doctor said her friend had been lucky.

Well, he might have been lucky, but she wasn't. Temple was leaving Galveston as soon as he could travel. Daisy's mind refused to dwell on it. "Say, Doctor, will I be able to take a cab home? By the way, how did I get here? I'm sure I didn't drive."

"By police car. I have a note on the chart that says a Corporal Phillips will be back to get you before he goes off duty at eight. Ah, looks as if he's here now." Motioning to the officer whose long shadow filled the doorway, the doctor scribbled a prescription for antibiotics. "I'll send a nurse to see you out," he said.

"We'll stop and get that filled on the way to your place." Phillips said. "How do you feel? You certainly look better than when I brought you in."

"Thanks. It's kind of you to put yourself out for me," Daisy said listlessly, "but there's no need. I'm sure you have better things to do. I'll call a neighbor."

"Weather bureau says we've got a major storm kicking up offshore. Thought I'd batten down the hatches at your house, since the chief pulled your night stake. Hurricane Ella shifted and is heading inland. They expect her to hit Galveston between 1:00 and 2:00 a.m."

"I haven't seen a newscast in days. I owe you, Corporal. The doctor told me to stay off my foot, so I will need help with the shutters. Frankly I doubt Mrs. Wyatt's the type to do second-story ladders." Her brows puckered.

"Uh—" he toyed with his hat "—the gray lady packed Rebecca's suitcase and scooted. You should've heard the to-do she made over the kid bein' a little dirty. Come to think of it, probably better you missed it."

"Do you know where they're staying? I didn't get to tell Rebecca goodbye." Fresh tears spilled down Daisy's cheeks. "I may not get to now, either, with the storm and all. And I—"

The corporal didn't let her finish her lament. "Speaking of which, shall we go? Here comes the nurse with a wheelchair and your checkout papers. I'll let you settle up while I bring my car to the curb."

Daisy nodded and tried to dredge up a smile, even though she felt as if her whole world had caved in. She'd tried to prepare herself for the Wyatts' going back to San Francisco, but if the emptiness that gripped her now was any indication, she hadn't succeeded.

During the drive, Daisy said very little. If Corporal Phillips thought her lack of spirit was caused by more than her injuries, he didn't let on. She roused herself enough to thank him again when he remembered to stop at the corner drugstore to fill her prescription. She'd slipped further into despair.

"Are you sure you feel well enough to stay by yourself tonight?" Phillips asked as they pulled into her driveway. From the way the treetops bent, it was obvious the wind had risen considerably in the past hour.

Daisy gave his question serious thought. Although her hesitation had nothing to do with the state of her health, but much to do with the state of her emotions. "I'll be fine," she said at last. "The ladder that'll reach the upper shutters is in the boathouse. If you'd throw everything in there that isn't nailed down, I'd be grateful. By the way, Corporal, has anyone on the force mentioned you're worth ten Chap Dentons? He doesn't deserve those sergeant's stripes. You do."

The corporal helped her hobble up the porch steps. "Sergeant Denton told me to say he's sorry for misjudging you."

"Well, it's about time."

"Say, what's this?" Bending, Phillips picked up a vase of pink rosebuds that had been wedged behind the screen. "Two dozen," he said. "Crystal vase, too. A lot of 'I'm sorry's here," he joked. "Tell me where you're going to settle for the night and I'll put them nearby. Anybody who spends this kind of dough on a lady deserves front row center."

"They're beautiful. But it's not my birthday or anything." Daisy ran a finger lightly over one pastel bud.

"You did just have a medical emergency," the corporal reminded her dryly. He might have said more, but a big gust of wind ripped the screen door out of his hands and whapped it against the siding. "Good old Ella's putting in her two cents' worth. I suggest you bunk downstairs near the door. Keep the phone and a flashlight close by. Looks like we're in for a humdinger of a storm."

Daisy hobbled inside. "I hope Sal lashed down the *Lazy Daisy*. Come to think of it—" she frowned "—didn't he walk in just as I did my swan song?" She snapped her fingers. "A party, he said. He didn't happen to say where it was, did he?"

"Tell a cop a thing like that? No way. Coletti was with a friend, and they followed us to the hospital. I think he felt responsible for you stepping on the glass. But for a big guy, he doesn't like blood. Left as soon as the doc said you were okay. Hey, I gotta close those shutters. I'll come back through when I'm done—make sure you're locked up tight."

"Thanks," she muttered, but already her thoughts had slipped back to the roses. Maybe they were from Sal, although they seemed pretty costly for him. No. She recognized the bold scrawl on the envelope. Temple had sent them. Daisy sank into an overstuffed chair that had been in her family for years and rested her aching foot on the matching ottoman. Even then she didn't open the card right away. She smelled the flowers and admired how they looked against the room's dark heavy furniture.

She opened the envelope slowly. So many rosebuds suggested at least an "I love you" on the card. As she tugged it out, she held her breath—but she needn't have. The card wasn't a declaration of love. It was the standard florist's get-well wish. Temple had scribbled his name and Rebecca's at the bottom. He might have been sending it to a stranger.

Daisy tossed the message aside. After all, what had she expected? He'd obviously called down from his hospital room and ordered the flowers from the same shop Rebecca had bought his daisies. She doubted roses meant anything to him. Except as a sophisticated way to give a lady the brush-off.

Or maybe he felt guilty because he suspected he'd stolen her heart. He certainly knew he'd spirited away her best friend. Lisbon was a long way from Galveston on anyone's map.

At least she still had her pets, she thought as Pipsqueak and Troublemaker hopped up on the chair and snuggled down one on either side of her. These two were good storm barometers. Even if they always hid under the couch during the worst of it. Oh, well, she'd waited out storms alone before.

Corporal Phillips came in through the back, locked up and asked it he could get her anything else before he left.

"Since you asked, I wouldn't mind having the TV turned on to a news station."

He did that. "Anything else?"

"No. You take off. I've been through hurricanes before."

"But not as an invalid."

"Invalid? I take back the nice things I said about you, Corporal."

He laughed. "Okay, I'm leaving. Don't open the door to strangers."

"Yes, Mother." Daisy rolled her eyes and they both laughed. But what she noticed after he'd left was that the house seemed inordinately quiet. Like a tomb, except for the voices of newscasters who predicted disaster from her TV. Daisy didn't know why the local station thought they needed to bring on every self-proclaimed expert who'd ever lived through a hurricane. And, of course, every single report was full of references to "the big one." Anyone who wasn't scared before, would be after.

She was about to hop across the room and change channels when the phone rang. Daisy grabbed it on the first ring. "Hello," she said, her voice breathless.

"Daisy?" Temple sounded surprised to hear her voice, or maybe his surprise was at the speed with which she'd answered.

"Temple." For a moment her voice failed. Then she murmured coolly, "Hey, thanks for the flowers. They're pretty." She decided she'd show him she could be as sophisticated as his other rejects. Only the quaver in her voice gave her away.

"Are you all right, Daisy?"

"Couldn't be better," she snapped. "Three rooms upstairs still look like a war zone, and the doctor ordered me to stay off my foot for five days."

"They're releasing me tomorrow. I'll come and help. Maybe we can salvage something." On a soft chuckle he added, "Me with one arm and you with one leg. Should be quite a team, huh?"

Daisy couldn't help laughing. "Depends on who gets to give the orders." She felt better already; he had that effect on her.

"Now that sounds more like the Daisy I know. By the way, I heard my mother blew into town. How are you two getting along?" He spoke it casually, but there was an underlying edge to his question.

Her good mood vanished. "As if you didn't know, she took Rebecca. They left while I was in emergency. I wanted to tell Rebecca goodbye, but maybe this is best. I wouldn't want to cry and make her feel bad, too."

"What do you mean, took Rebecca? Took her where?"

"To a hotel. Don't you know?"

"No, dammit. Mother insisted on coming. I told her you had a bedroom we might be able to rent for a few days. I didn't say anything about a hotel."

"You mean you didn't ask her to take Rebecca home?"

"Why would I? Daisy, I thought you...I thought we... Hell, I hate being stuck in this hospital. Listen, it's late, but I'll track them down and tell her to get back to your place. Dammit, Daisy, I had a lot I wanted to discuss with you now that I'm back among the living. Do you mind if I call back later to talk?"

"Were you planning to tell me that you'd hired Daniel?"

The phone line crackled with static. "So, he saw you? I didn't know—he hasn't come back here. Are you upset that he's leaving?"

"Yes. No. I mean, Daniel's his own boss. Actually I hope it works out for both of you. He sold his boat, you know."

"You *are* angry."

"I'm not. It strikes me as odd, that's all. There's no love lost between you two, and I can't help wondering why you'd hire someone you disliked."

"Hmm," he said noncommittally. "Are you all battened down? I don't much care for what they're saying on TV. Will this storm be bad?"

"Hmm." She answered him the same way. "When you locate your mother, tell them to stay put for the night. Miss Ella could turn out to be a record-breaker."

"What? Who's Miss Ella?"

"Our hurricane—the one you're calling a storm. Goodbye, Temple." She hung up and stroked Pipsqueak's ears. Maybe she *had* been a little miffed. But miffed or not, she worried about Temple and Rebecca. Outside, the wind had begun to pick up.

Daisy mulled over what he'd said—that he hadn't meant his mother to take Rebecca at all. So lost was

Daisy in her thoughts that she didn't pay any attention to the fact that Pipsqueak and Troublemaker had hopped down and slunk under the couch.

The lights flickered once, and that was what eventually pulled her from her reverie. But her new electrical system held. Something else to tell Temple when he called back. Daisy found she actually looked forward to their next chat. She'd make sure she was more clearheaded, though.

The windows rattled viciously. Daisy got up and hobbled over to turn off the television. While she was up, she took her medicine—her foot had begun to throb. She moved to the couch and plumped one pillow for her foot, then settled another at the opposite end for her head. She brought the phone close, waiting for his call, but even so, it wasn't long before her eyes drifted shut.

Surely by now Temple's found his mother, she mused, fighting sleep. There weren't so many hotels in town that he couldn't have called them all by now. She was disappointed, but he must have decided to skip calling her back.

The wind lulled her to sleep.

Suddenly the phone rang at Daisy's side and jerked her awake. Heart pounding like a jackhammer, she failed in her first attempt to find the instrument. It rang twice more. When she finally hauled it to her ear with a shaky hand, Temple was already midsentence.

"I know it's late and I probably shouldn't disturb you. But I found my mother. Or, rather, she found me. She's beside herself. Apparently Rebecca's having a nightmare. God, Daisy, I heard her screaming, and I don't have any idea what to do."

"Where is she?" Daisy's voice sounded groggy from sleep. "I'll go right now."

"Honey, you can't. Have you looked outside? Rain's pounding hell out of us from every angle, and there're eighty-mile-an-hour winds. It's only advice I want, sweetheart."

"What time is it?" Daisy rubbed the sleep from her eyes.

"A little after two. Why?"

"I'll call the weather bureau and find out when the eye of the storm is due to pass over the city. I'll have ten or twelve minutes to get to the hotel during the calm. Are they at the Galvestonian?"

"No. The Galvez. But you can't go. It's too dangerous. Daisy, I can't tell you how much it means to me that you'd even offer."

"Temple—think. The hotel sits close to the surf. The pounding waves may trigger Rebecca's memory of the accident. What if she remembers everything and goes to pieces?"

"Then *I'll* go. They can check me out of here now. You said the doctor told you to stay off that foot."

"You don't know hurricanes like I do, Temple," she argued. "Besides, I know which streets are safe. There'll be limbs down and streets flooded."

"You think that makes me feel better about your going out in it? Daisy, don't even think it. If something happened to you, I couldn't stand it."

She couldn't take time now to revel in the meaning behind those words. "It won't. I promise. Call your mother back and tell her to hang on. Tell her just to rock Rebecca and sing. Oh, what room are they in? I'll call her."

"Room 215, but—"

"Second floor? Great. I'll give you a jingle when I get there. And Temple, trust me. I love Rebecca, too, you know?"

For a minute there was more static on the line. Then in a voice ragged with feeling, he said, "I love you, Daisy Sloan. You sit tight, because I intend to tell you again and again. Rebecca's my daughter. I'm going, and that's final."

"No, Temple. Listen to me." Daisy's hands shook so hard she dropped the phone. She dared not think about what he'd just said. When she picked up the receiver again, she discovered the line had gone dead.

She rattled the plunger several times. Blast and damn! No dial tone, either. That meant she couldn't call him back. Nor could she call the weather bureau. She'd have to go on instinct.

Hopping on one foot, she made her way to the front door, opening it just a crack to listen. The wind howled across the porch and almost ripped the door from her grasp. Rain came down in sheets and soon soaked the arm and leg she'd braced against the casing to help her keep hold of the door. This might be trickier than she'd thought. But she loved Rebecca Wyatt and her father. All her life Daisy had dreamed of being part of just such a family. This was what family members did for one another. Amid laughter and love, they took risks. Right now, that meant braving Hurricane Ella to rescue her water baby again.

CHAPTER FIFTEEN

HURRICANES CAME with a howl peculiar to the beast. Daisy clung to the doorknob, using both hands to keep it from being wrenched away. She listened with a practiced ear for the slightest nuance that would indicate the approaching eye of the storm. The humidity was oppressive. Tendrils of hair clung to her forehead and neck. The instant she sensed a lessening of the wind's velocity or a decrease in the driving rain, she knew she'd have to move fast.

What was Temple doing now? she wondered. His threat to go out in this storm terrified her. Surely he wouldn't be so foolish. She had lived with hurricanes all her life. While he might have encountered a few at his tropical resorts, she doubted he'd learned the intricacies of navigating in one. The biggest problem Daisy saw was the need to hurry. Her ability to move fast was greatly curtailed by her injured foot.

There—a subtle drop in humidity, a slight decrease in the wind. Daisy whispered a quick prayer. Not for herself but Rebecca's. The moment she heard the rain slacken, Daisy opened the door and slipped out. The night was black, and the circle of illumination from her flashlight didn't reach far—but far enough to show ankle-deep water in areas that were normally dry. The tricky part when driving was not to let the car bottom out in a puddle and short the spark plugs. Ugh, her bandage had gotten soaked already, and she hadn't even reached her car. In fact, she didn't think there was a dry inch on her entire body.

Fat raindrops followed her into the vehicle. Water ran in rivulets down her face, neck and arms. But unless she missed her guess, there was less rain pounding on the windows now. She jammed the key into the ignition and thanked her guardian angel when the engine roared to life. Her hands shook. Based on experience and the rate this storm was moving, she figured she had ten minutes max to reach the hotel before getting caught in the eyewall, which was when the most severe winds whirled at gale force. More than once she'd seen drivers misjudge and their cars tossed about like toothpicks.

The streets were ugly. Poles were down. Streetlights out, and uh-oh—a tree uprooted from old Mr. Perry's yard had fallen across the road.

Daisy cursed softly, made a U-turn and backtracked. This cost her precious minutes. At the next street she discovered broken electrical wires dancing against the sky like Fourth of July sparklers, and she prayed again that Temple had listened to her about the dangers that awaited on the streets.

HE HADN'T.

Temple stood in a phone booth in the hospital lobby, trying to get through to the police dispatcher. The night nurse refused to sign him out without a doctor's order. She even took his wallet and car keys. Thank goodness she had to answer an urgent phone call before she thought of hiding his clothes. At any rate, he figured the police would be out in full force. Maybe one of the guys he'd come to know through Rebecca's ordeal would drive him to the hotel.

He had tried calling Daisy back after the line went dead. All he got was a computer message that said his call could not be completed. What did it mean? Was there trouble on the main line or had something happened at her house? He drummed his fingers on the phone housing and tried to picture the trees in her yard. They were big and old. Sturdy—he hoped.

"This is an emergency," he shouted at the dispatcher who'd come back on the line. "Can you patch me through to Phillips or Denton—whichever man is closest to the hospital right now? Yes, I'm aware there's a storm."

Dammit! She cut him off. For a moment he stared at the receiver. Then he slammed it onto the switch hook and headed down the hall.

He'd simply have to walk. Apparently Daisy had been right about the eye of the hurricane giving relief as it passed over the city. "Oh, no." The lobby doors were locked and boarded over. Temple recalled seeing a fire door in the basement, off the lab. A couple of the techs had sneaked out that way for a smoke. If the door wasn't bolted, he'd sneak out, too.

It wasn't, and as luck would have it, no one stopped him. Outside, it was almost eerie. Temple hitched his sling into a more comfortable position and angled across the parking lot at a fast jog. It was the absence of traffic noise that made it feel as if he were on another planet, he decided. No cars and no people out walking. His footsteps echoed, except when he landed in puddles, which he seemed to do with regularity. Before long, his shoes and socks were soaked, and his jeans to the knees.

He refused to think about his discomfort, or about how out of shape he was. Damn, but he was pushing thirty-five. Not exactly rocking-chair time, but too old for this jumping-over-tall-buildings-in-a-single-bound crap, he thought as he was forced to slow his pace and catch his breath.

Laughter and loud music blared from a row of apartments. Daisy had been right about the parties, it seemed. *Daisy.* A vision of her, smiling and tousled, flitted through his mind. Where was she this minute? What was she doing? Even after the way they'd left things between them in that hotel room, she'd said she loved him. The shocker was that he loved her back. And it gave him a new lease on life.

Uh-oh. Ahead where the streets intersected—a flood. He'd have to cross, go up a block and hope the next street over wasn't the same. How long since they'd started into the eye? How much time did he have left? The humidity sapped his strength, and Temple knew he was beginning to tire. His breath burned in his lungs.

DAISY COUNTED the minutes under her breath, the way she had when taking her father's pulse. One one-thousand, two one-thousand and so forth for fifteen seconds. But it served no purpose except to make her more anxious. She'd had to backtrack to Nineteenth Street because so many streets were flooded. If it was, too, she didn't know what she'd do. Already she'd doused her headlights to avoid a police car. They wouldn't give a hoot about Rebecca's nightmare; their job would be to send her back.

"Look at that," she muttered aloud. "Some crazy jogger crossing Nineteenth." Lord, but joggers were a breed unto themselves. At the corner, Daisy saw the man stumble on the high curb. She had a clear view, thanks to her headlights. He threw his head back and rubbed at his chest as if he were strapped for air. Did he need help? Was he having a heart attack or something?

Daisy knew that pulling over to ask wasn't the smartest move she'd ever made. He could be a looter trying for a fast getaway. On the other hand, if he truly needed help and she didn't respond, she'd never forgive herself. Cruising slowly up behind him, she hit the button that rolled down the passenger window and beeped her horn.

Surprised, the man whirled toward the sound. He threw his right arm up to shield his eyes from the light. Daisy saw that his left was in a sling. "*Temple!* Oh, my God, Temple!" she screamed, and slammed on the brakes so hard the car slid on the wet street and jumped the curb. The back of her car swung toward him.

For a second there, Temple thought some idiot was trying to run him down. A drunk? Who but a drunk would be out in a hurricane? Swearing, he dove into a doorway. Then, somehow, over his galloping heart, he heard a woman call his name.

Daisy. "Lord," he whispered. "She came out in this after I told her not to." By the time Temple's heart slowed—enough so he could make a dash for her car— she'd bounced the right wheel off the curb. In spite of having no traction on the wet pavement, she attempted to back up. Then she stopped and rolled down her window.

Temple stuck his head in. "Daisy, all you're doing is burning rubber. God, do you look good, though. Except that I'm not sure whether to kiss you or strangle you."

"Hurry and get in. We've got about five minutes till all hell breaks loose. I can't believe you're out here on foot, you idiot. Have you ever seen a tropical storm after the eye moves past?"

He hurried around to the passenger side. He had difficulty getting the door open and then climbing in, mostly because his left arm was useless and his lungs felt like they were seared.

Daisy didn't wait for his answer. She tore off down the hill before he had the door shut. "What are you doing on Nineteenth? Why didn't you drop down to Seawall?"

"Flooding," he said, trying to catch his breath. "Cars si-whickered, and poles down everywhere. I was going to angle across Church to Twenty-first."

"No good. Twenty-first is a mess. Nineteenth is our only hope."

"Then Nineteenth it is. Hit the juice when you get to the bottom and let her hydroplane through that standing water at the Y. Daisy, I—"

"Save it," she muttered. "Thank me. Kiss me. Kill me. Just wait till we get to the hotel to do it."

His laughter sounded like wind rustling through fallen leaves. "Never give a man three choices unless you're a genie who can grant them. Man, being a logical animal, will invariably go straight for the last option."

"Look." She pointed as her car barrelled through the deep water. "It's the hotel parking lot." She let the momentum carry them up into the lot. "I figure we've got about two minutes to get from here to the building—or forget choices." In the distance, they could hear the waves crashing against the seawall.

"Then let's hustle."

Daisy unbuckled her seat belt and pocketed the keys. "You go ahead," she said as he threw open his door and hopped out. "I can't walk as fast as you."

He rushed around behind the car to assist her. It was the first time he'd seen her bandaged foot. "Jeez, lady.

Sal said you'd stepped on a piece of glass. This looks more like you cut off your foot."

"It looks worse than it is." She tried to hop, landed in a pool and almost fell.

Temple grabbed her arm. Noting that the wind had picked up, he gave a frustrated growl, knelt and hoisted her over his good shoulder. He ignored her vociferous protests and ran toward the hotel entrance.

"Put me down." She pounded on his rear end with her fists. "I will not go into one of the best hotels in town slung over your shoulder like a sack of pecans."

"Quiet." Temple struggled to keep from dropping her on her head. "Pecans are lumpier and they don't talk back. So hush," he said.

Daisy's sore foot bumped his rock-hard thigh. A stabbing pain shot through her, bringing tears to her eyes. "Please put me down. Temple, you're hurting me."

But because he didn't think she could make it on her own, he only ran faster.

The hotel had a double entrance, as did many buildings in Galveston. Vapor locks, they were called—to keep the heat or air-conditioning in and the weather out. He grappled with the first door and kicked it closed just seconds before the high winds in the eyewall struck and shook the city with the fury of an angry Norse god.

As if absorbing the electrical energy that swirled around them, Temple set Daisy down, then slid the palm of his good hand into her damp hair and yanked her into a kiss. His lips softened the instant they touched hers, and they spoke of love.

Daisy leaned into him. She ran her hands up his chest and over his shoulders, then her arms fully encircled his neck. Their sudden embrace blocked out the noise of the storm outside—and created one between them.

A doorman, a tall gangly fellow, peeked through the upper doors and cleared his throat. It was obvious that he intended to lecture the vagrants—until Temple set Daisy down on her one sneakered foot.

"Daisy? Daisy Sloan?" The doorman sounded relieved to see someone he knew. His face brightened. "Ah—and this is your boarder. The guy from California?" he said hopefully. "His mother's in room 215. Boy, are we glad to see you. She's convinced we're all gonna die."

"That sounds like my mother." Temple shook his head.

"As you can see, Mickey, I'm here, but I'm not firing on all cylinders." Daisy indicated her bandaged foot. "Are either of your elevators working?"

"Nope. Too dangerous in case our emergency generator goes out."

She sighed. "Well, I don't relish being stuck between floors, anyway. Guess I'll hop. It's only two flights. Temple, you go on ahead."

"If it wasn't for the fact that we don't know what's wrong with Rebecca, I wouldn't mind getting stuck between floors with you," Temple whispered.

Daisy slapped at his arm, her face turning scarlet. "I'll hop," she said again. Which she proceeded to do, although each hop jarred her injured foot. By the time she made it to the foot of the stairs, she was forced to stop and rest. And Temple didn't go without her.

"Let me help." He looped an arm about her waist. "I didn't mean to embarrass you in front of your friend. Forgive me?"

She clutched the banister and stopped. "Friend? Oh, you mean Mickey? His dad and older brother are shrimpers. Mickey's allergic to shellfish, of all things.

Disappointed his dad. He'd planned to retire and turn the boat over to his boys."

"Well, life doesn't always go according to plan," Temple said.

"Are you thinking of your father, or Miranda and Rebecca?"

"Us, I meant. Do you believe in predestination?" He fixed her with a somber, blue stare. "Like certain things are meant to be and certain people are meant to meet— and fall in love?"

Daisy leaned on the banister and rested her bandaged foot on the carpeted step above. "I don't want to believe in that theory. If I truly believed everything that happened was preordained, then I'd have to admit God—or the Fates—didn't like me enough to give me a mother who'd stick around. You think someone decided before you were conceived to let you watch your father die? I choose to believe we make our own destiny."

"Then my destiny is you." Temple brushed a thumb across Daisy's mouth and replaced it with his lips a moment later. The kiss lasted long moments.

When at last he pulled back to breathe, Daisy gazed into his eyes with a look of bemusement. "Wasn't kissing me choice number two, Wyatt? That tells me you aren't a man of logic."

"No? It's logical to me. If you and I are the masters of our own fate, I need to give you an incentive to drop anchor in my port." Growing more serious, he said, "When we get upstairs, I don't know what we'll find with regard to Rebecca. What's clear is that you're the best thing that's happened to either of us since she was born."

Daisy reached up and brushed the fall of wet hair off his forehead. "I thought...the other night...that you didn't want me."

"Whatever gave you a crazy idea like that? No. Don't tell me. Can you manage a few more steps?"

As she glanced upward and groaned, Temple scooped her into his arms and dashed headlong up the stairs with all the fervor of a twenty-year-old—not stopping until he stood outside the door to 215. He set her down with great care and rained soft kisses on her face. "Give us a chance to work things out?"

Daisy smiled her most loving smile, but as he curled his hand and raised it to knock, she reached up and stayed his fingers. Drawing his hand to her lips, she kissed his knuckles and whispered, "I'm not as brave as you think."

"You leapt into the ocean to save Rebecca. You took on her ogre of a dad in court. You popped a man holding a gun upside the head with a sand bucket. I can't imagine what would frighten you, sweetheart."

"Your mother." Daisy tensed.

"My mother?" Temple couldn't help it. He laughed.

Before Daisy could explain about being intimidated by the Saks Fifth Avenue queen, the door in front of them flew open, and the object of her concern greeted them, looking positively frazzled.

Daisy couldn't believe this was the same woman who'd come to her house. The high heels had been kicked off, the suit jacket was wrinkled, the perfect hairdo limp. The woman's granddaughter—formerly sweet child that she'd been—sat on the couch, brows lowered and arms crossed, kicking her feet.

Temple and Daisy gaped. They spoke the girl's name sharply and together.

She looked up, smiled and launched herself into Temple's arms. "Daddy," she screeched, "and Daisy." She peered over her father's shoulder and said in an impish voice, "I knew you'd both come. I just knew it."

Mrs. Wyatt aimed an accusing glance at her son. "Honestly, Temple, I'm afraid I have to side with Glendon Davis. Rebecca is spoiled rotten. Things will change once we get her home."

"I don't wanna go home." Rebecca pulled Temple's face around with both hands, forcing him to look at her. "I like it at Daisy's. Can't I stay with her when you visit your old hotels? Pipsqueak needs me. 'Sides Daisy and me are gonna build a sand castle big enough for a princess." Her eyes clouded. "I mean, we'll get to if they keep those bad guys in jail."

"They will, honey." Temple kissed her nose. "But I don't know if you deserve to build sand castles. You frightened everyone with your behavior tonight."

"I'm sorry." She hung her head.

Daisy had dropped down on the arm of the chair and was resting her injured foot on the lamp stand. The slight shake of her head and her frown caught Temple's eye.

"What?" he asked.

"Kids deserve the truth," she said, "and I just wondered how long the police can hold those men without proof."

"Haven't you heard?" Temple frowned. "I had a call from the police right before the storm. They got a full confession from Shaw. I assumed you'd been notified."

"No. I had no idea." Daisy smiled at Rebecca. "You bet we'll build that sand castle. Maybe this time your dad will help." Daisy nudged Temple with her good toe.

"Rebecca is coming home with me in the morning," Mrs. Wyatt said as she took a seat on the couch. "What's all this about bad guys? Would someone care to enlighten me?"

"First of all, Mother," Temple admonished, "I want you to tell me what's going on. I don't recall our discussing your departure date or your taking Rebecca with you. My understanding was that you wanted to come for a visit." When his mother twisted her diamond ring and looked guilty, Temple set Rebecca down and said, "Honey, why don't you take Straylia into the other room and put him to bed. I think we adults need to chat."

Rebecca glanced from her father to her grandmother to Daisy, then she sighed. "Do I hafta shut the door? I promise I won't listen."

"Rebecca," he chided.

She pouted prettily. "Darn, kids never get to hear the good stuff."

Temple smiled. "When we're finished, I'll read you a story."

"I want Daisy," Rebecca said. "She's got funny stories about the water babies. She makes me laugh."

Love shone in the look Temple bestowed on Daisy. "She makes me laugh, too, honey," he said, "and I thought I'd forgotten how. But it's up to her, Rebecca. We can ask, but we can't tell Daisy what to do. And we can't throw fits to get our own way, either."

"I know," Rebecca said. "I won't do it again."

The fact that everyone, including Temple's mother, stared at her made Daisy squirm. "My stories are nothing special," she murmured. "But sure, I'll come in and we'll make one up. I'll pretend to be Mrs. Doasyouwouldbedoneby, and you can be Tom."

Satisfied, Rebecca hugged her and skipped off.

"So tell me about Shaw," Daisy demanded, the moment the door closed behind Rebecca. "By confession, do you mean he admitted to blowing up the yacht?"

Temple sat in the chair beside Daisy. He closed his eyes and smoothed a thumb and forefinger over his eyebrows.

"I'm sorry," she said softly, laying a compassionate hand on his shoulder. "It must be hard for you to talk about all this. I'll ask the police later."

"No. It needs to be said. It's just so hard to believe. Miranda and Rebecca were innocent victims. Domingo, too, in a way. Halsey Shaw was using DeVaca's resorts to store drugs. It was a slick deal. The big drug lords would bring their families for a vacation and set up a buy. Apparently it'd been going on for two years. Then Shaw got greedy. He started tapping Domingo's till and heisting jewels and got himself fired. About that time, Domingo's son figured out Shaw's game. He wanted to be cut in. Except it was Shaw who had the contacts, so the only way sonny could get in on the deal was to get his hands on the resorts—which meant eliminating his father."

"Then DeVaca was only being nice to Miranda, like you thought?"

Temple shook his head. "No. I was wrong about their relationship. If I'd known for sure, I would've moved on them earlier and kept them from taking the yacht. DeVaca's daughter claims her dad planned to marry Miranda, and that her brother saw the marriage as an added threat to his inheritance. He sent Shaw to blow up the yacht. By going shrimping in Rum Row, you foiled their plans. Shaw and a man named Lopriori had hung out in the Row for two days. You were so close to the yacht the second day, he thought he could get two with one blow, so to speak." Temple heard Daisy draw in a sharp breath. He clasped her hand. "I know—it's scary when I think what might have happened."

"When I heard them make contact with the yacht, I hauled anchor. They must've thought I'd kept going."

Mrs. Wyatt broke in for the first time. "We're grateful you didn't. I've never believed in rewards, but if anyone deserves one, you do. I hope Temple was generous."

Daisy stood and limped toward the door. "I think this is where I came in. I don't want a dime of his money, Mrs. Wyatt."

Temple reached out and grabbed Daisy's arm, pulling her into his lap. "Hush, Mother. Daisy taught me that there are some things money can't buy."

Mrs. Wyatt smoothed her skirt with a nervous hand. "I was only trying to help. The bottom floor of her house isn't finished. And I thought she could use some new clothes."

Temple looked horrified that his mother would be so rude. He circled Daisy's waist with his arms, hoping to hold her in place while he searched for a way to apologize.

But Daisy laughed. "Since Temple got shot and Rebecca regained part of her memory, I haven't been home long enough to do any laundry. I dug these things out of my ragbag, Mrs. Wyatt."

Temple jiggled her a bit. "Shouldn't you practice calling her Mother?"

Daisy avoided the woman's sudden frown, but the frown seemed focused inward. "What do you mean, Rebecca's regained *part* of her memory?" she asked. "Should she be in therapy or something? What part of her memory is still missing? Oh, this is awful."

Temple couldn't answer his mother. "I'm not sure, unless Daisy's referring to Rebecca not remembering Miranda or the accident. When you called and said she was having a nightmare, we thought she might have regained that part, too."

"Seems it wasn't a nightmare," said Mrs. Wyatt. "I found out she threw a tantrum because she didn't want to leave here. Glendon said we have to stop spoiling her."

Daisy touched Temple's jaw to get his attention. "You should visit Dr. Rankin again. I saw him briefly when Rebecca and I stopped to buy your flowers. He noticed her progress and said he'd like to run some tests. He mentioned a type of amnesia. I forget the name he used, but it's where the victim completely blocks out all memory of a particular incident. For instance, a painful experience."

"I read about that when I stopped by the medical-school library," Temple said. "Part of me would rather she didn't remember. Part of me wonders what I'll do when she gets older and her friends ask her about her mother."

Daisy's eyes darkened in sympathy. "You need to discuss these things with her medical team. Rebecca remembers her school, her friends, even her maternal grandparents. It's a good start. She's lucky she has you, Temple—family's important to you."

"Thank goodness, you're sensible, Miss Sloan," piped up Mrs. Wyatt. "Rebecca will do fine once we get her home."

Temple gazed at his mother for a full sixty seconds before he spoke. She began to shrink under his steady gaze.

"I'm not going back to San Francisco, Mother. Neither is Rebecca. We're staying here in Galveston." He eased Daisy off his lap, then rising, slipped his good arm around her and continued to gaze at his mother.

"Why, what do you mean?" the older woman blustered. "San Francisco's your home. Wyatt Resorts is headquartered there."

"It's your home, Mother. All I have is an apartment. A cold empty apartment. A home should have love and laughter, kids—plural," he said, slanting Daisy an oblique look, "and a pet or two."

Daisy ceased to look apprehensive as the light began to dawn.

"And a pony?" a young excited voice asked. Rebecca poked her head out from the bedroom, making Temple and Daisy laugh.

Mrs. Wyatt sank slowly against the couch cushion. "Did you invite me here thinking to spring a wedding on me? Temple Wyatt, how dare you? I didn't pack one thing suitable to wear to my son's wedding."

"She hasn't agreed to marry me yet, Mother." His gaze was on Daisy now, and her eyes widened in surprise. "I realize this isn't the most romantic proposal a woman could receive," Temple murmured. "Both of us are short a limb and half-drowned, as well."

He let go of her long enough to step to the bedroom door, grasp his daughter's hand and bring her into the living room. Then he knelt before Daisy and said, "I figure there's less chance of you turning me down in front of witnesses. So, here goes—Daisy Sloan, will you be my wife and the mother of my children?"

Rebecca jumped up and down and cried, "Yippee! This is better than a pony."

Daisy's eyes filled with tears. She scrubbed at them, her face blossoming into a huge smile. "I will," she agreed, "but the ceremony'll have to wait until I'm on two feet again. I'll be darned if you're going to carry me down the aisle over your shoulder."

Temple kissed her. He winked at his mother over Daisy's shoulder, pulling away only long enough to suggest the older woman do the honors of telling her granddaughter a bedtime story. "A very long, very detailed story," he said.

"I don't know any stories," Mrs. Wyatt protested.

"You might start with the tale of the Taj Mahal," he muttered as he molded Daisy to him for another kiss.

Mrs. Wyatt stuttered indignantly. "Who told you? Why, I never... How long have you known?"

It was obvious the answer to that question would have to wait a while. Temple and Daisy were totally immersed in one another.

"Rebecca," the older woman cooed, "let's go into the bedroom. Grandmother will tell you about the most beautiful dress. I saw it last week at a children's boutique. White organdy. Long, with puffed sleeves. The perfect dress for a flower girl."

"Grandmother, you're silly," Rebecca said, giggling. "Girls aren't flowers. They only borrow names from flowers. Daisy told me that." She spoke as if Daisy's word was all the proof she needed. "I think I'll be a water baby. They have pearl necklaces, and seaweed skirts."

Outside, the storm wound down and blew itself out. The two who had braved it out of love surfaced from a kiss long enough to smile conspiratorially.

"I'm afraid my mother's in for more surprises," Temple whispered. "Picture this—the queen of boutiques juggling cat, dog and kid, not to mention Sal Coletti, for two weeks while you and I go to Charlotte Amalie on our honeymoon."

Daisy did picture it for about two seconds. Then Temple saw to it that she had other things on her mind.

EPILOGUE

THE WYATT RESORT on Galveston Island was in its fifth year of operation. It had taken a year to build, with all its peaked roofs, curved lacy balconies and elegant chandeliers. From the day it opened, rooms were in such demand that Temple Wyatt was forced to move his office to the Strand. As he did, he recalled fondly how Daisy had tried to get him to lease space there that first night he'd moved in on her, lock, stock and baggage.

Sloan House was fully renovated now. The final touch would come on Christmas Eve when Daisy opened his special gift—the restored replica of the Cutty Sark. Temple couldn't wait to see her face. She'd never dreamed it could be repaired.

Temple glanced at his watch, then out his office window. Speaking of his wife, she should have been here twenty minutes ago. They were going to miss the kickoff feast for Dickens on the Strand if she didn't hurry. Temple loved the Victorian Christmas festival, but he didn't like these confining itchy wool waistcoats all the businessmen on the Strand had to wear throughout the festival. He did like seeing Daisy dressed up in her taffeta hooped skirt and short velvet jacket over a creamy lace blouse. She hated the bonnet. So did Rebecca. Like as not, they'd both be swinging them by the ribbons when they finally waltzed in.

Ah, thank goodness. There they were. First out of the car was Rebecca, quite the young lady. She still didn't remember the accident, but at the suggestion of the medical team, she'd been told quite a bit about Miranda. Temple took a wreath of flowers out to Rum Row every year on the anniversary of her death. Maybe next year he'd let Rebecca go with him.

His mouth turned up in a smile. Rebecca was having quite a time containing her three-year-old brother. Kemper Everett Wyatt, named for both Temple's and Daisy's fathers, had hit the birthing room feet first and hadn't stopped running since. His breech delivery had been hard on both Daisy and a very worried dad. Because of that, Temple had decided two children were enough. But on Halloween night, in the midst of a dozen trick-or-treaters, Daisy told him fate had other plans. How typically Daisy, to cuddle up behind him and drop a bomb like that when he had ten of Rebecca's friends ringed around the table—and him up to his elbows in popcorn balls. He grinned widely at the memory.

Jerking open the office door, expecting to scoop up his rambunctious son, Temple was astonished when Daniel Coletti walked in, with a classy-looking brunette on his arm. "Surprise!" Daisy chirped, herding the kids in behind the couple. Before Temple could ask the name of Daniel's latest—he'd come home each winter escorting a woman prettier than the one before—Daisy jumped in to say, "Temple, meet Maria Francine. She and Daniel are booked into the honeymoon suite at the Tremont."

"The Tremont?" Temple was more stunned by that than news of the marriage. "My new manager of the Wyatt Lisbon is staying at a rival hotel?"

Daniel laughed, translating in fluid Portugese for his blushing bride. He'd attained a polished look that complemented the top hat and cloak he wore. A small diamond still glittered at his ear, but seemed somehow more sedate in the presence of a well-groomed mustache and goatee. "I thought Maria would be more comfortable in the European atmosphere of the Tremont," he informed Temple. "Besides, old man, I wanted to surprise you."

"And you did," Temple shot back. "But call me old man again, and the joke will be on you, my about-to-be unemployed friend."

Daisy peeled off her gloves, put two fingers to her lips and whistled like a stevedore. "Merry Christmas, guys. You don't mean a word of this bickering. Give it a rest at least till Sal gets here. He called to say he's buying a new shrimp boat for his fleet—his sixth, I think. Oh, my word—Temple, stop your son. He's eating a crayon."

"Ick," Rebecca said. Being closest, she wrestled it from the pudgy hand. "Boys are so gross. I hope our new baby is a girl. Girls never eat crayons."

Temple and Daisy gazed at one another, linked hands and smiled. They were both remembering a time when life hadn't been so settled for the Wyatts. A time of danger, vicious storms—and little girls eating crayons.

Surveying his growing happy family, Temple thought his life couldn't be more perfect. "I love you, Mrs. Wyatt," he whispered.

"And I love you," she said. She didn't care who heard.

Weddings by DeWilde

*Since the turn of the century the elegant and
fashionable DeWilde stores have helped brides
around the world turn the fantasy of their
"Special Day" into reality. But now the store
and three generations of family are torn apart
by the divorce of Grace and Jeffrey DeWilde.
As family members face new challenges and
loves—and a long-secret mystery—the lives of
Grace and Jeffrey intermingle with store
employees, friends and relatives in this fast-
paced, glamorous, internationally set series. For
weddings and romance, glamour and fun-filled
entertainment, enter the world of DeWilde . . .*

*Twelve remarkable books, coming to you
once a month, beginning in April 1996*

Weddings by DeWilde begins with
Shattered Vows
by Jasmine Cresswell

Here's a preview!

"SPEND THE NIGHT with me, Lianne."

No softening lies, no beguiling promises, just the curt offer of a night of sex. She closed her eyes, shutting out temptation. She had never expected to feel this sort of relentless drive for sexual fulfillment, so she had no mechanisms in place for coping with it. "No." The one-word denial was all she could manage to articulate.

His grip on her arms tightened as if he might refuse to accept her answer. Shockingly, she wished for a split second that he would ignore her rejection and simply bundle her into the car and drive her straight to his flat, refusing to take no for an answer. All the pleasures of mindless sex, with none of the responsibility. For a couple of seconds he neither moved nor spoke. Then he released her, turning abruptly to open the door on the passenger side of his Jaguar. "I'll drive you home," he said, his voice hard and flat. "Get in."

The traffic was heavy, and the rain started again as an annoying drizzle that distorted depth perception made driving difficult, but Lianne didn't fool herself that the silence inside the car was caused by the driving conditions. The air around them crackled and sparked with their thwarted desire. Her body was still on fire. Why didn't Gabe say something? she thought, feeling aggrieved.

Perhaps because he was finding it as difficult as she was to think of something appropriate to say. He was thirty years old, long past the stage of needing to bed a woman just so he could record another sexual conquest in his little black book. He'd spent five months dating Julia, which suggested he was a man who valued friendship as an element in his relationships with women. Since he didn't seem to like her very much, he was probably as embarrassed as she was by the stupid, inexplicable intensity of their physical response to each other.

"Maybe we should just set aside a weekend to have wild, uninterrupted sex," she said, thinking aloud. "Maybe that way we'd get whatever it is we feel for each other out of our systems and be able to move on with the rest of our lives."

His mouth quirked into a rueful smile. "Isn't that supposed to be my line?"

"Why? Because you're the man? Are you sexist enough to believe that women don't have sexual urges? I'm just as aware of what's going on between us as you are, Gabe. Am I supposed to pretend I haven't noticed that we practically ignite whenever we touch? And that we have nothing much in common except mutual lust—and a good friend we betrayed?"

Fall in love all over again with

This Time... MARRIAGE

In this collection of original short stories, three brides get a unique chance for a return engagement!

- Being kidnapped from your bridal shower by a one-time love can really put a crimp in your wedding plans! *The Borrowed Bride*— by **Susan Wiggs**, *Romantic Times* Career Achievement Award-winning author.

- After fifteen years a couple reunites for the sake of their child—this time will it end in marriage? *The Forgotten Bride*—by **Janice Kaiser.**

- It's tough to make a good divorce stick—especially when you're thrown together with your ex in a magazine wedding shoot! *The Bygone Bride*— by **Muriel Jensen.**

Don't miss THIS TIME...MARRIAGE, available in April wherever Harlequin books are sold.

HARLEQUIN®

Don't miss these Harlequin favorites by some of our most distinguished authors!
And now, you can receive a discount by ordering two or more titles!

HT #25645	THREE GROOMS AND A WIFE by JoAnn Ross	$3.25 U.S./$3.75 CAN. ☐
HT #25648	JESSIE'S LAWMAN by Kristine Rolofson	$3.25 U.S.//$3.75 CAN. ☐
HP #11725	THE WRONG KIND OF WIFE by Roberta Leigh	$3.25 U.S./$3.75 CAN. ☐
HP #11755	TIGER EYES by Robyn Donald	$3.25 U.S./$3.75 CAN. ☐
HR #03362	THE BABY BUSINESS by Rebecca Winters	$2.99 U.S./$3.50 CAN. ☐
HR #03375	THE BABY CAPER by Emma Goldrick	$2.99 U.S./$3.50 CAN. ☐
HS #70638	THE SECRET YEARS by Margot Dalton	$3.75 U.S./$4.25 CAN. ☐
HS #70655	PEACEKEEPER by Marisa Carroll	$3.75 U.S./$4.25 CAN. ☐
HI #22280	MIDNIGHT RIDER by Laura Pender	$2.99 U.S./$3.50 CAN. ☐
HI #22235	BEAUTY VS THE BEAST by M.J. Rogers	$3.50 U.S./$3.99 CAN. ☐
HAR #16531	TEDDY BEAR HEIR by Elda Minger	$3.50 U.S./$3.99 CAN. ☐
HAR #16596	COUNTERFEIT HUSBAND by Linda Randall Wisdom	$3.50 U.S./$3.99 CAN. ☐
HH #28795	PIECES OF SKY by Marianne Willman	$3.99 U.S./$4.50 CAN. ☐
HH #28855	SWEET SURRENDER by Julie Tetel	$4.50 U.S./$4.99 CAN. ☐

(limited quantities available on certain titles)

	AMOUNT	$
DEDUCT:	10% DISCOUNT FOR 2+ BOOKS	$
ADD:	POSTAGE & HANDLING	$
	($1.00 for one book, 50¢ for each additional)	
	APPLICABLE TAXES**	$_____
	TOTAL PAYABLE	$_____
	(check or money order—please do not send cash)	

To order, complete this form and send it, along with a check or money order for the total above, payable to Harlequin Books, to: **In the U.S.:** 3010 Walden Avenue, P.O. Box 9047, Buffalo, NY 14269-9047; **In Canada:** P.O. Box 613, Fort Erie, Ontario, L2A 5X3.

Name: _____

Address: _____ City: _____

State/Prov.: _____ Zip/Postal Code: _____

**New York residents remit applicable sales taxes.
Canadian residents remit applicable GST and provincial taxes.

HBACK-AJ3

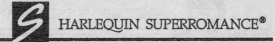

HARLEQUIN SUPERROMANCE®

The Baby Contract
by Lynn Erickson

Bettie Gay Bryson is pregnant and alone.

Late one night, she finds herself sitting in a police station in Tucson, Arizona, because her boyfriend—*ex*-boyfriend— robbed a highway convenience store. He escaped, leaving her to face the law.

Now the County Attorney's office—in the person of handsome investigator Greg Tyrrell—is offering her a deal. No prosecution, plus her living expenses paid—if she'll go undercover to help him trap the head of a baby-selling ring. She and Greg will be working closely together....

B.G. agrees. What other choice does she have? And this decision marks not only the beginning of her new life but the beginning of love.

> **An exciting and moving new novel by Lynn Erickson, author of *Aspen*, described by *Publishers Weekly* as "suspenseful and tumultuous...a sharply plotted page turner, abetted by loads of colorful secondary characters."**

The Baby Contract is available in May, wherever Harlequin books are sold.

Sully's Kids
by Dawn Stewardson
is

A story with a lot of romance and a little mystery

A story that will make you smile

A story with

CHILDREN INCLUDED

Lauren Van Slyke and Jack "Sully" Sullivan are total opposites. Lauren works for the family foundation that supported Sully's boys' home in the Adirondack Mountains. They're attracted from the moment they meet—but they see everything from very different perspectives. She's old money, he's no money; she's city, he's country. Love doesn't stand a chance, does it?

Sure it does—if Sully's kids have any say in the matter!

Sully's Kids is available in May, wherever Harlequin books are sold.

CI-1

BRIDE'S BAY RESORT

UNLOCK THE DOOR TO GREAT ROMANCE AT BRIDE'S BAY RESORT

Join Harlequin's new across-the-lines series, set in an exclusive hotel on an island off the coast of South Carolina.

Seven of your favorite authors will bring you exciting stories about fascinating heroes and heroines discovering love at Bride's Bay Resort.

Look for these fabulous stories coming to a store near you beginning in January 1996.

Harlequin American Romance #613 in January
Matchmaking Baby by Cathy Gillen Thacker

Harlequin Presents #1794 in February
Indiscretions by Robyn Donald

Harlequin Intrigue #362 in March
Love and Lies by Dawn Stewardson

Harlequin Romance #3404 in April
Make Believe Engagement by Day Leclaire

Harlequin Temptation #588 in May
Stranger in the Night by Roseanne Williams

Harlequin Superromance #695 in June
Married to a Stranger by Connie Bennett

Harlequin Historicals #324 in July
Dulcie's Gift by Ruth Langan

Visit Bride's Bay Resort each month wherever
Harlequin books are sold.

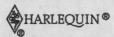

HARLEQUIN®

BBAYG